Thanks~!

Enjoy!

G^2

*A new assassin, a new terrorist,
can kill anyone, anywhere, anytime.
It's time for a new solution.*

SURGICAL

A Novel

by

Geoffrey Germann

This book is a work of fiction.
Names, characters, places, and incidents described are either products of the
author's imagination or are used fictitiously. Any similarity to actual locales,
events, or persons is purely coincidental.

Dedication

To my family

PROLOGUE

The cigarette shook in his host's hand, putting eddies and curls in the smoke trail as it lifted from the smoldering tip. The smoke carried upward like a living ribbon until it dissipated into the room already thick with the fumes. The host put the cigarette in his mouth, but the trembling persisted. The end danced in midair in a chaotic motion that reflected the owner's all-too-apparent instability.

A drag of tobacco should have calmed his nerves, soothed and steadied the shaking, but it didn't seem to have any effect at all. Maybe that wasn't the point. Maybe it couldn't soothe this malady. Maybe all it could do was keep him from going over the edge, from breaking down completely.

Maybe nicotine was the only thing holding him together.

Benjamin Gobran had seen this only twice before.

Once, it was a death row inmate.

Five years ago, he had had the distinction, he wouldn't call it an honor, of watching Lionel Cage put to death. That despicable excuse for a human being had killed nine people as he cut a bloody swath through the heart of the country. It had taken almost three years to get the conviction and another seven to work through the profuse red tape necessary to put the animal down. Benjamin was the district attorney at the time and his presence was required at the execution. Still, he took no joy in the event, nor did he feel any remorse in seeing that thing die.

Lionel Cage's cigarette had shaken the same way his host's was shaking right now. Back then Benjamin had barely noticed, but now he took a very keen interest indeed. The odd part was he had never known his host to smoke, never mind chain-smoke like some crack-addicted junkie halfway through withdrawal.

The second time Benjamin had seen something like this was during a tour of the post-traumatic stress ward in Arlington. It's been said that a human can only take about 200 days under combat conditions. Benjamin had the scarring experience of knowing the depth of that truth. Unlike with Cage, he'd been quite affected by the state of the war veterans at Arlington. He never forgot it, or them. No human being should ever have to endure that kind of hell, but looking at the Premier now, Benjamin knew that, regrettably, some did.

It didn't make sense, though. This was not a death row inmate or a war veteran fresh from the horror and gore of the killing fields; this was the leader of a stable Eastern bloc country. He was not at war with anyone and, until recently, he had enjoyed strong, stable relations with his neighbors. This state of anxiety, and the seemingly rapid deterioration of his mental state, just didn't fit with what Benjamin knew of the man and his circumstances.

The Premier took another drag on the cigarette. Benjamin didn't even want to think about what was going to happen when the supply ran out. "Thank you for coming, Mr. Gobran."

"Of course, sir," Benjamin said warmly. "We've always valued our relationship very highly."

"You've been confused by our policy shifts of late."

It wasn't a question.

"Yes, sir," Benjamin admitted. "It would be fair to say we've been hurt by them. We've always stood shoulder to shoulder with you, sir. We've always felt we were friends."

"And my actions of late have not been those of a friend."

Again, it was not a question as much as an admission.

"No, sir," Benjamin said. "Respectfully, no, they have not."

The Premier nodded wearily and took another drag of his diminishing solace. He exhaled in a stuttering breath, almost like he was shivering.

"Come with me, please," he said, rising from his chair and punching a button on an instrument panel set in the stately desk. "Have the Vice-Chancellor meet us in the new room."

He released the button, walked around the desk to the front of the well-appointed office, opened the twelve-foot double doors, and exited with Benjamin in tow. Two guards fell into place behind them. They walked through a series of hallways. Benjamin was soon lost and disoriented in the sprawling residence, but he dutifully followed.

At last they came to a nondescript door. A man, whom Benjamin recognized as the vice-chancellor, was waiting for them. What came next was a strange, and clearly well-rehearsed, ritual that Benjamin simply could not fathom.

The door opened to a room about the size of a small closet. The Premier stepped in and bade the Vice-Chancellor and Benjamin enter. The three of them squeezed into the very uncomfortable quarters, which were quite inappropriate given their stations. The Premier turned on a small ceiling light and one of the guards closed the door. The Premier produced a key, locked the door from the inside, and returned the key to his breast coat pocket. The Premier and the Vice-Chancellor felt around the space in the closet, over the walls and up to the ceiling. When it seemed they were convinced the space was secure, whatever that meant, they nodded to one another, again ritually.

The Premier produced a small remote control unit and pressed a button.

The side walls of the closet began to move away from the three men. The walls kept a tight seal with their neighbors but slowly receded, turning the closet into a hallway about fifty feet long. With the press of another button, the final wall, the wall opposite the door, began to move away from the men as well. Again, the wall kept a tight seal around its perimeter. In the space of a minute, the closet had expanded to a large room, about fifty feet on a side. With the push of a third button, solid blocks of what would serve as furniture rose out of the floor. When the process was complete, the room was furnished with spartan but adequate chairs and tables, and one large desk.

For whatever reason, the room had been carefully engineered and constructed to make absolutely sure there were no surprises therein. There could be no one and nothing in the space but what the Premier had designed. There was simply no way to gain access and nowhere to hide.

The Premier walked over to the desk and sat in the accompanying chair.

There were no windows and only the one door. In place of art work and ornamentation on the walls, there were several flat panel monitors set flush with the surface. Each had a tight seal around its perimeter. Some monitors displayed still

4

images, a replacement for paintings and photographs, some showed media feeds. The Premier didn't seem to take notice of any of them. Benjamin stepped away from his position in what had been the closet and walked through the large chamber.

He spoke quietly to the Vice-Chancellor, who kept abreast of him. "What is this place?"

The Vice-Chancellor, who appeared only marginally less close to his breakdown point, did not meet Benjamin's eye.

"The Premier built it to be a safe room, a secure retreat. Now he calls it the new room," he said.

"Why not the safe room?" Benjamin said.

The Vice-Chancellor glanced at him.

"There is no safe room," he said.

Benjamin walked over to the Premier's desk and sat down in the guest chair that had bloomed from the hardwood floor. The Premier produced an envelope from his sports coat pocket, removed the contents, and placed the document on the desk.

The Vice-Chancellor paced nervously in the background.

"I'd like you to convey my apologies to your President," the Premier said heavily. "It has been a very trying time for me and for my country."

That still didn't make any sense to Benjamin. To all outward appearances, this was not a trying time for his country. The only trying parts of his life were the ties to the United States that he had recently tested with his inexplicable, almost belligerent, policy and rhetoric.

"I cannot explain it further," the Premier said. "I can only offer my apologies for what has passed and try to set it right."

He tapped on a stack of paper.

"Premier-" the Vice-Chancellor said, his anxiety clearly elevated.

The Premier held up a hand to silence him then put his hand back on the stack of paper.

"This will repeal the policies I've put in place over the past year," the Premier said.

Benjamin couldn't believe his ears. He'd been sent to try to normalize relations with the Premier and his country. His charge was to understand the Premier's recent shift in position, to buttress relations that were in a state of diplomatic collapse, and, ideally, to soften the march toward belligerence the Premier had embarked on. Benjamin never thought he might be able to accomplish any significant policy shift, much less coax the Premier into a complete reversal, but here it was now, sitting on the table in the form of about five printed pages.

It was the accomplishment of a lifetime for someone in his position.

"Premier-" Benjamin began.

Again, the Premier held up his hand.

"Please do accept my apologies. Mr. Gobran, I've always valued my relationship with the United States and quite frankly with you personally. I know my actions have caused you great difficulty and I deeply regret that. Let us hope this can make some progress toward setting it right."

With that the Premier took a pen out of his coat pocket.

The Vice-Chancellor jumped in, almost hysterical.

"Premier, you cannot do that!" he demanded.

He charged over to the desk and leaned on the edge with both hands. Benjamin thought he would reach over the desk and grab the pen out of the leader's hand.

"Gregory," the Premier said, "I cannot live like this. This just isn't acceptable to me anymore."

The Vice-Chancellor fidgeted and raised his hand off the desk. Again, he seemed about to lunge forward and wrestle the pen out of the Premier's grasp. The Premier, with a sigh and an air of resignation, took the cap off the pen.

Then Benjamin saw what was perhaps the most haunting and horrifying thing he'd ever witnessed.

He heard something that sounded like a muffled firecracker, a distinct but subdued 'crack' coming from the Premier's direction and Premier's head hit the desk like a lifeless bowling ball. There was a loud bang when his skull struck the hard metal desktop and the Premier's body slid off raised surface and flowed out of his chair like water cascading downhill. The body settled on the floor with twisted arms and curled up legs, like a marionette with the strings cut.

Benjamin jumped out of his chair and vaulted the desk, scattering the Premier's document as he brushed the surface. He knelt beside the still form and shook the body.

"Premier?"

He checked the Premier's head. There were no signs of trauma, no blood, no wounds, nothing. He checked for a pulse. There was none.

Benjamin could only guess he'd suffered the most poorly timed coronary thrombosis imaginable.

Benjamin looked up.

"Did he...?" he began, but ended abruptly when he saw the Vice-Chancellor's face.

Benjamin had never seen such a mask of terror in his life. It seemed the Vice-Chancellor thought a ghost was responsible for the Premier's death and it was still in the room, drifting about, terrorizing him, chasing him down the path of his psychotic break.

"No," he begged, eyes wide and unblinking, darting from side to side. His skin was white and glistening with cold perspiration.

"No!" he backed away from the desk slowly, still looking from side to side in a bid to evade his ghost.

Then Benjamin heard it again, but this time it was not muffled.

A loud firecracker went off exactly where the Vice-Chancellor had been standing. There was a large spark in midair about twelve inches in front of the Vice-Chancellor's face. There was no debris, no shrapnel, no powder; none of the evidence one might expect of an explosion of that ilk. There was just a loud *bang* in the silence of the spartan chamber and a flash of light like a small fireball.

These came seemingly right out of nowhere.

There was no smoke, no residual flame, nothing to mark the event at all. After the fraction of a second it took to disappear, Benjamin could have easily believed it had never happened at all, or that he had imagined it, but the only other person in the room knew better.

The Vice-Chancellor ran for the door in a blind panic. He showed no decorum and kept no pretense. The manic break that had been threatening the Premier settled on him with its full weight and measure. He bolted across the room, waving his arms and begging like a broken child.

"No," he screamed. "No! No! God, no!"

When he reached the door, he grabbed the doorknob and began to twist and tug. He had either forgotten that the Premier had locked the door or he hoped the guard could open it. He pounded on the portal with his fists and began to kick the stubborn wooden surface in an impotent display of panic.

"No! No! God, no!" he screeched, venting an internal nightmare Benjamin couldn't even imagine.

Then, mercifully, it happened a third time.

Benjamin heard a third firecracker. The sound was muffled like the first, but came from the opposite end of the room. He heard the inexplicable report and saw the Vice-Chancellor melt just like the Premier. He went silent in mid-sentence and collapsed on the floor, a limp collection of bones. His head struck the hardwood floor, again with a resounding bang.

Benjamin froze.

He kept stone still, kneeling next to the body of the Premier as he had been. The echo from the Vice-Chancellor's collapse danced throughout the chamber like a cackling jester and finally faded to silence. Benjamin scanned the room, trying to divine what had happened, and how.

As the next instant dragged on for an excruciating eternity, Benjamin grew to a terrifying awareness of his position. The haunting words of the Vice-Chancellor settled with agonizing clarity, "there is no safe room," and for the first time in his life, Benjamin knew the maddening and precarious reality of the proverbial fish in a barrel.

CHAPTER
1

The foundation was cracking.

He could feel it, the subtle shift, the slight tilt in the now uneven ground, the almost undetectable slope.

It was small, but it had started. The steady bedrock that had given him his footing for so long was no longer reliable, no longer the staunch base on which he could depend.

It had started, and it would grow.

First, he would feel the almost imperceptible signs; a tiny quake and a passing quiver. Then he would hear the more noticeable signals; an audible creak and a telltale rattle. It would accelerate. He would begin to see cracks race across the once pristine structure. He would see the windows shatter and the walls buckle. Inevitably, the violent tremors and rending metal would announce the death throes of a noble giant.

Soon enough the entire structure would collapse around him. It would cave in on itself from the top floor down like an abandoned high-rise whose destruction had been carefully orchestrated, delicately engineered.

He could see it now.

It was coming.

But it wasn't a building.

It was civilization.

It was ingenious in its own terrifying way, the artful deconstruction of an ancient structure. It was exactly that: demolition applied on the most global scale. The assassination of a leader was one thing. That was enough to cause panic and uncertainty, but only in the short term. Inevitably, any country could find a new leader, a new figurehead, a new 'top floor.'

No, this was more than that and it was brilliant.

This cancer was insidious. It was slow-growing and infectious, so you wouldn't even see the symptoms before the affliction had advanced to the point of no return.

Horrifying!

And it chose its targets carefully, growing on non-critical organs to get its foothold before advancing to the subsequent level, and the one after that, and the one after that.

Which, of course, begged the question: who would be next?

Terror.

That was the root of it.

First make them aware of your power. Make them see that they are in your control, that they live or die at your whim. Show them that you can kill any one of them, anywhere, anytime. Hold it over their heads like an inescapable lurking vulture, the specter of death always just a breath away for any one of them, the leader, his cabinet, his family, his loved ones; anyone.

And we know how this works.

We've seen it. We've measured it. We've studied it. After centuries of war, we've boiled it down to a simple formula: 200 days. That's how long it takes. Two hundred days on the front line, with horror threatening every second, and the human psyche starts to break down, destabilize, disintegrate. The most horrifying of human conditions: death from the inside out. Madness.

A lot can happen in those 200 days. You can lay the greater groundwork. You can threaten and coax. You can steer and dictate. You can make demands, extract erratic behavior, cause policy shifts, strain relationships between nations and economies. With strings on the leader, you can begin the process of chipping away at that foundation, confusing the populace, alienating allies and neighbors, isolating each individual nation state.

And they have no response, no way to stop it, no way to find you, no defense.

Then what?

When the top floor, the exhausted, unstable, erratic, psychotic leader, has outlived his usefulness, who takes his place? When this broken marionette is removed, commits suicide, steps down, or you finally decide to kill him for whatever reason, who takes his place knowing what is in store for them? Very quickly, any leadership becomes untenable.

When the top floor collapses, the others quickly follow, because there has always been leadership. It is the foundation of every successful human society, no matter what the political environment, no matter what the ideology. Leadership is the nervous system of human civilization, from the high-functioning brain to the smallest of voluntary nerve endings. Remove that brain and no society can function.

Ten thousand years of civilization. The very fabric of our global society is constructed upon a hierarchical template.

Remove that structure, compromise the viability of that model and there can be only one result: chaos. The organism simply ceases to function.

And it had already started.

The first fissure had been the assassination of the premier of Moldova. Of course, that had been a long time coming, but neither Walter nor anyone else knew the nature of the case until well after the fact. Yes, they had seen the erratic behavior over the previous months. Yes, they had noted the sudden belligerence, the policies with the lilt of hostility toward now former allies, but just enough to raise anger and not suspicion. They'd been played perfectly to raise the rancor and acrimony between nations, but not so overtly that the players would write off Moldova as an enemy state or have the premier forcibly ousted.

Those actions had been carefully, brilliantly scripted.

He had read the classified reports from Benjamin Gobran, the secretary of state. They described the disintegration from within, both politically and psychologically. They described what was happening, but not how.

For that, he'd need different resources.

For that, he'd need genius.

The good news was that existed.

The bad news was he didn't quite know where.

Walter Rocaena was feeling the tremors as he stood staring out his fourteenth-floor office window in downtown Los Angeles. It was kind of poetic that in this place known for earthquakes and tremors, Walter was sensing a different kind of seismic shift, a more terrifying one.

Walter rolled a set of Chinese meditation balls in his right hand. They weren't as effective as a cigarette or a sedative, but they did soothe his nerves a bit, and he didn't smoke, nor was he ready for medication. Those were for weaker men.

He looked out through his ceiling-to-floor infrared-filtering windows over the city toward the west and meditated on the vast expanse of humanity that stretched from here to the sea, over thousands of miles of ocean, across Asia and the Indian subcontinent, across East and West Europe, past Iceland and Greenland, onto the east coast of North America, across the great expanse of his mother country, and back to his own state, city, building, floor, and office.

Somewhere in all of that, somewhere, the cancer was growing, plotting, scheming, and choosing its next target.

Somewhere.

One of the meditation balls slipped from Walter's fingers and landed on the Persian carpet with a subdued thud. He bent over to pick up the errant sphere.

That was when his life changed.

Just as he bent to retrieve the metal orb, Walter heard a loud crack, as if a firecracker had gone off just above him. The sound came from exactly where his head would have been if he hadn't bent over at that exact second.

The shock of the sound couldn't have hit Walter any harder if he'd been shot in the chest with a high caliber bullet. He fell to the floor from the impact to his nervous system, caught himself at the last second, and lunged away from the window. He rolled, regained his feet, scrambled to the corner of his office, and took refuge behind a large mahogany bookcase.

His heart beat in his chest harder than he'd ever experienced. His mouth went dry. His hands shook and perspiration began to soak through his business shirt.

Unfortunately, all that was irrelevant and he knew it.

Surgical

None of this made any difference—the jumping, the hiding, the hardwood bookcase; even a bulletproof shell if he'd had one would have made no difference at all.

There was no evading this enemy. There was no eluding this fate. Walter slid to a sitting position on the floor and rubbed a hand over his face. He closed his eyes and felt the abyss open below him, a deep and hopeless blackness that would claim him eventually no matter what he did.

There would be no second firecracker today, probably not tomorrow, maybe not until next week, but there would be another. Just as there would be instructions, demands, and threats, there would be more firecracker-like explosions when he least expected it. In the middle of the night, in the shower, in his car on the way home from work, all of these would come at the least expected, most psychologically damaging time.

This was day one.

It would be followed by 200 days of torture and misery and would end with his madness and death. The events in Moldova had shown him his fate.

The cancer had chosen him, and he had just over six months to live.

***

The isolation was the hardest part, particularly when he wasn't working. There were no friends, no family, no co-workers, no one who even knew his name; no one even knew he existed. He wouldn't have thought it would have been so difficult psychologically, but it was dramatic. It was easy to ignore the emptiness when he had his attention on an operation, but he couldn't work one hundred percent of the time and the prolonged lack of direct human contact was getting unbearable, even for an introvert.

The first few months weren't a problem, but it had been growing steadily as the seasons passed and he needed to develop strategies to combat it.

A five-minute chat with a stranger in a coffeehouse didn't make it. There was no depth, no sense of connection, no feeling of any permanence, and anything more than a five-minute conversation was out of the question. Even if that didn't put the other person in direct danger, there was no win there when he would eventually move on within a few days or weeks. Even he could see this emotional state was unacceptable and unsustainable.

Existing without roots turned out to be untenable, so he took up a second hobby. It was a little rude, a little invasive, but an acceptable compromise. Besides, wasn't it a good idea to check up on his flock?

He called it 'tagging,' and why not? There was no one to share the word with and so no debate or confusion about a double meaning. It was no more harmful than spraying a stranger with perfume, only this perfume no one but he could detect. It would wear off over the course of a few days or a couple of weeks, but it saved his sanity.

Surely they would grant him that if they knew; which, of course, they never could.

Here's how it worked.

First, he found a powder that would fluoresce under UV illumination. That wasn't hard. There were a lot of those. That's how black light makes posters seem iridescent. The trick was finding one that would fluoresce at a wavelength the human eye couldn't see. Second, he made a pair of glasses with very specific spectral filter. The glasses had a CCD array that would record in the UV, shift up a couple of hundred nanometers, and play back in the visible. Now if he dissolved the powder in clean oil and rubbed it on the skin, it left no trace. When he shined a UV light on it, there was still no trace to the naked eye, but if he were wearing his filter glasses, he could see the signature as clear as day.

So, on the occasion that an operation put him within arm's length of a 'client,' he would touch a hand or wrist and tag him or her with the fluorescent oil.

Rude, yes.

Cowardly, yes.

Even a little creepy.

But he found it was a toll he needed to charge.

It was extremely therapeutic to run into an 'old friend' on the street, even if that person didn't know it. Now Darren could walk about in the day and scan for people he 'knew.' It wasn't just a blur of anonymous faces. There were people out there that he cared about, personally. And who, he could reasonably presume, cared about him, even if they didn't know it.

Today, Darren sat in an alfresco coffeehouse just outside Bristol. He'd been in the area for a couple of weeks, mostly working the north end, where the crime rate was the highest. During the day, he liked to get breakfast or lunch in less troubled areas. They were more pleasant and it was better to frequent different areas in his different guises. It was better to leave as few connections between his personas as possible.

Darren wore his filter glasses almost constantly and clicked the UV flashlight that looked like a pen on and off habitually. A passerby would assume it was a nervous habit.

He liked alfresco cafes because he could scan the river of people as they milled past. He could scan hundreds, even thousands, in the day. After a few weeks in the area, it wasn't uncommon to identify one or two clients during breakfast or lunch.

Each blip gave him waves of joy, but he rarely spoke to any of them.

The waitress came over as Darren was staring out at the crowd.

"Would you like a refill?" she asked.

Darren came out of his reverie with a start and looked at his empty cup.

"Please," he said with a smile and pushed his cup to her.

He was beginning to develop a taste for European coffee and espresso.

As the waitress lowered the pot to provide his refill, Darren clicked his UV pen.

The waitress had a tag.

Darren's heart skipped a beat, but he choked it back.

He looked up at her. She was probably about twenty. She had her long black hair held in a bun with two sharpened pencils. The white sleeveless T-shirt she wore under her black apron revealed a set of bruises on her right shoulder, as if she had been grabbed by a merciless set of fingers.

Now he remembered her.

They'd met about a week ago.

"How long have you been here?" Darren asked.

The waitress started at that one.

"Oh," she said and smiled, "about a month."

"Do you like it?" Darren asked.

She smiled again.

"I like having a job," she said.

"Are you full time?" It was right about then that he realized how nice it was to be speaking English. He'd been around a lot of French and German for the past few months and that always made communicating a lot tougher.

"No," the waitress said. "Part time. I go to school north of here."

18

"Night classes?"

"Yes," the waitress said quietly. "Mostly."

Darren frowned.

"It's a bit unsavory up there at night, isn't it?" Darren asked.

The girl darkened and looked away.

Her left arm came up to the bruises on her right shoulder.

"I'm sorry," Darren said. "It's none of my business."

"No, it's OK," the waitress said. "There are day classes I could switch to. I've tried to change shifts, but there are two guys ahead of me and they don't want to trade."

Darren nodded and looked at her name tag. It said 'Sarah.'

"Do they go to school up north?"

"No."

"Well, maybe things will swing your way," Darren said. "I'll keep my fingers crossed."

She gave a weak smile and moved to the next table.

Darren got up, left some cash on the table to pay his bill, walked to the back, and found the first person with an apron.

He was a short, balding man of about forty with a name tag that said 'Richard.'

"Hi," Darren said. "Can I speak to the manager?"

"Is there a problem?" the man said with instant concern.

"No," Darren said. "Definitely not."

"I'm the manager," Richard said. "Can I help?"

"Yes," Darren said. "I don't mean to pry, but my friend Sarah works the day shift."

Richard brightened and nodded.

"She goes to school at night and, well, frankly I'm concerned about her safety in that neighborhood. I was wondering if she could switch to night shift. It feels like she'd

19

be safer working here at night and going to school during the day."

Richard shrugged.

"There is a pecking order," Richard said. "Technically, Sarah can't move until someone gives up their spot."

"Do they go to school up north?" Darren asked.

"No."

Darren handed Richard a stack of one-hundred pound notes. "Would this persuade them to trade with her?" he asked.

Richard gave an audible gasp. "Almost certainly," Richard said with satisfaction.

"Can I ask you to take care of that?"

"Consider it done," Richard said, folding the bills in his fist.

Darren nodded then turned and exited the restaurant.

He would give it a day then follow up to ensure that the change had been made. Richard seemed like a trustworthy guy, but nothing succeeds like redundancy.

The bad news was, despite the fact that he liked this coffeehouse, he could never come here again. He had compromised his anonymity so this location was now off limits. It was too bad though; it was an ideal perch to scan for tags.

The good news: this nice distraction had kept him from thinking about Corrine for the last fifteen minutes.

CHAPTER
2

Location is character.

A place, a physical space, has a personality, a temperament, just as a human being does. The Chinese call it Feng Shui and perceive it as the ebb and flow of energy. That art manages the personality of a space, and the manner in which people perceive and interact with it, by careful arrangement of the elements therein.

This applies to any room, building, street, or city block. Each one has a nature, a predisposition for invitation or rejection, for serenity or turmoil, for good or evil. And to these locations people flock according to their disposition: the homeless to the hidden places, the out-of-the-way corners, the neglected alcoves; children to their parks, fields, and play structures; businessmen to their offices, conferences, and board rooms. Of course, it could be argued that the inhabitants themselves imbue a space with its distinctive nature, but it is irrelevant. It doesn't matter which comes first.

Location is character.

So the patterns of human behavior march along these game trails of space and identity, hopelessness to the abandoned, joy and exuberance to the open and sun-kissed, industriousness and productivity to the quiet and sedate, malice to the shadows.

The pulse and flow of any city give rise to eddies and backwater currents where malevolence can collect, spaces that nurture selfishness, hatred, and violence: locations of low character.

Fortunately, despite predisposition, despite history and predilection, despite pre-existing proclivities, energy can be redirected.

Character can be taught.

"C'mon, man," Liam pleaded. "I hate this place. Let's move on. This one just sucks."

"What the hell is your problem?" Vach said. "The cops never come here."

"Do you know why the cops never come here?" Liam asked. "Because this place sucks, that's why."

"You're a pussy," Wall said. "No cops, no problems, end of discussion."

"Unless the place is a shit hole," Liam said.

"Shut up!" Vach admonished. "Here comes one now."

Indeed, he was right. From this vantage point in the shadows of the alley, Liam could see her coming; a fat purse, a bag of groceries, and an unsuspecting gait; a mouse in a trap.

That made him all the more nervous.

"Sweet and luscious," Vach drooled. "Come to daddy."

The fact that he wasn't talking about the purse or groceries turned Liam's stomach into knots.

"No, man," he said. "Grab and go. Let's get out of here."

"If you don't shut the fuck up, I'll shut you up," Wall said.

Liam had no doubt that he meant it.

When the quarry crossed in front of the alley, Vach and Wall jumped out to flank her. Liam reluctantly did his part. He'd have been in for beating if he let her escape, so he fell into place to complete the three-point trap.

The three took up positions behind, in front, and street side of the woman. The only way out was the alley itself and that was not an option. The young woman, whom Liam had to admit was lithe and youthful, stopped in her tracks. He could see the fear in her eyes, but not enough to suit his taste.

"Grab and go, man," Liam warned.

They wouldn't stop to shut him up in the middle of the score.

"No, I think we'll take this one nice and slow," Vach said, salivating."

"Yeah, this one's tasty." Wall reached his hand toward the woman with a disgusting version of tenderness.

Then he yanked it back like he'd just been stung by a bee.

"Ow!" he yelled. "Shit!"

"I told you this place sucks, man," Liam insisted. "Grab and go, man."

Wall walked over and punched Liam in the face with his good hand.

"I said shut the fuck up!" he screamed. "Now, come on," he called to Vach. Wall was now in a foul and violent mood.

"Let's get it on!"

He approached the woman, clearly intent on herding her into the darkness of the alleyway. Then he yelled again and recoiled from some unseen attack.

"Ow!" he yelled. "Fuck!"

23

This time he brought a hand up to the back of his neck and began rubbing. He pulled his hand away apparently checking for blood, but there was none.

"What the fuck is wrong with you?" Vach demanded.

"Something is stinging me!" Wall argued. "That's twice!"

"Bullshit," Vach said. "There's nothing here." With that, he heard a buzzing sound that seemed to come from all around. "What?" he said. "You hear that?"

"I told you, man," Liam protested, nursing his jaw.

"Shut up!" Vach and Wall screamed in unison.

"What?" Wall asked.

Then he began to hear it, too.

He looked around.

Nothing.

Granted, it was dark, but they could see one another just fine. If there were bees in the air, they should be able to see them too.

"C'mon, let's get the bitch inside," Vach said and started for the woman. "Ow!" He recoiled like he'd just been shot in the leg. "What the fuck?"

The buzz grew louder, filling the air with a thick threatening hum.

"Man, what the fuck is that?"

"This place is a shit hole!" Liam cried and started running.

"Man, get the fuck back here!" Wall demanded.

In a rage, he drew a pistol from the pocket of his jeans and pointed it in Liam's direction. That sting hit him three times on the wrist and hand and he dropped the weapon, wailing at the top of his lungs.

"Ow!" he screamed, and followed it up with a string of epithets.

Surgical

Having nothing on which to vent their anger, Vach and Wall glowered at the woman, who was clearly as confused and disoriented as they were, and bore down on her like a black tide.

"Man, I'm gonna…" Vach began.

He froze in his tracks when the hum in the air formed words. It was nothing like a human voice. It was too high-pitched and it didn't have the range a human voice would, but it started to stutter and skip. Words emerged from the droning sound, almost as if a swarm of bees had gotten organized and set the buzz of the swarm to trace out a message.

"Not too smart, are you?" the swarm said malevolently.

Vach and Wall looked at one another in terror before a swarm of stings hit them about the face and neck. To be fair, these latest stings had nothing of the intensity or stopping power of the previous attacks, but the psychological effect seemed to be devastating.

Vach and Wall ran screaming in opposite directions, repelled from the site of their would-be attack by terror and panic.

The woman stood slack-jawed in the middle of the sidewalk and gazed around, waiting for the malevolent force to descend on her.

"Sorry for the drama," the swarm murmured in an alien monotone whisper.

"What are you?" she asked.

"Hmm." The swarm gave an almost chuckle-like sound before it quieted and faded out.

A laser can burn human skin from hundreds of feet away. An infrared laser can do so without any visible trace. Since you can't see the source, there is no way of knowing where it's coming from.

Such a laser in pulse mode is even more formidable, but the danger of long-term effects is negligible. It's no greater a long-term threat than any burn or scald and does not have a propensity to increase the risk of melanoma.

Of course, you need to be careful to stay away from the eyes, but with the source mounted on a precision stage and a little clever face recognition software, that problem is easily avoided.

It's best to hit the skin, but it will burn through clothes easily. So, in the absence of having exposed skin, two closely spaced pulses, one to burn through the fabric and one to hit the target, are adequate to achieve the desired effect. A hit like that will almost always pull a mugger off a target.

Now, the stealth of such a weapon is a tremendous asset as a petty crime deterrent, but it can be limiting if the target is too dense or confused to get the message. And, of course, revealing yourself by saying 'Go away' kind of defeats the purpose of being stealthy in the first place.

That's when ultrasonics came in handy. Crossing two high-intensity ultrasonic beams can generate an audible sound at the intersection. The military has been using this technology as a non-destructive deterrent for some time, but some thugs are too thick to get the message, even if they're being stung by a laser and buzzed by an ultrasonic signal at the same time.

In such a case, modulating the ultrasonic beams to trace out a short message usually does the trick, and again, with that technology you can never tell where the sound is coming from so it can be pretty spooky.

The system works even better if you use software to trace a circle around the would-be victim. The computer can do all the work by simply zapping anything that moves across the virtual barrier.

Darren Kiel watched the confused but unharmed woman gather herself and continue on her way. With the night vision scope, he could see her clear as day from his perch atop one of the highest buildings in Bristol, England.

When he was satisfied her attackers were gone for good, he scanned the rest of the street, the entrances to alleyways, the nooks and crags of the inner city. He watched for movement in the shadows and kept a vigilant eye on any pedestrians who found it necessary to be out at this hour.

It was quiet for the moment. That was a good sign. It was also an indication that it might be time to find a new perch.

Darren began to pack up. He disassembled the rifle-like laser apparatus in small servo-drive motors and returned them to their form-fitting designated locations in the backpack-sized carrying case designed to accompany them. He stored the touch pad computer and tripod assembly in a second gym bag and left the roof quietly and inconspicuously.

The gear weighed close to one hundred pounds, but it was inconsequential to his primary piece of equipment: the exo-suit.

Darren's full body casement consisted of hundreds of thousands of micro joints, up to 1000 per square millimeter in some regions, each of which could bend and contort to any program he chose. In this case, Darren carried the one-hundred-pound burden of nonlethal sniper equipment about three steps, recorded the movement of those three steps for the exo-suit, and played back that program in a loop. The result was that the suit did all the work thereafter, mimicking Darren's original labor again and again. Darren, the driver, simply relaxed and let the form-fitting vehicle carry both him and the rest of the supplies to the stairs.

Once at the stairs, he did the same thing. He carried the burden a meager three steps then played back that program for the remainder of the descent to the street. With practice, it was only slightly more difficult than driving any other vehicle but with several distinct advantages; strength and speed being primary among them.

When Darren exited the building, he resumed the pre-programmed carry. He had meant to find a new perch and set up the equipment to police a new set of streets and alleyways, but he decided to stow the gear in a secure location and patrol on foot for the rest of the night. In this case, an abandoned and lockable chamber he discovered in an old city access tunnel below street level served nicely.

In addition to strength, speed, and the particularly convenient option to act as a pack mule, the suit had another distinctive feature. Each of the hundreds of thousands of addressable elements could be programmed to resist deformation. That is to say, if an enemy decided to hit Darren in the back of the head with a baseball bat when he wasn't expecting it, the suit would sense the impact, the deformation of the elements comprising the suit, and respond. The effect would be to instantly form a rigid shell along the head, neck, and back, protecting Darren from any injury and, in most cases, even awareness that the attack had happened. The specification of the movements that the suit would *not* allow was in the end its most lifesaving feature. It could stiffen, steel, and brace itself so quickly and with such force that it could shrug off a wide range of weapons, knives, and bullets, even high caliber or Teflon-coated rounds.

Although he was not invulnerable, the safeguards the exo-suit provided enabled Darren to address urban crime more directly and effectively than any other means he could contrive and still not have the work constitute a suicide mission.

It was with these tools that Darren had been patrolling the corners and back neighborhoods of Bristol and South Wales the last several weeks. Intelligence reports he'd been able to hack had shown an increase in Albanian gang activity over the last several months. Of course, it didn't matter if it was an Albanian gang or a group of rabid chipmunks; all Darren cared about was that the instances of robbery, rape, homicide, and most forms of violent crime had risen out of the base noise level. That meant it was a good time and a good place for him to visit.

The good news was it was working. That one thug who had said 'this place sucks' had done so for a very good reason. Darren thought he'd seen him before. His name was Liam and he had good reason to stay away from this set of city blocks.

He'd never seen the laser trick but he had enough reason to believe that this place sucked, at least for him; at least if he had any intention of hurting anyone. His friends probably felt the same way now. Thick though they were, they would probably think twice about coming around, and that's what it was all about: countermeasures and deterrents.

The best way to do this was sting and move. If crime started picking up, provide some countermeasures. If it moved to a different place, follow the activity and apply the countermeasures there. Stamp it out where it starts to bulge. Sure, it will rise again, but it takes time. It's not instantaneous, but by slapping down the outliers, by making it just a little less comfortable for crime to rise, the effects are substantial.

Keep the average as low as possible. Don't try to drive it to zero in any one area. Just keep the average as low as possible. It's not ideal, but it's sufficient.

As Darren walked down the street, he held to the shadows. He checked the usual haunts. He even strafed some of the particular stores that had been favorites for the thugs before he got here. One store owner got a glimpse of him before he ducked away, but it was quiet.

Quiet enough.

It was time to move on.

There was one section in Vilnius, Lithuania, that had been bringing the average up recently.

That would work.

CHAPTER
3

The store was in great shape. The windows were intact. The sidewalk in front looked like it had been scrubbed recently. Even the paint didn't seem too old, chipped, or defiled. There was a bench under the front window and fresh flowers grew in a wooden barrel next to it. It almost seemed like a serene little park.

Unfortunately, these were all bad signs.

If she had been stepping over broken glass or the storefront had been boarded up and full of graffiti, she'd have liked it better.

As it was, this didn't bode well.

She pushed the door open and heard the tiny bell announce her. She glanced around the well-lit store and scanned the fully stocked shelves for signs of disorder.

She found none.

She was too late.

Damn it, she thought.

Faye Skarsiksaan walked over to the elderly man smiling behind the cashier's counter. She looked him in the eye. He looked right back at her, steady and cheerful. It was another sign that she had failed.

"Hi," she said.

"Welcome," the man said. "Can I help you find something?"

She smiled at that one.

"Perhaps," she said. "How's business been lately?"

"Oh, pretty good," the old man said. "I can't complain."

"Better than a few weeks ago?" she asked.

The man darkened slightly. "You might say that," he said with a hint of suspicion.

She nodded. "Yes," she said. "Maybe you can help me find something."

The man brightened again.

"My name is Faye. I'm new in the area, but I'm looking for someone," she said. "He has an affinity for neighborhoods like this and he frequents stores like yours."

"Petruccio," the man smiled. "I've been here a long time and I know pretty much everyone who frequents this neighborhood. Do you have a picture? I could tell you if he works here or if I've seen him."

"A picture probably wouldn't tell you much," she said, "but I think you might know him. He has a tendency to make an impression. He usually wears a light full-length coat and a brown rain hat with a six-inch brim. He doesn't often let people see his face."

Petruccio's eyes shot open.

"*That* guy?" He beamed. "You're looking for *that* guy?"

She couldn't keep the grin off her face in the presence of his childlike response.

"Ma'am, a lot of people are looking for that guy," he said. "Both the good kind and the bad kind."

"Yes," she said. "Like I said, he does have a tendency to make an impression."

"Have I seen him? Yes," he said. "Can I help you find him? No. If you know him as you say you do, you know he doesn't seem to stick around very long. No one I know has ever even spoken with him."

Faye looked away, discouraged.

"What's your interest in him?" Petruccio asked.

"We have a mutual friend that needs, shall we say, his kind of help," she said.

"Ma'am, a lot of people need his kind of help," the man said.

"Yes," she said thoughtfully. "May I ask when you saw him last?"

"It might be a week since I've heard of him helping anyone around here," Petruccio said. "That's the longest it's been since he started a month or so ago. We were getting used to having him around. Well, some of us anyway." He gestured to the adjacent stores. "Listen, you know him, will he be coming back?"

"Has crime dropped substantially since he's been around?" she asked.

"Yes," the man said confidently.

"Then he probably won't be coming back," she said.

Petruccio looked crestfallen.

"I'm sorry," she said, "but he seems to move on to the next place once he's made an impact."

He nodded.

"I don't suppose you have any more information?" Faye asked.

"I'll be honest with you," Petruccio said. "As you said, a lot of people would like to find him, and many for the worst possible reason. I have no way of knowing which side of the fence you come down on, so even if I could help you find him, I probably wouldn't. You understand."

"I do," she said.

He nodded gratefully.

"Can I leave you my card?" she asked. "On the off chance that you do see him again, would there be any harm in letting him know I'd like to speak to him?"

"You said yourself he won't be coming back," he said. "Even if he did, it's not like I've ever gotten close enough to even hand him a card. He just disappears."

She shrugged. "A girl can always hope," she said.

"He's good at that, isn't he?" Petruccio said. "Hope, I mean."

"So I hear," she said as she handed him a business card. "Thank you for your time, and good luck with the store."

Petruccio watched as she turned her back to him and walked toward the door. Her coat had a strange set of features on the back. It looked like there were zippers on each side of her spine, like if she opened them she might have wings that would deploy through the back of the coat. He didn't have time to get a better look before she opened the door, the tiny bell announced her exit, and the portal closed behind her.

When she'd gone, he glanced down at the card she'd left. It had a single name on it, no last name, no company name, no address, no embellishment.

In the middle of the card, it simply read 'Walter.'

***

Faye exited the store and turned left. She quickened her pace, accelerating to a brisk walk away from the store and Petruccio in particular.

It was coming.

This latest failure had triggered it and it was coming for her now with a terrifying pace, an inescapable blackness gathered in her chest and throat and began to grow.

She would have stopped on the bench in front of the store to catch her breath and compose herself, but she couldn't stand the thought of Petruccio, or anyone else, seeing her cry, so she fled. Thank God the street wasn't crowded with people, choked with throngs of milling pedestrians. That would have boxed her in and smothered her. She would have been buried alive. The very thought pushed her further toward the darkness and fed the creeping panic inching up her spine and crawling down her limbs.

It hadn't always been this way.

There was a time when nothing in the world would have made Faye Skarsiksaan run scared.

Quite the opposite.

There was a time when the world would have run scared from her.

Two years ago, after five years as one of very few female Navy combat operatives, Faye had earned a reputation even her staunchest and most bigoted critics had to respect. She'd had dozens of operations, on land, sea, and in the air. The last two years of her enlistment, she'd commanded the missions and left both her allies' and adversaries' heads spinning with her focus, precision, and iron will.

At that time, they all wondered how she did it. How she managed to be so stone-cold unflappable. They all marveled at the way that seemingly nothing got her off her pins.

They didn't know her secret.

Ian was six months old when Faye took her first op, and she just couldn't believe how such a perfect, precious miracle of a living thing could turn her into such a savage lioness. It wasn't something she thought about, just something that was.

After Ian was born, Faye's life had only two defining parameters: making the world a better place for him and getting back to him when it was done. She would have moved heaven and earth to make those two things happen. That was why she was so fierce. That was why she was so cold, so tenacious, so uncompromisingly resolute: Ian.

Two years ago that had all changed. One phone call, one single moment, and everything had changed. In an instant God cut her soul right in half. It was a car accident and subsequent fire, both Ian and her husband Justin. They had to identify the bodies from dental records. She didn't have a chance to say goodbye. She didn't even have a chance to see the bodies. In that moment, the woman Faye had been ceased to exist. She was hospitalized for psychiatric reasons. She spent the next six months existing and wishing she didn't.

Faye's combat days ended with Ian's death, but the Navy doctors and brass were set upon helping Faye recover her life. They tried assigning her as an instructor, but it was a disaster. She was erratic and would fly into a rage one minute and a sobbing fit the next. The Navy quickly concluded that any position dealing directly with people was not going to work. They tried assigning her to a facilities management position, but the isolation exacerbated the depression. Luckily, the doctors were able to see the precursors to suicide and pull her out.

More out of desperation than anything else, the Navy decided they would try R&D. They ordered Faye to audit and inventory the research activities of one of their private contractors. They were a bit surprised when one of the board members, Walter Rocaena, suggested he assist Faye in person. That was more than a bit unusual, but if it meant Faye would get some extra attention and help to ensure her success, they were all for it.

Surgical

When the day of her first audit came, Mr. Rocaena greeted her in the lobby himself.

"Miss Skarsiksaan," Walter said with a smile and offered his hand.

"Mr. Rocaena," Faye responded. She held out her arm. Her hand dangled at the end of it. The shake made her hand feel like a limp fish.

"Walter, please," he said.

Faye mustered a weak smile but didn't look at his face.

"I appreciate your coming," Walter said. "I'd like to make this as interesting for you as possible. I know it may seem a little dry, auditing our engineering and design processes, but I'm hoping you'll find some value in it."

"I'm looking forward to it," Faye lied. "You're doing some critical work for our department and we're curious to get your status updates."

She was parroting word-for-word. They had coached her for this meeting. She knew what she had to do and she knew the words she had to spit out at each step. A tape recorder could do this job, but it was better than reading dials on a boiler.

Walter led her down a long corridor with glass walls on both sides. On the other side of the glass, there were demo bays for various projects including guns of various designs, corner shot weapons, smart bullets and armor piercing projectiles.

"This is the tactical section," Walter said, pointing to the various bays. "These are mostly our offensive projects. Down that way, we have defensive, ablative armor and that sort of thing."

He continued to usher her through the building.

"Down that way," Walter continued, "we have intelligence and transmission wearable tech. and that sort of thing. In the next building, we have aeronautics and guidance..."

As Walter continued, Faye began to wane. They were half an hour into the day and she could barely take any more. She was barely managing to keep her composure when Walter, quite suddenly, handed her a bottle of water.

She grabbed the bottle, shakily twisted off the cap, and gulped it down. When she pulled it away, the bottle was completely empty. She tried to fit the cap back on but she couldn't manage it.

Before it got embarrassing, Walter pointed her to a recycling bin and Faye threw the cap and bottle in.

"Actually, never mind all that," Walter said. "How about advanced Ian D.?"

Faye spun on her heel.

"What?" she demanded.

"Advanced R&D," Walter said nonchalantly, even though he had clearly not said that the first time. "Right this way, please."

Faye was still processing her confusion and contemplating calling Walter out for using her son's name when they stopped at a secure door. Walter put his hand on a biometric pad. "Walter Rocaena," he said in a distinct voice.

The door sounded a click and Walter pushed the portal open. "Please," he said as he ushered her in. "Miss Skarsiksaan, what if you could disappear?" Walter asked bluntly.

"What?" Faye asked, still off balance.

"What if you could be right there, hearing everything, seeing everything, reading every nuance and every gesture, every hint in everyone's body language? What if you could be physically present, but all of that information only went one way? As a field operative, you know the value of stealth, the advantage of surprise," Walter said. "What if you could gather intelligence unseen and unheard, and I don't mean remote surveillance. That's never perfect. I mean on the ground, but invisible, undetectable, impervious to the world's perception?"

Faye felt like she'd been walking through the desert for six months and now someone was dangling a glass of water in front of her.

"How?"

"We're working on two separate technologies," Walter began. "Over here is the audio portion." He pointed to what looked like a very large silver cube, about six feet on each side, in the middle of the otherwise pristine research lab. A man in a lab coat was just stepping out of the cube through a large door on one side.

"Ah," Walter said. "Ben?" Walter waved him over and the man approached.

"This is Faye Skarsiksaan," Walter said. "She's a contract auditor from our friends at the naval office."

"Good to meet you," Faye said with a genuine smile and a stronger handshake.

A wisp of a smile flashed across Walter's face but passed quickly.

"Good to meet you, Miss Skarisksaan," Ben said.

"Ben, would you mind sharing a little demo?" Walter said.

"Of course," Ben said.

The three walked over to the cube and Ben entered, leaving the other two outside. Then Ben took a long, deep breath and started singing. Well, that wasn't quite accurate. He let out a loud, high-pitched note, not quite screaming but not quite singing. From the deep breath, it was clear he was going to hold the note as long as possible. Then Walter closed the door with a thump and the room outside went completely silent.

It was completely silent!

There was no one else in the lab and, now that she thought about it, no incessant hum of cooling fans, no click of electronics, not even the background noise of the building's air conditioning. She could have heard a pin drop, but she couldn't hear Ben singing his note. She moved closer to the door. Not a hint, not even a whisper. She reached over and opened the door. The single note chorus poured out of the cube and almost knocked her over.

She closed the door again... Silence.

She listened closely... Nothing.

She could hear her own breathing, but not the slightest hint from the cube. Walter reached over and opened the door. The note came rushing out again, but Ben was just about turning blue.

"OK," Walter said.

Ben stopped singing and took a deep, much-needed gasp of air. After Ben had caught his breath, Walter pointed to the shelf inside the cube.

"Do you still have the whistle?" Walter asked.

Ben nodded and reached for a large brass whistle. "Ready?" he asked.

Walter pushed Faye back a few feet and nodded. Just for a second, they heard the loudest thing she ever heard. The whistle just about blasted straight through her ear drum before Walter closed the door.

Again... Silence; deep, penetrating silence.

Indeed, Walter had the only word that could describe it: impervious.

Walter opened the door. The whistle blasted out for just an instant before Ben cut the sound and spared them all the painful side of the demonstration.

Walter gave a nod and said, "Thanks, Ben," before he led Faye toward the next research bay.

Faye lagged and looked back at the box, then back to Walter. "How?" she said.

Walter smiled.

"Don't think it's easy," Walter said. "The materials are critical, but there's also an electronic feedback component to getting it that good. We're getting better at this all the time. People like to say there is no sound in space."

Faye nodded.

"Our techs like to say space is loud."

Faye laughed. It was a sound she herself hadn't heard in over a year.

"That's not the hard part though," Walter said and brought her to the next bay. "Visual," Walter said. "Yeah, that's the hard part."

CHAPTER
4

There were several techs in the next bay. Walter and Faye entered quietly so as not to disturb them. The techs all seemed to be milling around the central area surrounding... well, nothing. There were five of them and they formed a circle around ten feet in diameter. They were facing each other, studying something in the center of the lab that didn't exist. They cocked their heads and shifted their weight like a bunch of museum patrons studying a work of art, but there was nothing there.

Faye watched them as they contemplated the ether under bright light.

When the door closed behind Walter, all heads snapped in her direction and there was a palpable recoil. Faye got the impression that they would have immediately pounced on her and ushered her out but they hit a wall before they could act.

That wall was Walter.

Faye knew she was in a high-security area. She'd been given a map of the facility before she started the audit. Strictly speaking, she was not supposed to be here. This was a routine audit. She didn't have the clearance for this level. She was seeing things she shouldn't be seeing. One of the techs even had the stones to call Walter on it.

He looked at Faye and back to Walter with grave concern. "Sir?" he began.

"Noted," Walter replied. "I'm not stopping you."

The tech hesitated for a moment then gathered himself and made a beeline for the exit. Faye looked at Walter. Walter waved his hand in a gesture that told her not to worry about it then he directed her attention back to the research group.

The group seemed frozen.

"He's done his job," Walter announced. "Carry on."

Faye watched them for several minutes as they contemplated the ether under bright light. There was a stinging aura of discomfort about them but they soldiered on.

"Not bad; I've got three or four," one of them said.

"Yeah, I've got about the same," another said.

"Jones?" the farthest one asked.

One of the techs, apparently Jones, stepped back about five paces then approached the ghost again. He stepped back a second time and move forward toward it.

"Yeah, I think we're good on the primary axis," Jones concluded. "OK, Farrouk," Jones said, apparently to the ether, "let's try the next term."

Then a seam opened in midair and disgorged a sixth research tech. Just in that second, Faye could see the elusive shape the techs had been studying. There was something in the central area but by some miraculous trick of technology it was functionally invisible. Faye simply could not believe her eyes. She orbited the central area like the techs had been doing, but she couldn't see a thing.

She looked at Walter, held out her palm toward the ghost, and cocked her head.

Walter nodded.

As the techs groused and fidgeted on the sidelines, one of them even checked his watch, Faye stepped forward and slowly moved her hand in the direction of the object. Nothing, nothing, then, yes, there was something there, something giving resistance in midair. She still couldn't see it but there was definitely a physical object there, like a soft cloth.

Faye pulled her hand back and marveled at it.

"Would you like to take it for a spin, Miss Skarsiksaan?" Walter asked.

Faye couldn't have heard that right.

The techs looked at Walter like he'd just set the lab on fire.

One of them started to speak, but Walter interrupted him.

"It's meant to be mobile and it's meant to be used," Walter said to the tech then he looked back at Faye. "Would you like to try it?"

That glass of water dangled in front of her again, only this time it had ice cubes in it.

Faye looked at the techs.

They could barely contain their rage at the suggestion.

Faye felt something stir in her belly and at the same time something tightened in her throat. She nodded to Walter and Walter beckoned her to continue. Faye put both hands on the object and felt along the surface until she felt a discontinuity, the seam. She gently moved her fingers into the seam and pulled back. The object opened a fissure in midair. Faye kept pulling until it was large enough for her to enter.

Then she stepped in.

In that instant, Faye Skarsiksaan ceased to exist.

It was nothing like what she anticipated.

For some reason, she expected it be pitch black inside. How could it not be? Clearly the device was emitting as much light as it gathered. In fact, it had to be putting out as much light as was hitting it. Every photon that hit the back of the device must, by definition, be emitted from the front. There's no other way it could appear invisible. In such a case, there must be no light left to illuminate the interior; ergo, the interior must be pitch black.

But it wasn't.

It was absolutely luminous. Faye could see, clear as day right through the cloak, every square inch of the lab. In fact, it was better lit inside the cloak than outside. She could see things that she hadn't even noticed before she entered the sanctum of privacy. It took her a number of minutes to figure out that the device could generate more light than it intercepted. It could generate two images at once; one to transmit to the other side to simulate invisibility, and another to display on the inside. It could even amplify the light for the viewer inside.

There was a harness attached to a rack in the center space. The cloak was attached to the harness like an umbrella might be attached to a backpack. It suspended the cloak over the wearer, leaving the person's hands free. Faye looked at the harness reverently. She hesitated desecrating the device with her touch, but remembered Walter's words, "It's meant to be mobile and it's meant to be used."

Faye stepped forward, laced her arms through the harness, and buckled it on. She lifted the harness and the cloak from the rack and stepped forward. The cloak followed her like some high-tech divine halo. Whatever material they used was silent as a mouse, no rustling, no friction.

As she moved off the center podium, Faye noticed that the techs were looking at the place she had been, not where she was. She kept moving toward the door, right past the lab techs, and still they didn't notice. She suspected they didn't know the cloak was gone at all. Walter was tapping his phone like he was sending a text to someone.

At that moment, the lab door opened and two agitated men entered, one of them was the lab tech who had questioned Walter and exited the lab a few moments ago. The other wore the uniform of a security guard. They marched toward Walter as if they were about to arrest him for high treason.

Walter seemed unfazed.

Faye stepped right past both of them and made it through the door before it slid to a close. Now she was back in the audio lab, but who would even have known? She saw Ben sitting at his station but he didn't acknowledge her. Faye looked at the large silver audio chamber and drifted in that direction. Ben's phone chimed and he moved to pick it up. At that moment, Faye decided to risk opening the chamber door. She hoped Ben was distracted enough that he wouldn't notice.

This was a thorny problem.

They had gotten it almost perfect, but there were a few micro decibels that kept annoying him. Granted that was orders of magnitude below anything smaller than a large dish collector could detect, but they were still a factor of two off the theoretical limit and that was just annoying.

Ben was pulled away from his calculations when his phone beeped the signal for a text message. He picked it up. It was from Walter, presumably next door. It said, "let her be." Ben didn't know what that meant until the door to the isolation chamber closed with a barely audible thud.

Someone unauthorized had stepped inside.

Ben's first impulse was to race over and see who had slipped by him, but then he looked at the test message again.

He had his instructions.

Inside the isolation chamber, unseen, unheard, at last gone from the world altogether, Faye finally imploded like a dying star.

She dropped to her knees and screamed out all the pain and anguish that had lived bottled up inside her from the instant she had gotten that phone call months ago. The agony poured out of her like a faucet; every moment she'd shared with Ian and Justin flashed through her field of vision as she relived every moment of joy and pain she'd felt with them for the past six years.

Just now, just here, just when no one could see and no one could judge, when no one could touch her and no one could make a pathetic attempt to console her, here she reached out to what didn't exist anymore, because neither did she. As far as the world was concerned, she didn't exist at all.

Just here, just now, she could love. She could hate. She could scream.

She could heal.

Here in her cocoon away from the world, Faye began her rebirth.

It took a long time.

She was in no hurry.

At long last, she drew a breath through her throat that was sore and raw from crying. She managed to bring her exhausted, still-cloaked body to its feet and reach for the door to the isolation chamber. She hesitated for a moment, reflecting on who might see her exit, but then realized she didn't care. She opened the door, stepped out, and looked around.

The lab was empty.

Just luck.

Faye walked back toward the cloaking lab. She hoped Walter was still there because he was going to give her a job, even if he didn't know it yet, even if she had to kill him with her bare hands to convince him.

Faye had a solution here. She was not going to let it go.

Keith Norte, the security guard in the R&D wing, was furious and he'd been that way for... he checked his watch... far too long. The cloaking lab was one of the most sensitive areas in the complex. No one, not even a member of the board of directors, not even the chairman, was permitted to bring anyone in the cloaking lab without clearance, and that certainly included a low-level auditor.

They had drilled this into him from day one. It was infuriating to be sitting here waiting after a security breach of this magnitude.

As bad as that was, Mr. Rocaena was even more so.

"She's an invisible woman," he said. "How is searching going to locate her?"

So they waited, with nothing but Rocaena's advice and assurance that she'd come back; with nothing but his opinion that this was the best strategy.

Keith checked his watch again. "I'm going to call it in," he announced finally.

"Just give it another five minutes," Rocaena said. "If we don't resolve it to your satisfaction, you can drag me in with those." He gestured to the handcuffs on Keith's belt. "Surely that would make a good enough show to satisfy protocol."

Keith nodded and checked his watch. Either way this was going to be a satisfying five minutes.

At about the three-minute mark, the door to the cloaking lab opened of its own accord. It slid closed again just as independently. Keith checked his watch. At the four-minute mark, a woman appeared out of thin air on the cloaking platform. He recognized her as the auditor from this morning, although she looked exhausted and her face was red and wet, apparently from crying.

There was a fierce, piercing intensity in her eyes that he hadn't noticed earlier... and he would have if it had been there.

The woman stepped off the platform in what could only be described as an initial preparation for a charge at Rocaena.

Rocaena didn't flinch, but froze both her and Keith in their tracks with a single sentence.

"Mr. Norte, I'd like you to meet our new advanced stealth operative, Miss Faye Skarsiksaan."

It didn't take long for Faye to realize it was no accident. Walter had orchestrated it. He had done his homework. He had researched her and he knew this would fix her. She didn't know what in her psych profile or history had told Walter this would work, that this would make her whole again, but she didn't care.

She only knew that it had worked. It gave her some place to go, some place where she felt safe, some sanctuary.

It healed her, at least partially.

She never did thank him, not in words anyway. That would have been irrelevant. She thanked him by giving him his side of the bargain: the most devastating stealth operative imaginable. She never did anything illegal; well, not too illegal anyway. She wouldn't hurt or kill anyone who didn't deserve it, and he never asked her to. What he did ask her, more often than not, was to help other people.

Sure Walter always had his angle, his agenda, but she couldn't have cared less. He would point her like a gun and pull the trigger, and she would fire. She would execute the operation with fearful precision. Darren's girlfriend was a good example. At the time, she didn't know who either she or Darren was and it didn't matter.

Walter said fetch.

She fetched.

What exactly could have been the downside? Help a woman in the clutches of a drug-running street gang? Yeah, Faye had no problem with that.

She did have one condition; well, an ardent request. She wanted to keep the cloak. Ordinarily, Walter would have had her return it to the lab after each operation. Faye promised she would not use it for her own purposes. She would not use it at all outside her own residence. She would not abuse it. She told Walter it was for practice, so that she could become more versed in using it. There was some truth to that. There was considerable skill involved in being able to 'drive' the cloak, to maintain silence and invisibility. The more she practiced with it, the more skillful and efficient she became, but that wasn't the reason.

She needed to keep it.

Most of the time she just sat in her room under the cloak, silent, invisible, gone from the world. It was almost like sleeping for most people. When she was cloaked, she felt renewed, restored. It brought her strength back. It brought her power back. It got to the point that she spent more time in the cloak than out. The doctors would have said it was unhealthy, that she should try to spend more time in the real world rather than escaping it.

What the hell did they know?

She had tried so many other ways to combat her depression, her illness. Sodium valproate was one of the first things the doctors had tried. It made a dent, but it didn't cure her. The pharmacologists had tried plenty of cocktails over the stretch of months since the event. Either they didn't work at all or the side effects were unbearable.

This worked.

This healed her and was physically innocuous. It wouldn't make her hair fall out or give her cancer or drive her insane. It was just quiet, a meditative solution. It was no more harmful to her body than taking a nap.

What she didn't talk about, what she didn't think about, was why.

The simple fact was that she felt closer to Ian and Justin when she was invisible. She felt closer to them when she was farther from the world and she could hardly get any farther than when she was gone.

She never claimed she was perfect.

She claimed she was functional, and she was.

She could do Walter's ops. She could free a hostage. She could gather intel. She could infiltrate the lion's den when required. She could even play errand girl and go to Europe to find one of Walter's assets, but she never said she was perfect.

Every now and then it came after her, usually when she hadn't been cloaked in a while or there was nowhere to go to disappear, or if, God forbid, she was physically separate from it.

That's when she would get one of the panic attacks.

That was what came for her when she left Petruccio's store.

***

This one had stepped outside his radius. There was a pretty clear dividing line between where that guy operated and the areas that were beyond his reach, and she had crossed it. It was unlikely that, if he snatched her purse, that pain in the ass pseudo-cop would appear out of nowhere and make him regret it.

The funny thing was she seemed to be coming right at him.

She had turned off the main drag and walked right into the alleyway he was using tonight, like a rat walking right into a snake's den.

All the easier for me, he thought.

He shifted his weight quietly and readied himself for the sprint, just like a snake coiling for a strike. The woman stopped and glanced around. She seemed to be checking if anyone was watching, but she didn't notice him crouching in the shadows in the back of the alley.

Better and better. He smiled.

Then it got really weird.

She took off her overcoat, unzipped two compartments on the back, turned it inside out, and slung it onto her back like a pack. The straps deployed from the zipper compartments of the coat to secure it in that odd arrangement.

Then the weird went right off the charts.

The lining of the coat, now on the outside, peeled into several petal-like sections. The petals reached out and swallowed the woman whole, the way a waning flower might engulf a stamen.

Then the entire grouping vanished like a puff of dissipating smoke.

One second the easy target was right in front of him. The next, she faded out right in front of his eyes and the alley was empty.

What the f...? He rushed out of his hiding place to try to catch the woman, wherever she'd gone, but found absolutely nothing, no target, no purse, no trace, nothing.

He had begun to suspect that he was seeing things when an all-too-familiar jolt hit him from right out of nowhere. Several thousand volts scrambled every nerve impulse in his body and he hit the ground twitching and convulsing uncontrollably.

Just before he lost consciousness, he heard a female voice materialize out of thin air and descend on him like a blanket.
"That'll teach you to watch a woman while she's getting changed."

Then everything went black.

***

Better, Faye thought.

Once cloaked, her pulse began to slow and her breathing returned to normal. She took a deep breath and found her center.

She was home now, like a ghost or a soft breeze, passing through neighborhoods undetected, walking right by people without them even knowing she was there, listening, watching, just a breath away: her god-state.

Besides, walking the streets at night in an area he'd been patrolling was fine, but there was no reason to invite trouble once she'd stepped out of his radius. Not that she couldn't handle herself if one of these punks tried something, cloak or not, Taser or not, but there was no reason to court trouble when it could be so easily avoided in stealth mode.

Now, back to business.

Clearly he had moved on, and that was bad news. Her only consolation was that she knew where he was going, even if he didn't. The problem was she didn't know how long it would take him to figure that out, and time was not on her side.

CHAPTER
5

Driving took two days. Unfortunately, it was the only practical method of getting around. Flying was not an option. Even if he could smuggle the suit and other equipment on the plane, which was virtually impossible, he didn't like advertising his movements across the continent. Any plane ride would necessitate a pretty careful check of his passport, and that was something he'd just as soon avoid. Trains were an option, at least through much of Europe, but they weren't much faster and suffered from some of the same disadvantages. It was hard to smuggle equipment on and off the train, even if carrying it wasn't a problem, which it was.

No, driving was the best option. It afforded the greatest stealth and agility so he endured the inconvenience. Of course, having a trunk full of his 'accessories' wasn't going to make any border crossing easier, so he had modified his cars. There was at least one at every one of his hubs, with compartments to hide his accoutrements.

Surgical

It was electronic machinery, after all; not drugs, guns, or some other obvious contraband. The fact is they just weren't looking for what he was carrying. It wasn't hard to make the equipment look like part of the car and the suit didn't look much different than a set of ordinary motorcycle gear. It worked well enough; at least once he got settled into it.

Setting up the entire operation was something different. Some of the equipment, like the lasers and ultrasonic arrays, were pretty specialized components. Most countries didn't like importing and exporting technology at that level and the equipment he used to make and maintain the suit was handmade, so it wouldn't do to have to ship it around and risk losing it or damaging it.

The solution ended up being pretty obvious: he kept fully equipped workshops all over Europe, so one was always within striking distance. He traveled with a standard set of supplies, but he had the development and backup systems in a handful of major cities: London, Paris, Berlin, Rome, Stockholm, Vilnius, and Bucharest. He even had smaller versions in Madrid and Stockholm, but he found he spent less time there. Yes, there was some capital investment and it wasn't trivial to get all the stores required to equip each location, but once complete, the multi-based approach allowed him to operate as efficiently as possible. He could change cities and operating locations in a matter of hours while barely missing a beat. He had even started keeping apartments in secondary locations: Berne, Prague, Sarajevo and Athens, so he could move as quickly and freely as possible. It took over a year to set up and he had only really been hitting his stride for about six months now.

Vilnius never was all that convenient, ordinarily he might have chosen Warsaw or even Minsk, but Lithuania stubbornly bore one of the highest crime rates in Europe. That drew him eastward and made Vilnius the better choice.

Unfortunately, he'd been spending a bit of time there; enough that there was a new toy he wanted to try out.

***

"Gimme some."

The voice came from the left as they passed, but seemed to be directed at no one, like someone was talking in their sleep. That made it even worse.

There was a desperation in the voice, a craving Thomas found frightening, even more frightening than the near absolute blackness of the abandoned warehouse along the backstreets of Vilnius. He had been in this neighborhood before, but never this deep, and never by his choosing. It was the other three, Aldus, Jon, and Phaed. They kept coming here and he reluctantly came along. First, it had been the softer stuff, marijuana, ecstasy, rufees, but lately they had been going further, cocaine, crack, even crystal meth.

It was getting worse.

They were getting worse.

It wasn't just the drugs. It was them. They were meaner, angrier. They would punch him. They would insult him. They had started to mock him for not doing the drugs with them. First it had just been an offhanded comment, a little joke, a little jibe, but they seemed to be getting more serious now, more contemptuous of his choices. He had stopped protesting their desire to come here, to go further, to court danger. It only earned him their scorn and he didn't need any more of that.

When they first entered, Thomas couldn't see anything. He couldn't even see his own hand in front of his face, but as his eyes began to adjust, he could see the shapes moving in the darkness. He could see his companions, but there were others, large forms rolling in the corners among the garbage, small forms skittering between them.

An occasional blowing pipe pierced the blackness in the distance. The group made their way toward this spooky orange beacon.

Let's just get this over with, Thomas thought. *Let them get what they want then we'll get out of here.*

They continued into the bowels of this hell another hundred feet or so until Phaed finally called for someone.

"Booth?" he said quietly.

"Here," came a gravelly voice from the right.

Phaed reached into his pocket. "I have it," he said.

"Let's see," Booth demanded.

Phaed pulled a roll of bills from his pocket. Thomas didn't even want to think about where he had gotten it.

Booth held up a vial that Thomas recognized as heroin.

Jesus Christ! Thomas made the terrible mistake of letting out an audible gasp.

Booth looked at him. That was the last thing Thomas would have wanted.

"Who's the fish?" Booth asked, showing too much interest.

"No one," Phaed said. "C'mon, here, let's have it."

"Sure, whatever," Booth said.

He exchanged the bottle for Phaed's roll of bills and they turned to go.

"Don't you want to try it?" Booth asked.

"What?" Phaed said.

"Usually people try it first," Booth said. "I figured that's why you brought your friend there."

Phaed looked at Thomas then back to Booth. "Is there a problem with it?" Phaed asked.

"That's what people usually try it for," Booth said, flashing the devil's own grin at Thomas.

A bitter taste hit Thomas in the mouth just as cold sweat came to his hands. His eyes darted from Booth to Phaed to Aldus to Jon. Suddenly every one of them was wearing the same terrifying grin.

Then Thomas made his third and quite possibly final mistake of the night.

He ran.

He didn't make it far. Even as he turned, he ran smack into an enormous wall of muscle; one of Booth's friends, who had clearly done this sort of thing before. The wall of muscle pushed Thomas with an arm that felt like a tree trunk and Thomas fell onto his back.

Instantly he was surrounded. Aldus, Phaed, Jon, and the wall of flesh and bone held his arms and legs to the floor. Phaed rolled up the right sleeve of Thomas's shirt, covered his eyes, and held his head down. Thomas screamed and yelled, but it only seemed to make things worse.

"Here you go." He heard Booth laugh and draw closer.

Thomas couldn't see the needle, but he knew it was coming.

Then it happened.

Thomas saw a flash. Actually, it was a series of flashes, like someone had set off a hundred incredibly bright firecrackers in just a fraction of a second, but there was no sound. He would figure out later that it was actually white light, but so bright that it came right through the hand covering his eyes.

Everyone screamed: Phaed, Aldus, Jon, even Booth and his enforcer. The big one who had Thomas's legs pinned grunted and loosened his grip. Thomas didn't wait to figure out what had happened. He pulled his legs up and kicked with all his might. His feet came into contact with something solid that gave way just enough to fall like a giant sequoia and crash into an unidentified piece of furniture further back.

The group was still huddled around Thomas's torso, but they had loosened their grip as well. Thomas could tell they were looking around for the source of the disturbance, and not focusing on him.

Then the flash came again, a rapid-fire attack of light. The group yelled louder this time.

"Ow!" Phaed complained. "Shit! I can't see shit!"

Thomas yanked his arms away from whoever was holding them, pulled Phaed's hand away from his face, pulled his legs up again, and kicked Phaed full in the face. The hit was perfect. He nearly took Phaed's head off and sent him reeling back away from the pack.

Thomas scrambled to his feet. He could still see adequately in the darkness of the fetid warehouse, but apparently he was the only one. Everyone else was stumbling around like they were blind as bats; Aldus, Jon, and Booth most of all. Thomas's rage somehow eclipsed his fear and loathing just long enough for him to haul off and smash Aldus in the face with every iota of his strength.

He was pretty sure he broke Aldus's jaw in the process. Unfortunately, he did a pretty good job on his hand as well, but Thomas wouldn't figure that out until the next morning. For the moment, adrenaline washed away his pain.

He wasn't done yet.

Thomas walked up to Jon, dodged, and evaded Jon's fumbling, blind man's grasp. He waited for the right moment then kicked Jon in the groin with all his might.

John collapsed in a heap, writhing in agony.

With that, Thomas ran for the exit as fast as his legs, and barely adequate sight, could carry him. He ran out of the warehouse, away from the surrounding block, out of the neighborhood, and out of the lives of Phaed, Aldus, and Jon permanently.

He never saw any of them ever again.

From the rooftop, Darren watched a youth dart out of the warehouse like a high-velocity bullet out of a gun.

That was strange. They never got out that fast. This one must have had his eyes shielded when the flashes hit. Usually it took several minutes to clear the building, often much longer. Getting hit with that many lumens when your eyes have adjusted to darkness robs you of your night vision for a while, often even hours. If you get hit just right, a magnesium flash can cause snow blindness that lasts for days.

It really didn't matter; minutes, hours, or days, the occupants always stumbled out of the nest in a stupor. It was a good way to clear these reeking dens at least for a while, at least for the night. Just rouse them out of the cave and it's one more thing pushing the crime rate down.

Darren had already hit five of these with his new toy tonight. It seemed to be working pretty well, and magnesium was surprisingly easy to acquire.

It wasn't a silver bullet but it was a good tool, and it just felt right: darkness and light don't mix.

He had planned to give Vilnius his attention for another few weeks and collect a little more data; unfortunately, this was going to be a short stay. Moldova had unexpectedly gone a little crazy since the death of the premier and he'd have to cut his visit to Vilnius short for now.

***

It took almost two days to drive to Kishinev through Minsk and Kiev. Darren monitored the news and police reports the entire time. The death of a leader is always an unsettling event, but in this case it seemed to have unhinged the populace quite a bit more than usual. The police band was full of constant reports of looting and ethnic clashes. The news channels were reporting sporadic rioting in the center of the capital. Much of that was on too broad a scale for Darren to address in any meaningful way, but he could still help.

Hell, he could hardly hurt.

In this case the best thing he could do was orbit the city and try to stamp out small flare-ups before they got out of control. With that, he may be able to help contain spreading confusion and anarchy and keep it bottled up in the city.

In this case, it looked like anything would help.

Darren had never been to Kishinev; that was strike one. Being unfamiliar with the territory always puts you at a disadvantage. He also didn't have any backup equipment there. The nearest cache was in Bucharest, about 200 miles away. Granted, that wasn't the other side of the world, but it was a few hours by car and if Moldova got much worse, that would make the border crossing questionable. All in all, not the best situation, but at least he could give it a try.

Darren approached the outskirts of the city around dusk on the second day. He could see several plumes of black smoke rising from the city and he could hear gunshots ring out from that direction. He chose a safe-looking bed and breakfast as far from the madness as reasonable, paid cash for a room, grabbed a hearty meal, and suited up.

It was going to be a long night.

Darren left the laser and remote equipment packed away for the moment. He guessed he was going to have to apply less subtle measures, and unfortunately he was right. The first night was a constant stream of petty crime. Darren intercepted half a dozen in the first hour and things didn't let up until around 4:00 AM. According to the news reports, the problems persisted throughout the day and night, but Darren chose to keep to night patrols to maintain some anonymity and to give his body and equipment some rest and recovery time.

The second night was worse. The crimes were farther out, and they were bolder and more violent. Darren pressed closer to the activity, trying to stem the blood flow both literally and figuratively. The activity got more dense and the weapons got bigger. He even saw a rocket-propelled grenade attack on one occasion.

It was starting to look like a war zone.

The third night wasn't any better, but Darren was beginning to find his footing. He swept in an arc one mile from the center of the action and just kept moving. He was still taking matters hand-to-hand and block-by-block. The situation called for the direct approach, at least for now.

Around 2:00 AM Darren heard a window shatter about one hundred yards behind him. It was followed by an alarm going off. Based on the tone of the glass and the blare of the alarm, he guessed it was a storefront, not a car. He turned around, moved up to the nearest intersection, and looked around the corner.

About 100 yards ahead, he saw a group of five, seemingly well-armed, men climbing into the, now missing, display window of the jewelry store.

"Shit!" he spat.

Darren selected the run command and the suit covered half the distance in about ten seconds. That was a relative trot, but it gave Darren a chance to assess the threat a little more effectively. By the time he got closer, two of the men had come back out of the store, presumably to stand guard. They took up positions on either side of the storefront.

The seven-ten split is always a tough shot to make.

Surgical

Darren held close to the inside of the sidewalk and kept to the shadows as much as possible. He hit the gas and flew up to the men at about forty miles an hour.

The first one barely saw him coming. He was just turning his head when Darren's outstretched hand slammed into his temple. The second man had another twenty feet of warning, the width of the storefront, but in this case that only gave him an extra quarter of a second to react.

That wasn't enough.

He hadn't gotten his gun above his waist before Darren landed another blow, sufficient to knock him out, and zipped past him in one motion. Darren slowed up when he got about fifty feet past the jewelry store. That was just about the time the two men hit the pavement, unconscious.

With two down, Darren turned and approached cautiously. He peeked into the store through the smashed portal. He saw two men holding what looked like empty cloth bags and a third man holding a sawed-off shotgun at the chest of a much smaller man who had his arms in the air.

Darren looked up. The building was two stories high, about twenty-five feet tall, and there was a ledge about halfway up.

OK, he thought. *Let's try this.*

Darren jumped to the ledge then took a second leap to land on the roof.

CHAPTER
6

Joris Kemble stood to his full height of six foot three and yelled at the diminutive man before him. He bellowed in his most intimidating voice as the man cowered and shook.

In circumstances like this you had to dominate the situation, overwhelm the target. He'd learn that in the military before his dishonorable discharge, and he applied it here. First, case the joint. Make sure you know what you're getting into, where the money is, and how to get it. Second, come after hours. Who would be stupid enough to come during business hours anyway? There were too many variables, too many possibilities for patrons and passersby to get involved. Third, choose an optimal moment. The chaos in Moldova had provided the perfect opportunity for that. Fourth, come in force. He brought the other four men to make sure he had sufficient 'boots on the ground' for any contingency. Lastly, wait until all but one worker, probably the owner, had left.

Five to one; Joris liked those odds.

Now, move fast!

Rush the place like a tidal wave. Don't give him time to react. Make him get the safe open before he even knows what's going on. This was a critical step.

The man was shaking like a leaf. That was good, but not if he was too scared to function.

"Open the safe or you're dead," Joris barked, waving his gun in the man's face.

The man hesitated.

"I'll do you one better," Joris threatened. "We know where you live. We know who works here, your daughter and your wife. Open the safe or we'll kill them, too."

The old man cracked.

He turned and walked toward the safe.

"Check the front," Joris ordered.

Gillray peeled off and went to the front of the store. The old man finished dialing the combination and pulled the door handle.

The door was still locked.

"Open it!" Joris screamed in the man's ear.

"I'm trying," the man wept and began again.

Gillray returned with a confused look.

"What?" Joris demanded.

"Nelson and Roe," Gillray said. "They're out cold."

"What?" Joris asked.

The man stopped working the safe.

"Get it open!" Joris screamed with all the menace he could muster.

The man began dialing again.

"What do you mean they're out cold?" Joris asked again.

"Out," Gillray said. "No blood. No wounds. I didn't hear any gunfire. They're just out."

The safe finally opened. Joris threw the old man aside and called to Heath.

"Clean it out," he ordered. "Fill the bags."

Heath got to work.

Joris stepped over the man. He paid the cowering form no mind. He was of no use and no threat anymore.

Joris brought his gun up in a two-handed grip and stepped behind a support beam nearest the front of the store. He jerked his head from behind the beam just long enough to get a look, but not long enough to give anyone a shot.

Indeed, Nelson and Roc were out and there were no signs of the assailant.

"Heath?" Joris called.

"Done," he reported.

"Good," Joris said. "Out the back. Move!"

Joris, Heath, and Gillray filed toward the back of the store the way Joris had taught them: alternating point every few meters and clearing each corner as they went. They finally reached the back door and Joris kicked it open. It almost flew off the hinges from the blow. He peeked out for just a fraction of a second.

The alley looked clear, but something was going on so they needed to be cautious.

Joris nodded and Heath shot out the back door to the opposite side of the alley.

He took up a position behind one of the dumpsters and from that vantage point checked both directions of the alley.

No movement. He nodded.

Joris looked at Gillray and he followed Heath, this time taking a position a few meters further down the alley.

Same result.

No sighting, no movement.

Joris came out hugging the wall on his side of the alley. With the three of them out, each covering a different vantage point, there should be no way anyone could sneak up on them.

They started down the alley in the direction of the escape van. They could see it at the end of the lane, but proceeded slowly, taking no chances.

They were about twenty meters from the jewelry store exit when they heard a sound coming from that direction. It sounded like someone had thrown an object because there were several follow-on sounds, like a rock skipping along the tarmac.

The men froze.

Joris knew better than to run at an obvious distraction, but someone was here and it didn't take a genius to guess it was the same force that had taken out Nelson and Roe.

Then Joris saw movement from above. Whoever it was had thrown something from the roof. The object traced an arc toward Heath.

"Heath, move!" Joris ordered.

To Heath's credit, he was quick. He got out of his cover before the object hit. When it did, there was no explosion, but one might have sworn there would have been. A series of blinding flashes came in rapid succession, but there was no sound. Joris recognized the color temperature: magnesium.

This guy had military hardware.

Heath ran out of his corner and made a beeline for the next dumpster.

He wasn't quick enough.

There was a deafening whistle and Heath hit the ground like he'd run into a trip wire. He tumbled to the pavement, apparently semiconscious.

"On the roof," Joris called, and took up position under a broken fire escape to preclude attack from above.

Gillray responded with a spray of gunfire in the assailant's direction.

When the echo quieted, Joris heard no other sound.

The van was only fifty meters away, but that was too far to make a run for it.

Joris saw another object fall from above, this time toward Gillray.

"Gil, freeze and close your eyes!" he ordered.

Gil complied. Again, there was a series of bright flashes, but he held fast to his cover. When the silent attack subsided, he sprayed the roof line with gunfire a second time.

There was a pregnant moment of silence as Joris waited for the next object.

He didn't get what he expected.

This time a large object, a man, leaped from the roof above him and soared across the alleyway to the opposite rooftop. It was at least an eight-meter gap, but the man seemed to cover it without even exerting himself.

Joris wasn't fast enough to get his weapon up before the figure cleared the distance. Worse still, when the jumper was about two-thirds of the way across, when he clearly had a line-of-sight position on Gil, Joris heard that same loud whistle.

The man cleared the distance and disappeared over the opposite roof line. Unfortunately, whatever he was using hit Gil while the assailant was in midair. Joris could see Gil collapse behind his cover.

Two down.

Four if you included Nelson and Roe at the front of the store.

Joris was alone.

"Fuck," he spat and brought his weapon up to cover the roofline.

He had no intention of lowering it again. He scanned back and forth, just waiting for the figure to appear again, even just for a second.

It came, a large object in a high arc.

Joris didn't hesitate. He opened fire, getting off five rounds from his semiautomatic before the object got halfway across. The object fell like a meteor from high orbit. It dropped toward the pavement, accelerating as it went, and smashed into the street at a staggering velocity. When it hit, it sounded like a high-speed traffic accident and shattered into a thousand pieces.

Only then did Joris recognize the object: an old air conditioner unit.

This time the distraction had worked.

There was a noise behind him. It sounded like a man landing on the street, impact then footfalls. Joris turned, but whoever it was had made it behind the alleyway cover and into the shadows.

Either there were two of them or this guy had jumped eight meters to the pavement and never skipped a beat.

Joris was still processing the event when the alleyway cover started rumbling. The guy was pushing one of the dumpsters in his direction. There was a loud bang then another, then another as the enemy slammed his dumpster into the next and the next, stacking them up and driving them forward like a runaway train. How someone could push a set of dumpsters like that was beyond Joris. He must be immensely strong.

Joris jumped from the shelter just before the stampede could run him over. He rolled then came up shooting at the locomotive at the base of the dumpster train. He couldn't see the enemy, but the cover fire gave him time to move. He emptied one clip and was drawing the next while racing for the next cover point when the figure emerged for a split second. All Joris saw was the dark silhouette of a man in a hat, then something hit him; something ungodly loud and pitched at a frequency that seemed to cut his legs right out from under him. Joris staggered, fell forward, and slammed right into the side of one of the green garbage cans.

Now he knew what had hit Heath and Gillray, but Joris wasn't either of them.

He shook himself and managed to regain his feet. He was still groggy, but not so much that he didn't know where to shoot. He brought his weapon up with his left hand.

Something blocked it.

It was the guy in the hat.

He was standing right there in front of him.

Joris must have been more dazed by the weapon than he thought. He couldn't imagine how anyone could have covered the distance in the instant it took him to get to his feet. Even at that, Joris wasn't easily set on his heels. He threw a vicious blow at the stranger's face, a lightning quick shot that would have made his combat training specialist proud: shoulder snap, hip twist, the whole nine yards. He had knocked out plenty of men with a single blow of that quality.

The stranger didn't even flinch.

He didn't budge.

He didn't make a sound.

The only thing Joris heard was the distinct crack of two of his fingers and his wrist breaking on impact. His blow bounced right off the stranger's chin like he'd just punched a Sherman tank.

Joris screamed in pain, anger, frustration, and shock. He crumpled to the ground, cradling his wrist. He was just about to marshal himself for another attack when he felt a hand on his shoulder. Joris was about to react when the jolt hit him, several thousand volts from a Taser. Too familiar a sensation, but it was the last thing he remembered before losing consciousness.

Surgical
***

Reynard sat in his proprietor's chair and tried to stop shaking. He was alive, thank God for that much, and his wife had not been there. She was visiting her sister until the trouble in Moldova had subsided.

Thank God for that as well.

He looked around his pulverized store and his empty safe and tried to keep from crying.

It was all gone.

One minute of violence, one shattering event, and it was all gone. Twenty-five years of his life, his livelihood, all gone.

But he was alive. He was unharmed. He sat there for a long time in shock until the futility of staying settled upon him and he believed his quivering knees could take the weight of his body again.

Then he rose to his feet.

Just then he heard a noise from the back of the store. It was the rear door opening and closing. He heard footsteps approaching, not storming in the way thieves would, just walking at an unhurried pace. Reynard's heart rate climbed back into the triple digits. The footsteps approached. Finally, a man pushed aside the curtain that served for a door to the rear office and stepped into the light. He wore a wide-brimmed hat, which kept his face in shadow, and a light full-length coat. Past that, Reynard saw nothing of the man.

The stranger walked up and deposited three full sacks on the counter; the three sacks the thieves had loaded and carried out.

Reynard looked at the sacks then back to the stranger.

The figure said something in a strange electronic voice. It sounded like English, but Reynard couldn't be sure. Then the coat and hat walked to the front of the store and exited through the smashed window.

The door was still locked.

That was the last Reynard saw of him.

***

"Dr. Kiel, you are not an easy man to find."

Darren spun around. He was sure he hadn't missed any of them, but the evidence of his ears was undeniable. He scanned around carefully, eyes darting back and forth, checking every shadow and every unconscious body.

Nothing.

"Easy, Darren, it's me," a voice said from right out of thin air.

At that, Darren saw a flutter right in front of him, like the air had suddenly become too heavy with humidity and a cloud had condensed for just a fraction of a second. Then, as quickly as it had formed, it vanished. For a moment, Darren thought he'd imagined it.

"Who?" he asked.

Then the cloud formed again, this time more clearly defined. It had color and shape. The form of a female body with blonde hair was just discernible for an instant before it winked out again.

"Fade," Darren said finally.

"Faye," the voice corrected. "Good to see you again."

"What do you mean again?" Darren said. "I didn't see you last time, and I can't see you this time."

"Occupational hazard," the voice said. "There is nothing wrong with a little anonymity."

He was still scanning around, trying to lock down her position, but the voice kept drifting about, like the buzz of a fly he couldn't get a bead on.

"Nice to meet you, Darren. We have never been formally introduced."

72

The sound of a voice coming out of nowhere and drifting around him would have been a great deal more unnerving if he didn't have the suit. At least it gave some measure of protection from this unsettling unknown.

"If we're going to talk, can you at least stand still?" Darren complained.

"Sorry," the voice said. "It's a habit."

"How did you find me?" Darren asked.

"By the trail lacking bodies," Faye said. "We can track crime rates just as easily as you can, but for us the trick is to watch the rates drop suddenly then try to get there before you move on. I missed you by a couple of days in Wales. I didn't bother to chase you to Lithuania because I knew you'd be headed here."

"How?"

"C'mon, Darren," she said, "your moves are more obvious than that. Since their Premier was assassinated, the crime rate has nearly tripled here. That's like cheese to a mouse for you."

"What do you mean assassinated?" Darren said. "The reports said cancer. His health was one of the reasons he had been acting so erratically."

"Do you believe everything you hear?"

"You're still drifting," Darren said.

"Darren, forget about my drifting, for Christ's sake. Do you want to know why I'm here?"

"I was getting to that."

"Get to it faster. You seem to have a problem getting to the big picture."

"What's that supposed to mean?"

"I mean you take on these thugs one at a time, but you seem to be blind to the larger causes of crime in the first place. What the hell good does it do to stamp out some gang activity in some two-bit neighborhood when it is just going to grow back after you leave?"

"Not that it's any of your goddamn business," Darren said, "but you might want to see the effect on people's lives at ground level before you start judging from the ivory perch. I would talk about crime rate response and recovery times and an optimization of applied countermeasures, but let's get to your big picture. What the hell do you want, anyway?"

"Look, Walter sent me to find you. He has a problem and he needs your help."

"When you talk to him, tell him you did a shitty job of asking me for it," Darren said.

"I'll tell him you were too self-involved and myopic to make a decision for the greater good. Sound like anyone you know? Your dad, for example?"

"Fuck you," Darren said as he turned from the latest direction of the voice and started walking.

The voice continued to orbit about him as he went.

"Look, forget about what I think; we're talking about Walter. Are you going to help or not?"

"Forget about the big picture and look at the specific details for a second," Darren said. "When someone says 'fuck you,' you can, usually, take that to mean 'no.'"

"Not even if it's life or death?"

"Life and death are what I do," Darren said. "It's all life and death, every day."

"I mean Walter's life or death."

Darren stopped walking.

"Someone is trying to kill him."

Darren thought about that for a second.

"That's unlikely," he said.

"Why?"

"Because in today's world, if someone wanted to kill him, he'd probably already be dead," he said. "I am talking to an invisible woman, remember."

There was a pause.

"What's really going on?" Darren asked.

"It's a little complicated."

"It always is," he said and started walking again.

"Look, this is important."

"All this is important!" Darren yelled. "And your attitude that all this is beneath you is reprehensible. Every one of these people values their life, just as much as you, just as much as Walter."

"But they aren't as valuable, are they? Think about it," the voice said. "Walter made you and Walter made me. Walter made the people who do all this good, save all these lives, fight all this crime. Walter is a high value asset to the world as a whole. He creates 'good.' He is more than just a citizen. He is a savior. Take it from one who knows."

"If I were an elitist, I wouldn't do the work that I do," Darren said.

"Then let me put it to you another way. You are trying to stem the blood flow of a ruptured artery with a Band-Aid. I'm not saying you aren't helping, but this isn't going to cut it against what's coming."

"What's coming?" Darren said.

"I'm asking you to help suture the source shut, to solve the problem at the root, not the extremities. All of this is just a symptom of a larger problem, and if that isn't enough to convince you, I can tell you that whatever has driven the crime rate to triple in Moldova is the same thing that is threatening Walter."

Darren stopped a second time.

"Again, what's going on?" he asked.

"Look, this can be a win-win for you," Faye said. "One: you get to help a person; two: that person happens to be Walter; and three: this particular operation has far-reaching implications. It will address the problems you focus on, like where we're standing. It just addresses them less directly."

Darren hesitated.

"Come back to meet with Walter for a day, then he can explain; by all the evidence, he'll do a better job than I have been able to. I can have a plan ready to take you back within the hour. If it doesn't work out, we can always have you back the next day."

"No," Darren said. "I'll go, but I'll find my own way. Tell Walter I'll meet him in two days."

"Thank you," Faye said mutedly. "We'll see you then."

Darren stood where he was and listened as Faye, presumably, moved on and left him to his tasks. Of course, he heard nothing, just as he had when she approached, and just as he had while they were talking.

The realization that he had no way of knowing whether she was still here or not was more than a little unsettling. For the moment, Darren decided to let it go. There was no reason to suspect that Faye would stay just to spy on him, but longer term, this was not going to work. Friend of Walter's or not, the prospect of an invisible person lurking about was simply not acceptable. He made a mental note to devise a way to detect her.

He would probably never need it, but that was true of ninety-five percent of his assets.

'Probably' just wasn't good enough.

CHAPTER
7

It was great to see the original workshop firsthand again.

Darren had kept a close watch on it through remote cameras and net-accessible control systems. He had even occasionally visited through one of the remote suits. By synching his own exo-suit from any of the other workshops throughout Europe to the movements of one of the suits stored in the L.A. area workshop, Darren could see and feel his presence here. He could even check on and maintain the half-dozen vehicles in the hypogeal garage, also thirty feet underground and a quarter mile to the north.

But it wasn't the same as actually being here, feeling the dust and breathing the air. It was good to hear his own footsteps here again.

Today Darren had entered the workshop through the faux-abandoned garage that hid the entrance to the working subterranean one and took the tunnel sled that conveyed him to the workshop through the quarter-mile long tunnel.

Entering the workshop through the original entrance wasn't convenient since it was still covered with the rubble of the house Darren had blown up to prevent anyone from discovering the workshop and garage.

Fortunately, that had worked. The equipment had gone undiscovered all these months and since activity around the blast site and surrounding estate was close to zero, it was a good bet that it would go on for a good long time.

It was all here for him should he ever want it, but today all he needed was a ride.

The Ducati would do just fine.

Darren approached Walter's office building and rode into the secure underground garage through a familiar route. A security guard straightened when Darren approached and waved him on without stopping him.

Walter's garage was, usually, next to empty. Today Darren counted four other vehicles, all fairly nondescript. Walter's acquaintances often preferred to keep low profiles. Darren drove to the far end and parked the bike near the private elevator with which he was well acquainted. When he approached the elevator, the doors opened and he walked in.

It was a quick, solitary trip to the fourteenth floor.

Darren exited the elevator and walked past the unattended reception desk to the single office on that floor. He knocked on the door.

Faye opened the door to greet him.

"Darren," she said. "Come on in."

The door swung open and Darren stepped in. There were three other people in the room; Walter and two men Darren didn't recognize. The first was standing next to Walter, a man in his mid to late-thirties. He wore a well-tailored suit and had an equally well-tailored haircut. The other, Darren guessed, was in his late forties, a somewhat portly, bearded man sitting on the couch against the right-hand wall.

Walter looked like death warmed over. He sat at his desk slouched and exhausted. He was thin and pale as if he'd been fighting a serious illness for a long time. There were dark circles under his eyes that accented his gaunt, sunken cheeks. His hair was unkempt, at least for Walter. There were several hairs out of place that hung over his forehead, breaking up the perpetually chiseled look of his brow and hairline. His tie was not loose, but also not snug around his neck the way it always used to be. It was a picture of a man beginning to crack around the edges.

Darren marched in and made a beeline to Walter's desk. Walter rose weakly. His suit was clearly too big for his diminished frame. He extended his hand and Darren shook it firmly, but more tenderly than he might have.

"Thanks for coming, Darren," Walter said in a voice that lacked his characteristic boom.

"My pleasure, Walter," Darren said. "I'm sorry it took so long. If I had known…"

Walter gave him a dismissive wave. "You're here now." It looked like he was about to say something else but was suddenly winded and needed to sit down.

"I'm sorry," he said. "I haven't had much sleep recently."

Darren looked at the man standing next to Walter. The man extended his hand. "Brigham Otway," he said. "I'm a friend of Walter's."

Darren shook the offered hand.

"This is Martin Ives," Brigham continued, indicating the man sitting on the couch. "He's also a friend of Walter's."

The man got off the couch and Darren walked toward him. They shook hands at the halfway point, but the man never met Darren's eyes.

"Pleasure," Darren said.

"Likewise," the man said unconvincingly.

"And you've already met Faye," Brigham said.

Darren and Faye nodded at one another.

"Shall we get started?" Brigham asked.

Everyone nodded and found a place to sit down. Brigham tapped a few buttons on Walter's desk and the lights dimmed, the curtains closed, and a projector brought up the image of a middle-aged man on a screen embedded in the far wall.

"Bashiveux Keenan Siomak," Brigham began, "premier of the Republic of Moldova for the last three years, was assassinated in his state residence two weeks ago. His vice-chancellor was killed within seconds of him."

"So much for that health issues report," Ives said.

"Correct," Brigham said.

"How do you know he was assassinated?" Darren asked. "If we can't trust the health issues report, how did we know we can trust this one?"

"Benjamin Gobran, the United States secretary of state, was personally present when the Premier was assassinated," Brigham said. "He provided a detailed report that is, shall we say, not widely distributed. But we also have the forensics reports on both the Premier and the Vice-Chancellor. Let's just say it's pretty clear these deaths were not from natural causes."

"Actually, let's not just say," Darren said. "What was in the report?"

"The cause of death in both instances was massive brain trauma," Brigham said. "The brain tissue was charred, pulverized, like an explosion had been set off inside each man's head. I can show you pictures if you like."

"Pass," Faye insisted.

"What was it? Some sort of explosive bullet?" Darren asked. "If the assassin was good enough to shoot them in the head, why go the extra mile of using an explosive bullet?"

"Well, we're getting a little ahead of ourselves now," Brigham said.

"Let them go," Walter said.

"There was no bullet," Brigham answered. "There was no entry wound in either case. There was no external trauma whatsoever. From the outside, the men appeared perfectly fine. It was only when the forensics did the autopsy that they found the extensive tissue damage."

"Then someone must have planted it," Ives said. "Someone must have injected the men with some micro incendiary and triggered it remotely."

"Negative," Brigham said. "There were no signs of any debris or chemical residue in either body. That was checked and rechecked by three different forensics labs, including the best forensic lab in the United States. There was nothing. We're confident of that."

"No entry wound," Ives said, "no debris, no chemical signature at all? These men's brains just spontaneously exploded from the inside out?"

"It gets worse," Brigham said.

Ives, Faye, and Darren looked at one another.

"The men knew this was coming," Brigham said. "The assassin made himself known months before the event."

There was a stillness in the room.

"And they took every precaution imaginable," Brigham said. "The Premier had a safe room constructed to protect him from the assassin. There were no windows, only one door, which was guarded 24/7, and the walls were sealed and made of steel-reinforced concrete. The bunker could have withstood a small nuclear device, but all that seemed to be completely ineffective."

"Let me understand this," Darren said. "This guy effectively had these men in his sights for months."

"Yes," Brigham said.

"They were unable to find him," Darren continued. "They were unable to hide from him. They were unable to stop him by any means?"

"Yes," Brigham said.

"And he made this known to them?" Darren said. "They knew they were at his mercy?"

"Yes." Brigham began to fidget and looked at Walter. Darren looked at Walter too. His talking seemed to have exacerbated Walter's condition. Something was going on here.

"That speaks to the problem here," Brigham said as he pushed a button and brought up another slide. It was a list of events and dates. "His precarious situation put the Premier in a compromised position. Although virtually no one knew what was happening, the assassin, or in this case, terrorist, was able to extract policy changes and behavior from the Premier under constant threat of instant death.

"This is a list of the actions and policies of the Moldavian government that we believe were direct results of this threat against the Premier's life: military exercises near sensitive borders, trade embargos that seemed to accomplish nothing but increase tensions both internally and with allies of Moldova, missile tests that 'accidentally' strayed into the volatile provinces in neighboring regions, shifts in military personnel, and troop deployments that suggested aggression; the whole list seemed to have been specifically constructed to lower the flashpoint in this region of Western Europe."

"A real leader would never tolerate that," Faye mumbled. "He'd rather die than compromise his country."

"Easy to judge," Walter said, "but this threat wasn't just against him. His cabinet, his staff, his wife, his children, everyone he knew, anyone he loved, was under this threat. Besides, even if he did commit suicide or goad the terrorist into ending it, the next leader steps up and the whole process starts again, quite probably with a weaker man."

"Walter's right," Brigham said. "I don't know anyone who claims to be an expert in Moldavian politics, but the current interim leader is, by any measure, weaker and less experienced. We can only speculate on how that choice occurred, but it seems a safe bet that this assassin was orchestrating the choice with selective pressure on the cabinet. The end result is that the country now has a diminished leadership, which puts the entire region further at risk. The internal effects are even more apparent. Crime has risen to an alarming level. The citizens are nearing panic. It's the closest thing to anarchy we've seen in a long time. And it's getting worse."

Darren looked at Faye.

You were right, he thought.

"Has he targeted the current leader?" Darren asked.

Brigham paused and took on a grim look.

"No," he said heavily, then looked down at Walter.

Walter raised his hand.

"That would be me," he said.

Darren and Ives jumped out of their chairs.

"What?"

"Where?"

"How?"

"It started about two weeks ago," Walter said, "right after he was finished with the Moldavian premier."

"What started?" Darren asked. "How do you know?"

Walter looked up at Brigham. Darren and Ives followed suit.

"The threat has a distinctive signature," Brigham said. "According to the report from our secretary, there was a spark, a small explosion in midair, when the Premier and the Vice-Chancellor were assassinated. He heard this spark, this bang, between the time the Premier and the Vice-Chancellor died. To read the account, it seems that the assassin is able to cause these explosions, these discharges, and he kills by detonating one of them inside the target's brain."

Darren felt his skin go cold.

"Anyone, anywhere, anytime," he said.

"Yes," Brigham said.

"Including any one of us right now."

"Yes," Brigham said.

Darren stepped back and rubbed a hand over his face.

"I'm sorry," Walter said, "but the time for fucking around is just over."

"Did you consider the consequences to anyone in this room before you dragged every one of them directly into the line of fire?" Darren said in a raised voice.

"Yes," Walter said. "I did, and given the same circumstances, I'd do it again."

"Not just now, but any time hereafter. The minute we stepped into your office, we put ourselves on his list, on his radar, at his mercy," Darren said.

"Like I said, the time for fucking around is over," Walter said.

"That is not your decision to make!" Faye said. "How dare you put our lives at risk, drag us into this without warning, without consent!"

"If I took the time or the risk to negotiate consent from all of you, it may have been too late," Walter said. "As I understand it, Faye had trouble convincing Darren in the first place. How much luck would I have had with any of you if you knew the circumstances?"

"Walter, that wasn't your decision," Darren said.

"Apparently, it was," Walter said. "It was my decision to get you here by any means necessary. Why? Because it's required. It's as simple as that."

"To save your skin," Faye said, "you put us all at risk."

"To hell with my skin," Walter said and stood from the chair, half in a rage. "Haven't you been listening? This is not about my skin. Countries are at risk here, entire regions are being manipulated toward war and destruction, toward anarchy and collapse. You want to do good? This is the way to do it. You're here now and you're in it, whether you like it or not. No, I didn't waste time trying to convince you. I made the correct decision because it was required. When you've had a chance to think about it, you will come to that conclusion on your own, but for right now, there are more important things in front of us."

Ives, who seemed remarkably calm, returned to his place on the couch and sat down. He seemed to stop and think for a moment then he looked up at Brigham and Walter.

"He would have to see them," he said. "In order to target them, in order to hit them with something like that, to hit them with anything, he would have to see them first."

"Yes," Brigham said.

"Inside a sealed room," Ives continued, "in a secure location, behind fortified walls, with no windows or doors, in the middle of a patrolled government compound."

"Yes," Brigham said.

There was a pause.

"He sees like I do," Ives concluded.

"Yes," Brigham said.

***

Two years ago:

Alone.

What part of 'alone' did they not understand? It was the worst part of working with people. It was the worst part of working at all, this proclivity for selective hearing.

Machines.

What part of 'machines' did they not understand, and how much clearer did he have to make it? Machines were quiet, obedient, predictable, and productive. They have virtue. All you have to do is give them attention and respect. All you need to do is treat them well. They make excellent partners.

What the hell did people have? Bad breath, BO, sweat, rudeness, selfishness, hatred, temper tantrums?

What part of 'machines' did they not understand?

'Annual review'?

They had to be kidding. He had work to do. What the hell good did an annual review do for anyone? He understood the job better than anyone, so what value could this possibly have? If they wanted to know more about the project: read the annual report. Other than that, he just wanted to be left alone.

Still, in order to appease these useless jellyfish, Martin Ives began the march toward his supervisor's office at one minute to the hour, because it took exactly one minute to walk there.

Of course, when he got to the door, his supervisor was running late, again. What else would you expect? Martin knocked on the door and the portal swung open. There were two men inside. His supervisor didn't notice, the asshole. The other man checked his watch crisply and showed irritation.

"Damn it," the man spat and immediately darted for the doorway Martin occupied.

He looked Martin in the eye for the most fleeting instant.

"He's all yours," the man said. "Sorry for running over."

He squeaked past Martin without brushing him or even requiring that Martin move and then he was gone.

Martin checked his watch

It was six seconds past the hour.

Martin's supervisor, Lawrence Carryl, waved Martin in.

"Well, that was quick," Lawrence said, noting his guest's quick exit.

Martin gave no reaction.

What followed was about half an hour of incessant droning from this ineffective parasite. He went over some of the events of last year, half of which he got wrong. He listed some of what Martin had worked on, most of which he got wrong. He discussed some aspects of Martin's project as he tried to show he was involved and knowledgeable. He failed miserably on both counts.

"Well," Lawrence said, "all in all, I'd say you've met our expectations for the year."

That was, of course, nonsense. His supervisor had changed course three times in the past year and Martin had exceeded the stated goals each time.

"Well," Lawrence said, "if you could sign that you agree with the assessment, we'll log that we covered it in your annual review package."

Martin made no move at all. Lawrence never finished anything in half an hour. One hour was his minimum time block. Martin sat and braced himself for the second half. The good news was Lawrence began to look uncomfortable, the way he did when something was slipping out of his perceived control, his pathetic and minuscule fiefdom.

"Well," Lawrence began. It was the only way he knew how to start a sentence, "there's been some discussion about reassigning you."

Martin cocked an eyebrow one-quarter of the way up at that.

"Well, there is a project they feel you may be suited to," Lawrence continued. He slid a folder over toward Martin. Martin picked up the folder and scanned through it. He had to resist both eyebrows going up. There was no sense letting Mr. Useless get a read on him. He enjoyed Lawrence's discomfort too much.

"Well, of course, this is not mandatory," Lawrence squirmed. "It's just a discussion. We don't want to reassign you if you're happy where you are and we certainly…"

"When?" Martin asked. It was the first thing he'd said since entering the office.

"Well, the discussion was 'as soon as reasonable'," Lawrence said, "but there's no rush. Like I said, if you're happy where you are…"

"Now?" Martin asked.

"Well, let's not rush into it, Martin," Lawrence was sweating. "This would entail a change of supervisors."

"Who?" Martin asked.

"Well, actually," Lawrence said, "the gentleman who just left, Brigham Otway."

Martin stood up.

"Upstairs?" he asked.

"Well, yes, but he was clear that you should take all the time you need to…"

Martin grabbed the assessment sheet on Lawrence's desk, turned on his heel and walked out the door. He gave no goodbye nor did he acknowledge Lawrence at all. He crumpled the assessment sheet and tossed it into a waiting trash can on his way upstairs. He found Brigham's office and knocked on the door.

"Come," came a steady voice.

Martin opened the door.

Brigham looked up from his desk.

Martin held the folder up.

An efficient smile crossed Brigham's lips.

He gestured to a waiting chair.

Martin closed the door and sat down.

One year later, Martin was on his way to another annual assessment.

***

Martin had argued the point but Brigham had insisted, and Brigham never insisted.

Never.

He'd given Martin the freedom and isolation he craved, and in return Martin had moved the project along. Within the last year, he had done what Brigham asked, and met or exceeded project goals. Now it was time to present the results to the board.

Martin would have preferred an acid bath.

Indulging his desire for isolation had an unfortunate side effect. It worsened the condition. After a year of laboring in his preferred state, he had a pretty serious case of agoraphobia, as well as a near-crippling case of anxiety when dealing with people, never mind speaking in public, never mind in front of the board. But Brigham had talked him down.

"Just focus on the work," he said. "Ignore anyone else in the room and just speak to me, like we rehearsed. If you focus on the presentation, once you start speaking, it'll all be over before you know it."

By the time Martin had climbed into the limo Brigham had sent, endured the ride to the office, climbed out of the car, made it to the elevator ride, and met Brigham, he was practically hyperventilating.

"Excellent," Brigham said with palpable confidence. "That was the hard part. Now, there's the door. Just go in and start talking. Ignore everyone else. They're not expecting you to engage them and the lights are off in the rest of the room, so just go in and start gabbing."

Martin's breathing was still too quick and heavy. He could barely talk and if this kept up, it was clear he would pass out before he even got a good start.

"Actually," Brigham said, "forget that. Just start now. How did it all start? What did we practice?"

"You gave me a set of specs on an early version," Martin puffed.

"Good," Brigham said. "What else? What early version? Pretend I have amnesia."

"The early version only used single pulses and was really low resolution," Martin said.

"How low?" Brigham asked. "Why was that a problem?"

"It limited the range," Martin said. "They could only go twenty or thirty feet."

His breathing had started to regulate.

"OK, we're getting ahead of ourselves," Brigham said as he drifted toward the conference room door. "Tell me about the goal. What were we trying to do to begin with?"

"Remote surveillance," Martin said, holding Brigham's attention.

"Like radar?" Brigham asked.

Don't act stupid, Martin thought.

"No," Martin said, "like a nonlethal X-ray, but much better."

"Why better?" Brigham asked, opening the door to the conference room without losing eye contact with Martin. "What advantage do radio waves have over X-rays?"

Then he opened the door wider.

"Radio waves can travel through walls, buildings, even entire city blocks without stopping," Martin said.

Then he realized that it sounded a lot like the beginning of the presentation he and Brigham had rehearsed so many times it was nauseating, so he went to the next point like he was playing a voice recorder from his own head.

"Some wavelengths of radiation can go through whole planets without noticing, but that's not useful if there's no interaction at all."

Martin still had his eyes on Brigham as he entered the conference room, but he soon started pacing at the front of the dark room, staring at the floor as he did. He continued his well-rehearsed monologue.

"In this case, we chose a wavelength of radiation that will only lose one percent when traveling through a standard building wall. The figure is more like two percent if the wall is concrete or some higher density material."

Brigham was still listening.

"If you think about that for a second," Martin continued then he saw a diagram come up on the main presentation screen right in front of him. Fortunately, it was the slide he needed, so he started pointing and kept talking, "that means it will go through one hundred walls and still maintain thirty-six percent of its initial intensity."

The slide changed and Martin began speaking to the new slide.

"Now here is the important part. Let's say the one-hundredth object is a person, and when the radio wave hits that person, it reflects one percent back, just like it would if it hit another wall."

The slide changed again.

"That one percent will come back through those one hundred walls, and again thirty-six percent of it will survive the trip. If you do the math, that means 0.13 percent of the original signal comes back."

The slide changed again.

"The good news is we can detect that. Zero point one percent is actually a great deal of signal. We can construct a high-resolution image using a lot less than that."

The slide changed again. Martin was now speaking to the screen directly. At least they shared a common interest.

"Now, in order to separate the image of that person from the signal bouncing off the other ninety-nine surfaces, we use a pulsed source and time the detection window for the depth and distance we wish to interrogate. That part is similar to a medical ultrasound image. The only real difference is we are using light, more specifically radio waves, instead of sound."

The slide changed.

"When we first began this work a year ago, the technology was limited to single pulses. That means you could only really track one image at a time. It was two-dimensional, like a picture."

The slide changed to show the grainy image of a single person. It was the same image Brigham had shown him a year ago, a picture taken through only three walls and thirty feet of distance.

"We have since refined the sources and the pulses we use. Now we can imagine entire volumes, a room, for example, and track any of the elements simultaneously. What used to be a two-dimensional image is now a volumetric three-dimensional image, like a hologram. We have a demonstration set up."

At that, the slide changed again. It showed a gray-tone image of a crowded room. The assembled group looked like dull, colorless mannequins, just one continuous surface tracking the full outline of the faces, clothing, and hair, but the resolution was excellent. The faces were clearly identifiable, even without their skin tone and eye color.

"This is a remote image of this room. It is being taken from our working prototype in real time."

At that, Martin saw his own image on the screen, his own gestures and his own face. He heard a great rumble as the assemblage did the same. Everyone in the room flinched and either stood or squirmed in discomfort at the revelation. Then, with every doll-like figure on the screen moving and every accompanying sound audible, Martin turned around, suddenly aware of his audience.

The dark room hid them all from him, but the awareness of so many anonymous creatures in the dark hit him like a swarm of ants on his skin. He looked at Brigham as a cold sweat broke from his epidermis. Brigham saw his face, sprung out of his chair, and ushered Martin from the room. He gave Martin the paper bag he'd been carrying to ease Martin's now full-tilt hyperventilation.

The presentation was over.

The point had been made.

CHAPTER
8

"Jesus!" Faye breathed.

"Cute," Darren said. "Very clever. How far can you see?"

"A mile is never a problem," Ives said. "Two is, usually, do-able. Five is, usually, pushing it."

"So you can see anything from up to five miles away?" Faye asked.

"Yes," Ives said.

"Inside the Supreme Court, the White House, anywhere?" Faye said.

"Yes," Ives said. "Virtually anywhere. The only exception would be any chamber that is specifically constructed to isolate against radio waves, but those are few and far between. In this day and age, when everyone wants cell access or wireless access, insulated rooms are not common."

"Jesus Christ!" Faye said.

"Was the premier's safe room insulated against radio waves?" Darren asked Brigham.

"I have no information on that," Brigham said. "I'll check into it, but it's possible that it wasn't. He may not have known what to look for, but let's not get ahead of ourselves. First, Ives may be able to see from a distance, but he can't kill from a distance. The technology is purely surveillance. Second, even if the premier hid from the assassin in some dark secluded room, that wouldn't solve the problem. He would have to come up at some point. No leader can hide forever. Third, all this presupposes the assassin is using the same radio technology. We don't know that. Let's not base our actions on questionable assumptions."

"It's highly likely that he's using the same basic approach to do surveillance," Walter said. "Highly likely."

"Why do you say that?" Brigham asked.

"How else would he do it?" Walter asked.

Brigham paused and appeared confused.

"The fact that I don't know how else it might be done doesn't mean there is not another way," Brigham insisted. "We need to keep an open mind to the possibility that we still have no idea what we're actually dealing with."

"Noted," Walter said dismissively. "We can keep it in mind, but we need to start somewhere and this is a highly probable assumption. Highly probable."

Walter's last words trailed off like he was preoccupied with something.

"Then I would guess you'd want to start setting up safe rooms here," Darren asked, "and design a way to insulate your car against this as well."

"No," Walter said quietly.

"What?" Darren said. "Why not?"

"Because I'm not going to be here," Walter said. "None of us are."

He looked at Brigham, pushed another button on the desk, and a new slide came up; a map of Western Europe. The country of the Czech Republic was highlighted.

"Prague, the Czech Republic, two weeks ago," Brigham said. "There have been 'inexplicable discharge events' within the Prime Minister's personal chambers, his office, and main living quarters. One close cabinet member has died recently, reportedly from a sudden heart attack, but our sources tell us that is not true. We're still trying to get our hands on the forensics reports but we're pretty confident the assassin has chosen his next target. We believe he used the cabinet member as an example."

Darren let out a deep breath.

"Why the Czech Republic?" he asked. "Why Moldova, for that matter? Why not Bosnia? Why not Serbia ? If he wants to start a war, why not choose a country already close to the brink?"

"Because he wants a bigger war," Walter said. "Bosnia, Serbia, the eastern border of the Adriatic, those countries are already shaky. If they get shakier, it doesn't change the fundamental equation. No, he wants to draw out the conflict to engulf a larger region."

"Moldova, Czech, Hungary… that region is full of good choices. Some of them have been pretty stable, so if they start acting erratically, it's much more disruptive. They also form a bridge, a bulwark between less peaceful states like Bosnia and Serbia, and more stable states like Poland to the northwest, Bulgaria, even Turkey on the Mediterranean side. If you unhinge the broader region, the whole continent will begin to shake."

Darren took a deep breath and stared at the map. "The premier of Moldova was killed about a month ago."

"Yes," Brigham said.

"And, let's say, several days later, Walter's threatened in the same manner," Darren said.

"Yes," Brigham said.

"Now, a few weeks after that, this assassin is back in Western Europe and has his sights on Czech," Darren said.

"Yes," Brigham said.

Darren looked around. "Doesn't that seem strange to anyone?"

There was no response.

"Even if he did want to target Walter, the equipment needed to pull off this kind of operation can't be trivial," Darren said. He looked at Ives. "What does your equipment look like?"

"I've managed to get it into a standard shipping container," Ives said, "so it's about the size of a Mack truck."

"Exactly," Darren said. "And I'd guess that it's pretty complicated. You wouldn't want to ship it across borders or deal with customs issues on equipment like that."

"Hell no," Ives said. "You could never get across borders unless you shipped it a piece at a time, and even then it would be dicey. Something would always get held up."

"Exactly!" Darren said. "So, unless we're missing something, it would be virtually impossible for him to get this equipment from Europe to here and back within that time frame."

"So clearly there must be two units," Walter said.

"Or two different assassins," Darren said.

"Or many assassins," Faye said. "Possibly there is an entire division of them, all equipped to carry out these kinds of missions. Maybe several on each continent, to solve the shipping issues you mentioned."

Darren's chill rose to another level.

"But we don't know of any other activity," Darren said. "You haven't heard of any other threats, other people targeted like this?"

"No," Brigham said.

"It could be that Walter was the first in North America," Ives said, "but we can expect this to grow. Next we may be hearing about events all over the world as this grows, and more and more of them are built and put into action."

"Maybe," Darren said, still looking at the map. "Walter, you had one of these incidents. Were there any others?"

"No, just the one, but it was unmistakable."

"I don't doubt that," Darren said, "but you've had no communication since, and no demands?"

"I presume he went back to Czech, but strangely enough I haven't found that to be of much comfort."

"I don't doubt that either," Darren said. "Where did it happen?"

"In the office," Walter said. "I was standing by the window and dropped my..."

"By the window?" Darren cut in. "By one of these windows?"

"Yes," Walter said. "I was standing by the window and dropped my meditation ball. When I bent over to pick it up, there was a loud bang above me. It was pretty clear that if I hadn't bent over, it would have been the end of me."

Darren squinted and cocked his head. "This is making less sense all the time."

"Why?" Brigham asked.

"Why the window?" Darren asked. "Why not the desk, the bathroom, the bedroom at home? And why the botched head shot? From what you told me about Moldova, he wouldn't go for Walter's head, at least not at first. And if he did, he certainly wouldn't miss. And even if he did miss, he would just take another shot. You've already said he can see anywhere."

"I think you may be over-thinking this," Brigham said. "Maybe that's part of the campaign plan. Remember, he's a terrorist. His best weapon is fear, and the random, inexplicable, erratic nature of harassment helps keep the target off balance."

"Maybe," Darren said, "but I still have a problem with the window. That's a standard line-of-sight position that a traditional sniper would use, not this guy who can see through walls and into sealed-off saferooms."

"In the end, it's not really relevant," Walter said. "Whether there are one or many, and whether their modes of operation vary, the only pertinent point is the situation in Czech because that's the one that's destabilizing. If we are going to address this, it seems that the best place to do so is where it's happening, and that means Prague. We've had one event here. Reports are that they get one every couple of days there."

"Have fun," Faye said.

Walter looked at her.

"You asked me to find Darren and I did that," Faye said. "You asked me to convince him to come here so you could effectively force him to help, get him into the line of fire so he'd have to fight your battle. I've done that, too."

"That was not an exhaustive list," Walter said.

"I'm no more invisible to the assassin than you are," Faye said. "The cloak doesn't work at the wavelengths you're talking about. I'll be just as vulnerable, just as much a sitting duck as anyone, as all the rest of you. The second you step off the plane in Prague, who's to say he's not going to just blow your brains out on sight?"

"Obviously we're going to need to be cautious," Walter said and looked at Darren and Ives. "She's right in that, if we make ourselves known, there's nothing to stop him from hitting the switch that second. We'll have to be smarter than that."

"Unless he already knows," Darren said. "Who's to say he's not watching and listening right now?"

"I took a gamble bringing you all here," Walter said. "I know that. I also know that a face-to-face was the only way. A teleconference or any remote meeting would not do it. It's too easy to turn it off and walk away. Now that we're here and you can all see the danger, I expect your help. I think it's reasonable to say we've cleared the first hurdle because if he was listening to us right now, we'd all be dead."

Walter looked at each in turn. "That gives us an opportunity."

"Again," Faye said, "good luck."

"Faye," Walter began.

"No, Walter!" she yelled. "Ives can stay hidden by his very nature. He never has to set foot outside his crow's nest. Darren has a death wish anyway. He lives for the one on one. I'm not putting my neck on the line with no protection."

"You have more protection than the rest of us," Walter said. "The cloak may not be perfect, but it's something. I expect your help."

"No!" Faye said.

"I wasn't asking," Walter said.

"Good, because I wasn't answering," Faye said. "I was telling you."

Walter straightened and took a deep breath. "Obviously I cannot force you," he said.

"Good," Faye said. "We agree on something."

"So, if you want to step out, you are, of course, free to do so," Walter said.

"Good," Faye said and started for the door.

"But leave the cloak," Walter said.

Faye froze.

"What?" she breathed.

"Leave the cloak," Walter said.

It wasn't a request.

"Are you nuts?" Faye asked.

"What do you think?" Walter asked, stone-faced.

"You can't even use the cloak. You can't even operate it," Faye protested, clearly on the verge of tears.

"All true," Walter said, with all the emotion of a granite monolith.

Faye glowered at Walter to the point that Darren thought she might charge at him and rip the skin from his body. Finally, she pulled the coat tight around her, turned away, and retreated to the far end of the office where she paced like a caged panther.

"Walter," Ives said, "what good is going to Prague if we have no idea how to fight this? What are you suggesting? How do you propose we stop him?"

"I don't have all the answers," Walter said, "but I know that sitting here watching the world fall apart around us is not acceptable."

Darren drifted toward the window behind Walter, the one through which Walter reported being targeted. He stood roughly where Walter had indicated and began examining the portal.

"We really have nothing to go on," Ives continued. "Even if he is using the same surveillance technology I use, how does that help?"

"If you knew that someone was using the same technology to look at us, what would you do?" Walter asked.

"I'd set up radio wave sensors to detect the wavelengths I suspected," Ives said. "Whenever the surveillance started, the sensors would record the intensity and direction of the wave. With a couple of hits like that, I could pinpoint the source."

"Sounds like a good place to start," Walter said.

"Knowing how he sees the target doesn't help us even if the suppositions are right," Ives said. "Walter, he can kill with a thought. He can drop everyone in the room in a matter of seconds. We have no idea how he is managing that."

Walter looked down at his desk.

There was a silence.

"I might," Darren whispered.

Walter turned his head toward Darren.

"What?"

"I might," Darren said, still looking at the window. Then he turned from his reflection and looked at Walter and Brigham. "Do you have a laser lab in the building?" he asked.

Crack!

The spark came in midair without warning and without leaving a trace. There was no debris, no smoke, no evidence that it had happened at all.

Darren looked up from the demonstration.

"Like that?" he asked.

Brigham looked astounded.

"Exactly like that," he said. "The reports describe it exactly like that."

"I didn't actually see the spark," Walter said, "but the sound and the signature feel the same."

Walter, Brigham, Faye, and Ives stood shoulder to shoulder in the cramped laser lab on the seventh floor of

Walter's office building. They huddled around the table and watched Darren demonstrate.

"What's happening," Darren began, "is that the laser focuses so tightly that it's ionizing the air. There's no fuel, nothing tangible at all to cause the explosion. The laser is just so intense that it rips the electrons right off the air molecules. Yes, if you had a piece of paper or something else at the focus site, it would be even louder and more violent."

Darren looked around for something then he began rummaging through a set of drawers. He came back with a handful of microscope slides.

"And," he continued, "this effect can happen right through solid objects."

He placed five of the glass slides in the path of the laser beam before the ignition site and fired the laser again. The effect was the same.

Crack!

"Jesus Christ," Faye breathed.

"Could this go through walls?" Brigham asked.

"That would be trickier," Darren said, "but if Ives can do it, yes, theoretically it's possible."

"How would you do that?" Ives asked.

"You have to weaponize the surveillance approach," Darren said. "The technique you described is very passive. You send out a signal and you detect what comes back, but if you use that same wavelength, the one that goes through walls, and focus it down at the end; yeah, I think you could get the same effect."

Ives took off his glasses and rubbed his hand over his face. "I don't see that," he said. "This laser has a wavelength around one micron so it's easy to focus tightly. The surveillance equipment is more like 1 meter, over a million times longer. It doesn't focus like that."

"You mean you don't focus it like that," Darren corrected, "but what if you had a very large source, or you had several beams like your surveillance beam and focused them all at the same spot at the same time?"

Ives paused.

"There are surgical techniques that operate that way," Darren continued. "In that case they use very short wavelengths, but the effect is the same. By crossing a number of beams, you hold the intensity low enough to keep from harming healthy tissue, but by crossing and focusing the radiation, you can target and kill cancerous tissue selectively. It's the same thing here: surgical assassination."

"Christ Almighty," Faye whispered and shook her head. Then she looked up at Walter. "Now I see you why you wanted him here."

Walter smiled. "How do we stop it?" he asked.

"Faye is right," Darren said. "Her cloak wouldn't work against this kind of radiation. The fibers in the cloak will conduct visible and infrared radiation, but not something in Ives' range. You'd need an awfully fat optical fiber for that so stealth won't work. The only other way, as we mentioned, is to hunker down in the radio isolation chamber, but, of course, that has its own drawbacks."

"So," Walter said, "we need to get him before he gets us."

"Which is not trivial," Darren said. "Even if this is right, something on which I certainly wouldn't want to bet my life. Remember this is just one working theory."

"You have others?" Faye asked.

"I'm with Brigham," Darren said. "The fact that I may not know another way doesn't mean there isn't one. Another thing that's still bothering me is the displacement of the attacks. One scenario we haven't discussed is a space-based approach. What if the source of these attacks is in orbit? That would explain how he was able to target Walter and then get back to Europe virtually the next day. If there's a satellite that can hit any square centimeter on the earth's surface, the equation changes again."

"He'd still have to come through the floors and roofs of buildings," Ives said, "so the radio frequency supposition is still sound."

"It's not space-based," Walter said. "Darren's theory is the most likely," then followed with a whisper, "highly likely."

"Are you willing to bet your life on that?" Darren asked.

Walter continued to stare at the laser table. "Yes," he said heavily. "Anyway," he continued, "I expect all of you here to be involved."

He looked at Faye, but her resistance was clearly gone.

"The plane leaves this evening," Walter said. "We'll be in Prague until this is over one way or another."

"Actually, Walter," Darren said, "I have a few errands to run. I'll meet you there in a couple of days."

"Can I presume that means two, not five?" Walter asked.

"Two should do it," Darren said.

"That should be acceptable," Walter said. "It'll take Ives and the rest of us a day or two to set up anyway. Any other exceptions?"

There were none.

Walter reached into his coat pocket and pulled out a small envelope. He handed it to Darren, who looked at the envelope quizzically but took it anyway.

"Thanks for coming, Darren," he said. "We'll see you in a couple of days. Please don't be late."

"I won't be," Darren said. "I'll see you all then. Good luck."

He turned and left the lab.

He was about halfway to the elevator when Brigham came up behind him. "Can I share a ride down?" Brigham asked.

"Of course," Darren said.

On the elevator ride down, Darren began to assemble his headgear in preparation for another ride on the bike.

"I wanted to say thanks again for coming," Brigham said. "Walter... thinks highly of you."

"The feeling is mutual," Darren said, "but I'm not the only one. There were a lot of talented people in that room, and we all know Walter had a lot to do with them realizing their potential."

Brigham nodded.

"How long have you been working with him?" Darren asked.

"Since well before you." Brigham smiled.

"So what's your niche?" Darren asked.

"I'm not extraordinary, if that's what you mean," Brigham said. "I can't see like Ives. I can't disappear like Faye and I can't perform feats like you. I'm just a utility worker. Walter has only two hands. I do what I can to help with the mundane things, to make it easier for him to operate. I'm a gopher, basically."

"That's one helluva room to be a gopher in," Darren said.

Brigham shrugged.

There was a pause.

"I don't think so," Darren said.

"What do you mean?"

"There were no ordinary people in that room," Darren said. "Walter wouldn't bring anyone to this party who didn't add value, and substantial value at that."

"I'm telling you," Brigham said, "I don't have any unusual abilities."

"*That* I'm positive is not true," Darren said. "There are lots of different kinds of abilities. You're here for a reason. Look at the people in that room. What does that tell you?"

"Honestly," Brigham said, "it tells me I don't belong there."

"Do you have so little faith in Walter that you think he'd have you here for no reason?"

"Not no reason," Brigham said. "It's just that I think he's mistaken on the reason in this case."

Darren smiled, but under his mask it was impossible for Brigham to tell.

Then Darren did something he probably shouldn't have. Some time ago, he'd fitted the ocular sets in the mask with sensors to record spectral information. He got the notion while he was looking for tags with his glasses and UV pen. In this case, he mounted the UV lamp on the mask and put more sophisticated analysis sensors near the eye sets. In fact, they fit well right above the eyebrows. Now Darren could flash a UV beam of several different wavelengths and record the spectrum of anything the beam hit. Of course, when he pointed it at a human, he kept the intensity low but it was still enough to get very detailed chemical and forensic information from any surface he chose to target.

When Darren scanned Brigham for chemical signatures, he picked up a residue around Brigham's nose and upper lip. It took only seconds for the spectral library to identify the chemical signature: benzoylmethylecgonine.

That seemed very odd, until he did a search for the common name. Cocaine.

Damn, he thought, but said nothing

"Well, whether Walter has overestimated your contribution or not," Darren said, "can I assume that you're smart enough to know a good thing when you've got one, and that you're going to give every iota Walter asks of you?"

"Yes," Brigham said, stone-faced and determined. "I think that's the real reason Walter keeps me around. We both know I can't add value like the rest of you do, so I just do everything I can to close the value gap with what 'ordinary' abilities I do have."

"Something tells me that'll do," Darren said.

The door to the elevator opened and they stepped out.

"Good to meet you, Brigham," Darren said. "Stay out of trouble and I'll see you in a couple days."

"Good to meet you too, Darren," Brigham said.

Darren walked over to his motorcycle and pulled out the envelope Walter had given him. In true Walter-like fashion, the envelope contained exactly the information Darren needed to complete his errands. Given that, he would have no problem meeting them in Prague on schedule.

CHAPTER
9

In a lot of ways, it was easier in prison.

You didn't have to think about the details of daily life. The meals and shelter were provided for you. The wardrobe and bedding were determined without your input. You didn't have to think about those things. You didn't have to provide for yourself. You didn't have to muster the energy just to move through the day.

You didn't have to be your own driving force.

That made it so much easier.

Inside you didn't have the challenges and pitfalls you did outside. You didn't have the dangers.

All that made it easier, but it was more than that. First, the playing field was even. There was no affluence being paraded in front of you. There were no luxuries to speak of and so there wasn't a constant set of temptations, an endless series of trophies, to compete for. There was no sense of the carrot being dangled in front of you, just out of reach. Second, there were no women. Well, to be fair, you could put those into category one. But lastly, there was no freedom, so even if there were resources and prizes to be acquired, the lockdown nature of the pen made it virtually impossible to maneuver, to get an angle on the others around you.

In the pen, you just did your time. That was your only job.

Outside it was different. There were baited traps everywhere: cars, cash, real estate, all of it. It just made you drool: the ultimate piece of cheese in the ultimate rat trap. And if you fell for it, if you made a grab without being smart about it: Wham! They cut you off at the knees.

What cruel son of a bitch made up this game?

The best strategy here was start small and start smart. In this game you can't go from pen to penthouse in one step. They'd never buy that. But if it looked like you made the transition in believable steps... Well, at least it was a start.

Besides, what was the alternative? Flipping burgers as an ex-con? The end doesn't get any deader than that.

Joseph Kiel had always liked cars, the modern suit of armor, so when a contact in the penitentiary had mentioned an operation on the outside, Joseph was all ears. It was a clever business model. The first part was the standard hot wire and peel, but with all the low jack and tracking technology today, it took all of one minute for the owner to track the car and intercept the thief. The clever part was the operation didn't give them that one minute. The company basically bagged the car in an electrostatic sack. They had a semi-truck that was radio-insulated. Once the target car was mobile, they simply pulled it into the bed of the truck and shut the door. Once inside, the car couldn't communicate: no cell, no internet, no low jack, nothing. Once in the bag, literally, the car just dropped off the grid and the team whisked it away to a secure location. Then, still in the bag, mind you, they could strip it down, remove and disable any tracking hardware, reassemble the car and move the product.

It took a little finesse to launder the VIN number and move the merchandise, but they had the process in place to get it clean. The cars they targeted stayed in the $100k range so the profits were getting pretty impressive.

Modern cars defined the man, his value and his status.

Joseph had been out for almost a year now and he was starting to feel like he was getting his footing. He had even gotten his own car and apartment recently. It was a big step to get out of the ex-con halfway house.

Joseph was on recon tonight. There were five units they had been targeting but he needed to get their routines down cold before the team planned a move. The safest time was always the wee hours of the morning, but it was important to quantify the window, so Joseph had to be patient. It took weeks, sometimes even months, to plan a successful grab. It was tough being that disciplined, but the operation had taught him that skill, and he wasn't the only one. The entire team had their skills. It was the only way they had managed to build up such a successful business.

Joseph logged the time and GPS location of one target then walked a few blocks to locate the next. He would do this several times a night to develop an adequate map of each car's pattern. It was about 2:00 AM and he was about to start the second round when he turned around and his heart froze.

About 100 yards away, there was a guy in a long coat and a floppy rain hat leaning against a street light post. The silhouette of the figure was shockingly stark for someone Joseph knew was more practiced at keeping to the shadows.

His first thought was to turn and keep walking, to pretend he hadn't seen him, but that probably would just have made matters worse.

The music was here. He might as well face it.

Joseph twitched his head at the alleyway across the street. In the dark, no one would have been able to see the motion from 100 yards away, particularly when that someone was standing under a bright streetlight and Joseph was shadowed in the darkness, but Joseph suspected that this figure couldn't have seen it more clearly if Joseph had waved a set of semaphore lights.

The figure pushed away from the street light and slid across the street to the alleyway Joseph had indicated. When the figure had melted into the dark nook, Joseph drifted in that direction as well. There was an infuriating mix of anger and joy in him as he approached his judgment.

Joseph turned his back on the alley and faced outward toward the street then he lit a cigarette and leaned back against a wall at the corner of the alleyway.

"Good to see you, son," Joseph said, still looking out toward the street.

There was a pause as the shadow choked back the response Joseph knew was coming.

"Go on. Let it out," he said.

"What the fuck are you doing?" the shadow said.

Oddly, Joseph felt a tug at his lip and he smiled at the sound of the voice.

"Good to see you, son," Joseph said again, this time the sarcasm was apparent.

"What the fuck are you doing?" the shadow repeated.

"None of your business," Joseph said. "That's what I'm doing."

"A few years in prison hasn't taught you a thing?" the shadow asked.

"This is an old conversation," Joseph said then he dropped the cigarette, crushed it with his foot, pushed off the wall and started to leave.

"Wait," the shadow said with a sigh.

Joseph stopped and straightened.

"I'm sorry," the shadow said. "It's good to see you, too."

Joseph sighed, reached for another cigarette, and returned to his place on the wall.

There was a long silence.

"I was in town and I wanted to say hi," the shadow said.

Joseph nodded. "How have you been?" he said.

"Good," the shadow said. "Productive."

Another twitch and a smile came to Joseph's face. He almost wished the shadow could have seen it.

"Where have you been?" Joseph said.

"Europe," the voice said.

"What brings you back?" Joseph said.

"A project," the shadow said.

"Can I help?" Joseph asked.

There was a pause.

"No," the shadow said. "Thanks."

Joseph nodded.

"I'm assuming we can't have that lunch," Joseph said.

"I'm still wanted," the shadow said.

Another pause.

"I just wanted to say hi."

"Try to see your mom," Joseph said.

"I was sorry to hear about the divorce."

"It's probably better," Joseph said.

"Good to see you, Dad."

Joseph felt a tug at his throat at that one.

"I'm sorry, but the carjacking ring will be gone by morning," the shadow said. "Find another job."

Joseph didn't know whether to yell, curse, or turn around and try to punch the orator, but it was irrelevant.

Joseph knew the shadow was already gone.

***

The parking lot was empty. It usually was at 5:00 AM, or at least nearly so. That didn't make it safe. That just made it less lethal. Trouble had a tendency to spring up quickly around here so Corrine Daniels had developed the habit of staying alert. Of course, that was usually difficult at this hour, particularly when she had worked a double shift.

She always splashed some cold water on her face before packing up to leave, but today she could feel the fatigue dragging her down, dulling her reactions, diluting her lucidity. She had her keys at the ready, her purse good and tight under her arm and her coat zipped and buttoned before venturing out to her car.

It was deathly still.

She could hear every squeak of her shoes on the rain-wet pavement. She walked the one hundred feet to her car and pushed the unlock button on her key fob while she continued to scan for any movement, any trouble. When she got to the driver's side door, she yanked on the handle, but the door did not react and she lurched forward from the force of her own arm.

The door was still locked.

Corrine raised an eyebrow. She could have sworn she'd pushed the unlock button, but it was irrelevant. She unlocked the door with the physical key, checked the back seat carefully to make sure she had no unwanted passengers, climbed in and relocked the door.

Still looking around, she fastened her seat belt, slid the key into the ignition, pressed the clutch pedal with her left foot, and turned the key.

The engine gave a sluggish groan and quieted.

"Oh, no," Corrine breathed.

She tried again and got nothing but an even more sluggish complaint from the engine.

"Damn ..." Corrine began.

After one more try, she reached up and turned off the headlight switch with her left hand. The switch had been left on for the entire duration of the double shift.

"Mother f...," she spat and leaned on the wheel.

She collected herself for several seconds before stomping down on the clutch and twisting the key in the ignition so hard, she thought she might snap it off. In fact, she meant to.

"Son of a bitch!" she screamed before all hell broke loose.

Suddenly the vehicle lurched forward like someone had just slammed into it from behind. There was no sound but Corrine's car jumped forward about five feet. She instinctively pulled her hand away from the ignition and her foot off the clutch, but that just made matters worse.

She heard the tires skid on the pavement and she pitched forward so violently that the seatbelt had to restrain her from hitting the steering wheel. The car bucked back and forth for several seconds. When the motion finally settled down, the only thing Corrine could hear over the thumping of her heart was the rattle of the car engine.

It had started on its own.

Corrine looked behind to see what had hit her but saw nothing. She jumped out of the car and examined the back bumper.

There was no damage. She stood in the middle of the empty parking lot. There was no one, no movement, and no sound save for her own car engine.

In her experience, small miracles had only one name.

"Darren," she whispered and looked to the shadows.

"Darren!" she yelled into the night. "Darren!"

There was no answer.

"I know it was you," she whispered, "and I know where to find you."

It was a two-hour drive.

She would have tried another way but, of course, that was part of the problem. There was no other way to reach him.

The good news was that Corrine's previously weighty fatigue had been washed away, eclipsed by her determination at the present task. She was sure it would come back with a vengeance soon enough, but she'd have her satisfaction by then.

Dawn was just breaking when she reached the supposedly abandoned estate and drove up the cracked driveway to the flattened remains of Darren's house.

It looked much the same as she remembered, strewn planks, charred foundation, brooding fireplace chimney and all. It was more peaceful though. Still air and dew graced the site with a solemnity that brought her pulse down a notch. Orange light creeping over the horizon was just beginning to touch the upper reaches of the chimney, giving the site a church-like quality. She was glad there was no wind. It would make it easier to talk.

She walked up and stood next to one of the trees, one she knew contained microphones too small to see but which Darren monitored continuously.

"You could at least have said hello," she said to the tree.

There was no response.

"I know you're not going to *not* answer me," she said with a little more edge.

"I'm sorry," the tree answered.

She had to admit it was glorious to hear his voice again.

"You are here," she said.

"I said I would be."

"Are you actually here or somewhere else?"

"Somewhere else, and moving on fast."

"But not so fast as to not stop by."

"Well, obviously I can't deny it. I hadn't planned to, but…"

"You couldn't have stopped for five seconds? Just to say hello, here's a jumpstart, gotta go."

"Would that have made it better? Just blink in and disappear? I don't think that would have made it better."

Corrine said nothing.

"Look, I'll admit it was pretty juvenile to just watch and not say hello, but then I saw your car wouldn't start and I couldn't just leave you there so I tried to get away with it."

"Well, thanks for the jump anyway."

Silence.

"You say you're moving on. Does that mean you're running?"

"Working."

"No one works 24/7, not even you."

"The fact that I'm working is not the reason I didn't stop. The fact that I '*work*' is the reason I didn't. You know what happened last time."

"We both live entirely different lives now. That past is far behind. It seems it's taking it too far to avoid any association, to zip around at 4:00 AM when no one else is around, just out of paranoia. I hope you're not living your life that way."

"Kind of."

"Darren…" she began.

"It's not paranoia, Corrine. It's caution."

"Look, I'm not saying I don't appreciate your being careful, I'm just saying there is such a thing as taking it too far. I'm not talking about me. If you treat everyone in your life this way, I think you're going overboard."

"Do you remember my friend Adam?"

"Yes."

"He was killed."

Corrine gasped.

"I'm sorry," she said. "I didn't know."

Silence.

"I don't know what to say," Corrine said. "I wish you were here."

"Just try to understand I can't not do this, and as long as that is the case, it's not reasonable to involve other people."

"There is a difference between being involved and just having simple human contact."

"Honestly, Corrine, we haven't spoken in a long time. I'd really rather not argue about this."

Corrine took a breath.

"How are you?" Darren asked.

Corrine smiled.

"Honestly?" she said. "I'm lecturing you about working too hard, but I could probably stand to take some of my own advice."

"I was glad to see you left Mercy. Your current assignment is not as much of a war zone. Not that I've been checking…"

"No, I get it. I was glad to get out of there. The Orchard is nothing like it was. It's a lot better, a lot more civilized, a lot less violent, but I still wanted to move on. This one is a few levels above the hell the Orchard used to be and the staff is pretty good. After this, I'm thinking of specializing, maybe pediatrics."

"That's great."

"Yeah, we'll see. My office is on the same floor as the maternity ward and I find myself being drawn in that direction."

There was a silence. It sounded like Darren had a question but he hesitated to ask it, something about which she was curious but didn't want to know the answer.

"Your turn," Corrine said with a smile. "Where have you been and what have you been doing?"

"Corrine…"

"You know mine, Darren. You've checked up on me and I've told you my story. Now give."

"Umm…"

"Darren, we're on the phone, on a secure line. You can't call this involvement, and you can't check up on me without it going both ways. Give!"

Darren took a breath. "I've been spending a lot of time in Europe."

"Why Europe?"

"At first it seemed a good place to flee since I had gathered a little too much interest from L.A. law enforcement and wanted that to cool down. Then I started doing a little more research, and it seemed like a good area to operate in. The problem last time was that I was concentrating on a single area. That tended to bring a lot of unwanted attention and subsequent trouble. The strategy these days is to hit and run. I'll stay in one area for a week or two, try to make an impact, then move to the next area. The local effect is measurable, if less dramatic. The overall impact is better and sustainable."

"So you're operating in a much wider area in general?"

"Yes."

"And that means you can more easily maintain anonymity?"

"That was another goal, for obvious reasons. I'm concentrating a bit more on stealth now. Many cases don't even know there was an intervention, never mind how it was done, never mind who did it. It's safer that way, for everyone."

"That does sound safer, and securely anonymous."

Silence.

"Safe enough to act like a human being when you're not doing it," Corrine said.

"Corrine…" Darren began.

"Darren, listen. I understand your caution. I understand your fear for those you care about. I even understand guilt for your friend Adam and whatever else happened. All of it is reasonable, but it does not add up to making the solitary life justifiable."

"Corrine…" Darren attempted again.

"I'm not expecting to convince you here, now, but I want you to reflect on this. Consider all the steps you've taken and the changes you've made. Consider the realistic risk of saying hello to a friend at 4:00 AM on a continent thousands of miles from where you've been operating, where people don't even know you've been, where you have no identifiable enemies, and even if you did, they would have no idea who you are much less where to find you."

Silence.

Corrine took a breath.

"You're so good at planning," she said, "your toys, your tactics, your strategies, your interventions. Maybe one of the reasons you don't stop and say hello is that you didn't have it scripted. You didn't have a plan for that contingency. Darren, you don't always have to have a plan. Sometimes you can just see what happens."

More silence.

"I thought you said pediatrics not psychiatry," Darren said.

It sounded like there was a smile in there somewhere.

"Boys and their toys," Corrine said. "There's a lot of overlap between fields. Just think about it."

"I always think about everything."

Corrine smiled.

"Yeah, you do, don't you?" she said.

"This is not an excuse," Darren said, "but I do need to go."

Corrine nodded.

"I don't know why I'm telling you this," Darren said, "but I'm about to get a lot more focused on a particular area. A friend of mine needs help with a specific problem and it sounds pretty important. That's going to run counter to a lot of the anonymity we just talked about."

"Now I'm worried."

"Sorry."

"No, I'm glad you told me."

"Take care."

"You too."

The channel went dead.

"And stay safe," Corrine said.

CHAPTER
10

Darren met the group in Prague two days later. The good news was Darren had given Walter some basic equipment for the operation. The bad news was, although he kept an apartment here, Prague was hours from his nearest real workshop. That would limit how effective he could be if this got dicey.

"So, what's the plan, Walter?" Darren asked.

"Ives is set up, so our surveillance throughout the capital building and Minister's house is pretty solid. He also has a detector for each of us to carry so we can know if the assassin may be watching."

Walter gave Darren something about the size of a large wallet.

"If we detect the radiation, doesn't it mean he's watching, by definition?" Darren asked.

"Yes, but it may not be you," Ives said. "There is a depth component to this technology. If you are half a mile out, but he's watching something a mile out, you may be standing in the beam but he won't know it unless he pulls in his focus, or in this case, sets up the timing differently."

"Can you see two things at once if you chop the beam; effectively look at two positions simultaneously?" Darren asked.

"Yes, but I don't," Ives said. "It's like using a telescope. You can see your target very well, but there's a lot going on around you that you may not see if you don't look for it, and you can't look at everything at the same time."

Darren nodded. "We hope," he said.

"I am going to talk to the Minister," Walter said.

"Just like that?" Darren asked.

"It has to be in person," Walter said. "You can't make a connection like this over the phone."

"The assassin knows who you are," Faye said. "If he sees you talking to the Minister…"

"We've got to start somewhere," Walter said. "If I can convince the Minister that we have to help each other…it'd be a beginning."

***

He had begun preparations some time ago, well before this devil had begun to haunt him, well before the noose had begun to tighten.

That was a good thing.

If the plan hadn't been well under way, it would have been impossible to execute under the watchful ubiquitous eye of this harbinger of death. He was too thorough. He was too meticulous. He knew Sergei's every move, sometimes it seemed his every thought so it was a blessing that the plan was virtually running on autopilot by the time the nightmare began four weeks ago.

Sergei periodically checked the progress electronically, mostly by monitoring the balance of his offshore accounts, but almost never spoke of it to anyone. If communication was necessary, he'd usually text. On the rare occasion that texting was insufficient, he would arrange a face-to-face discussion while he was on a government jet 35,000 feet in the air and carrying nothing that he might usually take along.

Either the devil didn't know about his preparations, or he didn't care.

Either way Sergei only needed another couple of weeks. The GDP, agricultural, and manufacturing reports were due out next week along with a plethora of quarterly reports from companies Sergei was close to.

That had been his plan since he was twelve, not explicitly of course, but there was a natural progression to these things and Sergei was close to the inevitable conclusion of his professional path.

He'd even arranged the exit strategy, a flight in the middle of the night via a plane chartered through a third party, virtually untraceable. Sergei and his family would simply disappear in the middle of the night, never to be seen or heard from again. He would escape this devil and the investigations into his business practices that would be coming soon enough.

Just another couple of weeks.

He needed to appease the assassin for another couple of weeks before he could forget about all this and spend the rest of his life alternating between Switzerland and Costa Rica.

Of course the family would protest, but in the end they simply didn't have a say. His wife, Letitia, would fall in line. His son, Matthias, didn't have the will to resist an insistent mouse never mind a strong-willed father. His daughter, Lyly, wouldn't agree with a winning lottery ticket but she would comply even if she needed to be gagged and bound. Sergei estimated that was a distinct possibility.

At any rate, it was firming up. None of the demands the terrorist had placed on him were sufficient to get him thrown out of office in the next three weeks and none of them put a block on the flow of money from state funds to his own safehouse accounts so, the situation was satisfactory for the moment.

This latest development did concern him, however. This meeting he'd been effectively forced to schedule at 6:00 AM, a time when the entire house was, usually, asleep including himself. Enough people had told him it was important that he had granted the meeting, but the details had been vague and that made Sergei not only suspicious but impatient.

"Mr. Rocaena," Sergei greeted him with a nod.

"Mr. Prime Minister," Rocaena replied. "I apologize for the late hour and I appreciate your seeing me."

"It is late, Mr. Rocaena," Sergei said. "What is this about?"

"Forgive me, sir," Rocaena said. "This is a matter of some delicacy. We chose the hour for that reason. I understand you have an unusual problem."

"I don't know what you're referring to," Sergei said. "And in the interest of time, please be more specific."

"I understand that there have been threats on your life," Rocaena said.

"That happens every day for a man in my position, Mr. Rocaena," Sergei said. "That is not new, nor a reason for this meeting."

"I understand this particular threat is more real, immediate, and omnipresent," Rocaena said. "The reports are that he can see you anytime and seems to be able to threaten you with impunity."

Now Sergei's blood began to boil. Few people knew about his situation, and none of them had the audacity or foolhardiness to discuss it so unabashedly. It was reckless.

"Where do you get this information?" Sergei demanded.

"Personal experience," Rocaena said. "We have a common enemy."

"Then you are either a liar or a fool," Sergei said, "because no one who has direct experience of this threat would discuss it openly. Anyone who knew what this assassin can do would know that it is suicidal. Good evening to you, Mr. Rocaena."

"Sir?" Rocaena, surprised at the dismissal, began to speak.

"Good evening, Mr. Rocaena," Sergei ordered, "or do I need to get security involved?"

Rocaena sat in the chair with his mouth open for several seconds before collecting himself and standing up. He looked like he was going to say something then decided the better of it and simply walked to the door.

Sergei watched him leave without another word.

Walter left the Prime Minister's office seething, but he allowed the guards to escort him out of the building without protest.

When he finally exited through the front door, the valet waved his limo forward. When the car stopped, the valet opened the door. Walter threw himself in the limo and sat down with all the impact he could muster then he shuffled to the far end of the vehicle, opened the door and got out again. He put on a furious look, which he did not have to falsify, opened his mouth like he was going to yell at the valet, stepped aside so Faye could get into the car unimpeded, and closed his mouth as if he had thought better of berating the valet. Then he climbed back into the car.

Darren, in the role of chauffeur, pulled away from the Prime Minister's residence. He left the grounds and began the inevitable battle with early morning commute traffic in the center of the city. He made his way toward the district that housed Faye's quarters.

Even before they cleared the grounds, Ives called through the comm link. "OK," he said. "It looks like that worked. Faye, you got the placement about right."

Faye said nothing.

"The good news is I can hear what's going on in the office," Ives said. "The bad news is he picked up the phone a few seconds ago. Here he is."

Ives switched the channel so everyone on the line could hear. The team could hear the Prime Minister just fine, but, unfortunately, not the voice on the other end.

"Yes," the Prime Minister said. "This is Sergei. Sorry to wake you, but you asked me to call to inform you if anyone approached me about you. Yes. This evening. His name is Walter Rocaena. He's an industrialist from the United States. He claims that you have targeted him as well and that we have a common enemy. He wanted my help in catching you."

There was a pause.

"I didn't tell him anything," the Prime Minister continued. "I said he was foolish to be approaching me like this and I threw him out of my office. I told him I didn't want his help."

Another pause.

"He left a few minutes ago. No. I don't know where he's staying. No. I don't know how to contact him."

Pause.

"By limo."

Pause.

"Just a second."

"Shit," Walter spat. "Darren, stop."

"What?"

"Stop! Everyone out!"

Darren stopped the car in the middle of the street. Everyone jumped out.

The group scattered.

Of course melting away wasn't a problem for Faye, and Darren was pretty much in his element, but Walter was a little less well prepared. He wound his way between semi-stopped cars to the sidewalk and entered the slow-moving river of humanity.

"Ives, keep me tapped," he called.

"XH6743G," the Prime Minister said to the assassin on the line.

It was the license number of the now-abandoned limo.

Unfortunately, that means he'll be able to reasonably surmise that we bugged the prime minister's office, Walter thought. *Why else would we abandon the car in the middle of the street?*

"What?" the Prime Minister asked. "How am I supposed to do that? I just told you I don't know where he's staying."

Pause.

"On what charge? What's the pretext for hunting him down?"

"Spectacular," Walter spat.

"Walter?" Darren called over the comm line, "would you like an escort to your quarters?"

"Where are you?" Walter asked.

"I'm probably a couple of hundred yards southeast of the limo."

Surgical

"Well, I went north," Walter said. "Come north and we'll figure out a way to rendezvous discreetly. Keep some distance and monitor me. I don't want it to look like we're together."

"On my way," Darren said.

"Faye," Walter called.

"Yes," Faye said.

"We're going to wind our way toward your quarters," Walter said. "You can keep heading that way. I don't think we'll need you, but stay on call."

"Got it," Faye said.

"Shit!" Ives spat. "Walter?"

"Yes."

"The Minister just released an APB with your picture and description, including what you're wearing."

"That son of a bitch," Walter said. "Faye, where are you?"

"West," Faye said.

"Head north," Walter said. "Ives, pick a rendezvous point halfway between us and find some place I can disappear. Faye, they're going to have every traffic cam and ATM looking for my face. You're going to have to cloak me and get me to a secure location."

"No, Walter," Ives said. "Turn left and stay in that alcove. Have Faye come to you. The longer you stay on the street, the more you give them a chance of spotting you."

Walter complied. He glanced around and found the nook Ives suggested. He pulled up his collar and kept his face hidden as he walked over to the hiding place and took a position behind one of the dumpsters. It smelled like garbage and urine. The stink of the place almost made him gag as he tried to remain still and blend into the surroundings. Fortunately, there were no other street people in the alcove to potentially give away his position.

Then he heard the sirens, all too close. He hadn't gotten one hundred yards from the limo before ducking for cover, and that may not have been enough.

Red and white lights flashed from the direction he'd come and converged on the abandoned limo.

"Shit!" Walter said. "Ives, they're too close."

"Walter, you can't move now," Ives said. "If you think that corner is risky, it's nothing compared to the street out in the open."

"Faye," Walter called.

"About two minutes," Faye said.

The police had left their vehicles now and begun searching the street. Apparently, they'd surmised Walter had not had another car waiting so they began a foot search of the immediate vicinity.

Walter could see flashlight beams cut through the air in lethal arcs. The beams began to fan out from the limo site in all directions, most notably his. The problem was there were sirens coming from all directions now and they all seemed to be getting closer.

Ives was right.

There was nowhere to go.

Walter could see the heads of the cops waving the flashlights now. The foot traffic that he needed to help conceal him had dispersed and evaporated before the sweeping sickle. Walter tried to shrink further into the fetid hole.

"Faye?" Walter whispered.

"About 30 seconds out, Walter," Darren called.

"Going radio silent," Walter breathed.

As the crowds continued to thin, he could see the full silhouette of the approaching policemen. There were three of them. As they swept their flashlights back and forth, white light splashed into his hideaway with loathsome intensity. Walter slouched and tried to look homeless.

That was problematic when he was wearing a $2000 coat.

The cops seemed to be zeroing in on his location. They were no longer drifting in a random walk. Unfortunately, Walter's alcove was the only recessed point on the street. It was a natural hiding place, and the police were now funneling toward it.

There was virtually no one on the street to hide Walter now. A few drunken strays staggered around in front of the police, but the intervening space was otherwise clear. Walter held his breath, but one of the search team must have seen him because he locked the flashlight beam directly on the alcove and made a beeline in Walter's direction. He wasn't twenty feet away and coming at a brisk trot when Walter felt something brush against him.

It felt like a soft breeze.

Just at that instant, one of the drunks bumped into the approaching patrol officer. He knocked the flashlight away from Walter's alcove and almost knocked over the cop. There was an irritable scuffle and a brief moment when the drunkard stood directly between the cop and Walter.

At that instant, a seam opened up in midair right in front of Walter. He stepped in and the seam resealed.

The cop pushed the drunkard to the ground, pulled out his nightstick, and smashed him in the head with a vicious blow. He wound up for a second strike but realized that the nightstick had broken in half. The drunkard grabbed his head and curled up into a ball screaming. The cop tossed the broken nightstick aside. Walter could hear it clatter against the pavement. The cop stepped over the writhing form of the homeless man and again trained his flashlight directly into Walter's hideaway.

It was a strange sensation.

Walter could see the light beam full on his chest but as he looked back, he cast no shadow on the graffiti-filled wall. He put his arm around Faye and silently kissed her on the cheek. Faye smiled, but held her hand on Walter's shoulder very firmly.

The cop came closer.

He wasn't three feet from them, with his flashlight scanning every square millimeter of the alcove. He scanned back and forth, right over the two of them, but gave no indication that he saw anything but the fetid air and garbage. He pulled away slowly and moved past.

Faye and Walter were in no hurry to wade through the wall of police patrolmen. They waited until the search party had moved on before they came out onto the street and began to carefully and deliberately trek to Walter's quarters.

"Moving," Faye whispered.

At that, the drunkard the policeman had clubbed rose, apparently unharmed, and fell into place, shadowing Faye and Walter. It was only then that Walter noticed the drunkard was wearing Darren's signature coat and rain hat.

CHAPTER
11

Parisi Behrmen couldn't escape it. This had to be done, and he was the one it had fallen upon. It was likely the end of his career. He just prayed it didn't end up being more than that. People who failed the Minister had a way of being kicked to the curb, if not disappearing altogether, and this was an unforgivable failure. He had no explanation. Well, none that the Minister was going to hear. He had no excuse that the Minister would take into consideration. The Minister had a nasty habit of not being swayed by the facts in a given case if those facts were inconvenient to his personal agenda.

In the end, Parisi simply needed to face the music and pray.

He walked up to the office and girded himself for the moment. The fact that dawn was breaking and they had all been up the entire night wasn't going to make this any easier or the Minister any more generous.

"What do you mean you lost him?" the Minister yelled. "How could you lose him? He had barely left the grounds. His car was less than a mile from here."

"He wasn't in the car," Parisi said. "He abandoned it in the street. He got out and melted into the crowd. He slipped through our sweep."

"How could he slip through your sweep?" Sergei yelled louder. "He couldn't have been one hundred yards from the car. You had dozens of officers. There's no way you could have missed him!"

"Sir, I have no explanation for how that happened," Parisi admitted, "but if I may, I'd like to inquire as to how he knew we were coming."

"What?" Sergei asked.

"Sir, he abandoned the car just minutes after he left your office. He started running even before we had a chance to mobilize. Did he know you were going to arrest him, and if so, why not arrest him at the gate? Why not even before he had a chance to get in the car?"

"What are you saying?" Sergei demanded.

"Sir, I'm saying that the decision seems to have been made after he left the grounds, and he seems to have been made aware of it in real time, even before the police."

Sergei was silent for a moment.

"Sir, the circumstances lead me to question if he might have a listening device in your office."

Sergei paused then seemed to erupt in an even greater rage.

"Find him!" Sergei ordered. "I don't care if you have to call in the military to do the job you obviously aren't competent to perform. I want this person found. He is a terrorist and this is a matter of national security. Do you understand?"

"Yes, sir."

"Get out of my sight," Sergei said.

Parisi spun on his heel and exited the office. It was just possible that the Minister was distracted enough that he forgot to fire him.

The phone rang seconds after the police chief had exited and the doors closed.

"He's right," the voice on the other end said. "Rocaena must have planted something when he was there."

"How could he?" Sergei began.

"It doesn't matter," the voice said. "Have the room checked. Tear it apart if you have to, just make sure you find whatever he planted. In the meantime, find another room to use, but keep your phone with you."

Sergei groused. He felt like a dog whose obedience collar had just been snapped.

"Put all your attention on finding and eliminating him," the voice said. "Check the airport and find which plane he came in on then search any car service he might have used to get to wherever he is staying locally. He won't be easy to find, so try to dig up someone competent enough to run him down. Any of your usual imbeciles won't do."

Sergei would have spat at him for the insult if he hadn't been in the proverbial cage.

"If you don't make progress on this by tomorrow, I'll need to take steps to motivate you."

The phone went dead with that all-too-common threat.

Sergei was getting used to this specter haunting him in this way, but at least two things were new here. First, why did he care about this man? The way he was reacting, Rocaena seemed to present some kind of threat to the ghost. Sergei couldn't imagine how that could be, but he was clearly reacting to this development. Why would it be so important to find him? How did this devil even know him? Second, if the devil was distracted by Rocaena, that could only be good for Sergei. He would have that much less attention to focus on making Sergei's life hell. If the circumstances had been different, Rocaena might have helped Sergei: the enemy of my enemy and all that.

***

"Son of a bitch!" Walter almost screamed as he exited Faye's cloak, finally, to walk freely in his quarters. They had walked almost two miles from the limo to a location he could trust, for the moment, was secure.

Darren came to the back door a few seconds later as Faye uncloaked and began to pack away her gear.

Walter took a deep breath and tried to gather himself. "Thank you both," he said, almost as an afterthought.

Faye and Darren nodded.

"You too, Ives," he said to thin air.

"Of course," Ives acknowledged.

Walter began to pace, a habit Darren knew better than to interrupt.

Faye was not as attuned. "Now what?" she asked.

Walter shot her a glare and Faye fell silent. She looked at Darren, who simply shook his head. He still had his mask on so there was no facial expression to interpret, but the gesture carried the message clearly enough: be quiet and let him think.

"Obviously that asshole isn't going to make this any easier," Walter groused, mostly to himself. "Now we have two problems to deal with, and when they find the bug, we'll be another step backward: blind and deaf."

"And hunted," Faye said.

Walter looked up then continued pacing. "What do we know?" he asked.

"That the Minister isn't going to help," Ives said. "He'll rat us out any chance he gets."

"That the assassin isn't going to stop," Darren said. "If anything, I'd guess he'll be more motivated now that he knows you're here. He'll be looking for you."

"We know we can't cope with the situation blind and deaf," Faye said.

Walter was silent then he pointed at Darren. "You said he wasn't going to stop. What is he not going to stop?"

"Terrorizing the Minister, destabilizing the political environment, making disruptive demands."

"… and watching," Walter finished.

"Reasonable assumption," Darren said.

"He doesn't have to watch," Ives said. "He's got the Minister on a leash. A simple phone call can accomplish anything he wants. He doesn't need a weapon when he has the Minister in his pocket."

"Technically true," Walter said, "but if you were the assassin, would you fly blind?"

There was a pause.

"No," Ives said.

"I'm betting he won't either," Walter said. "He has to check in. He has to watch. He has to keep tabs on the minister. You don't have an ability like that and not use it, particularly if you believe you're invulnerable. Why would he not use the surveillance if it's available? If I were him, I would feel compelled to."

"Fine, so he'll be watching," Ives said. "That doesn't do us much good."

"Well, let's make it do us some good," Walter said. "We need to find him. It's as simple as that. We need to find him, and we can surmise he'll be watching. How can we use that to our advantage?"

"The question itself implies that we need to detect the surveillance wave," Darren said.

"Can we?"

There was a pause.

"Not without a sensor," Ives said. "There has to be a way to detect it. There's nothing in the office that I can use to pick up the signal."

"We'll have to get one back there," Walter said, looking at Faye.

Faye rolled her eyes. "Of course," she said resignedly. "Then can we track the signal and find him?"

"No," Ives said, "not with anything you could carry, and certainly not with anything you could hide. Nothing I can lay my hands on out here, and quickly, would provide the precision that we need. I can give you something that can detect the signal but it will be rough, and it won't tell you what direction."

"What about two?" Darren asked.

"Same problem," Ives said. "No way to detect the direction."

"No," Darren said, "what if we had one in the office and one a few hundred yards away? I can carry it. I can move it around. Then we should be able to get some direction information, even from a simple detector."

"That could work," Ives said, "but there are two problems. One: it'll be pretty rough. The further away you get, the potentially greater precision we could have to detect the direction, but that leaves problem number two: it'll be slower. We have to orbit the office with a pretty long radius and search around. That'll take time, particularly if you want to avoid raising suspicion by doing loops around the parliament building at ninety miles an hour."

"It'll have to do," Walter said. "We need to find this bastard, and even though the Minister is worthless, we need to stop this terror reign. Ives, work on putting together something Faye can take and hide. Am I correct in assuming that even if it's an office or two away, it should still be sufficient?"

"Should be," Ives said.

"Make a few; one for the Minister's office, one for his home, and maybe we'll pick another haunt or two. Then make one for Darren to carry. From there, we'll have to go fishing and hope we get luckier than tonight."

***

The ability to pick locks is one of the requisite tools of the stealth operative. In fact, you have to be very good at it. All the stealth technology in the world cannot grant a human being the ability to walk through walls, at least not yet, so, to be effective, you have to be able to defeat the standard barriers that restrict access to anyone else. There are also alarm systems that accompany any self-respecting modern lock and those need to be circumvented as well.

There was one advantage Faye had that others didn't: time. Ordinarily, you couldn't just park yourself at someone's back door while security personnel patrolled the grounds, but Faye could. She could take her sweet time working even the most stubborn lock. The only thing she had to be careful of was having the door knob too far inside the cloak. If anyone noticed that the door knob was missing or, in this case, had become invisible, that would raise a few eyebrows. Still managing the visibility of the doorknob was quite a bit less challenging than trying to act like she belonged on her adversary's porch picking a lock at 1:00 AM.

Still, it wasn't easy. Deadbolts were always a pain and of course she needed to be quiet as a mouse. The good news was that once she finally did work her way through three locks and two alarm systems, Ives could tell her the optimal moment to slide through without anyone seeing. That was one convenience she usually didn't have. Ordinarily there was always a risk of an armed guard on the other side of the door catching her flatfooted the minute she decided to step in.

Usually when that happened, they were so confused by a door opening on its own that Faye could get close enough to taze them out of the equation. There were exceptions, of course. One time the guard had been wise enough to shoot first and ask questions later and quick enough to put nine bullet holes in Faye's cloak and a crease across her rib cage before she was able to deal with him. The only one more pissed off than the guard was Faye, who had to limp home, needing repairs. It was not her best day.

By comparison, today was a cakewalk. Faye took care of the locks. Ives took care of the milling patrol around the Minister's residence. Faye placed Ives' sensors judiciously in the living room and bedrooms. Ives got her out. Faye relocked the doors and exited the grounds through the back entryway.

Smooth as silk.

Now she just hoped the sensors would help save this rat bastard's life.

Unfortunately, they wouldn't find that out for another two weeks.

***

Two weeks was too long.

It had been two weeks since Rocaena had approached the Minister, and that sniveling worm hadn't made the slightest progress on finding his target, not that it was all that surprising. He was incompetent and self-centered, after all. It made him easier to control, but less useful, a good one to practice on but hardly a big game player.

Still, Rocaena was out there and certainly trying to track him down. The annoying part was he was clever enough to have a shot at it, particularly if given enough time. Well, two weeks were already too much time to give him.

It was time to cut this game short and move on.

Just so it wouldn't be a total loss, he had one more job for his mostly-useless pawn. Maybe he'd go out with a bang.

***

The message froze Sergei to the core.

Had he read that correctly?

"Kill the president. You have 24 hours."

A bitter wave of panic washed over him like an electric current on a raw nerve ending.

He couldn't have read that correctly. How could the assassin possibly be asking him to kill the president? That didn't make any sense. When the shock wore off and he realized this was a genuine order, Sergei began to consider his options.

Even making an attempt on the president's life was out of the question. Still, any debate on the subject was futile. This devil had no reason to negotiate, and no history of doing so. Any time Sergei tried to discuss his demands, the demon made his implacability painfully clear.

The first time Sergei had questioned his orders, the assassin had nearly blown his left arm off. There was an explosion inside his left shoulder that felt like a gun shot out of nowhere. There was no entry wound and no exit wound. In fact, there was no evidence at all. That was the genius of it. If the assassin had targeted his leg, Sergei would have developed a limp that would have raised questions. If he had targeted Sergei's right arm, it might have affected Sergei's ability to function, sign documents, shake hands, etc. Again, that would have raised alarms, but the Minister could get along without his left arm, at least in the short term, at least until the wound healed. There was an ugly bruise that developed over a week later, a sign of deep tissue damage, but it wasn't anything a long-sleeved shirt couldn't cover.

The second time Sergei questioned his orders, the assassin wasn't so merciful. He killed Sergei's undersecretary, the closest thing he had to a friend in the Czech government. After that, Sergei learned never to question his tormentor, unless it was to ask for clarification.

No clarification was required here.

The instruction was clear as day; even the schedule had been set. The first rational question Sergei never asked was: why didn't the assassin just kill the president himself? It would be quicker, cleaner, and have zero chance of failure. But, on reflection, Sergei realized that was probably the point.

The assassin wanted it messy. He wanted it disruptive. He wanted it to reek of scandal and chaos and uncertainty. He wanted it to be destabilizing, and what could be more destabilizing to a country than having its president assassinated by one of his own cabinet members?

The question was: what now?

If Sergei went through with it, he would either be killed himself or caught and jailed for the rest of his life. If he defied the assassin, the result was obvious; Sergei was dead, along with everyone he cared about.

In the end, there was only one option, whatever the risk.

***

Lyly was sound asleep when all hell broke loose.

Surgical

The door burst open with a loud bang and flashlight beams poured through the portal and cut through the darkness.

The guy next to her, she didn't remember his name, screamed like a girl and scrambled toward the headboard. It was the furthest point from the door.

Lyly was barely aware of him as she too screamed and clutched the sheet and blankets to her body.

One of the burly forms stepped into the room, approached her partner's cowering form, produced a Taser and jammed it into the boy's chest.

The target flailed spasmodically for several seconds and went limp.

It was pandemonium.

Lyly scrambled from the bed in a bid to make it to the door. She didn't get two feet before another burly form stiff-armed her and knocked her back onto the bed. Before she knew what was happening, the same heavyset faceless assailant climbed on top of her and used the very blankets she was clutching to pin her down with her arms against her chest.

Feeling like she'd been encased in set concrete, Lyly opened her mouth to let out the loudest scream she could muster.

The sound never came.

A second man clapped a cloth over her mouth that had been soaked in chemicals and reeked of a hospital ward. Lyly choked on the gag for only a handful of seconds before consciousness began to seep away.

Her last thought was her most certain and most coherent: this had something to do with her father.

CHAPTER
12

One of the problems with working nocturnally was that it wasn't the body's natural state. Darren had mostly gotten used to it, but it was never preferred. Being in Europe, then back in the US, and back again in Europe, and mostly working in the daytime, had confused the matter further. That's why it was particularly annoying when the phone rang at 3:15 AM.

"Darren, the Minister's moving," Ives said.

"What?" Darren said, still shaking off the cobwebs.

"He's moving," Ives repeated. "I'm not sure what he's doing, but he's packing, and he and his wife are up and about."

Darren was still groggy. "Is the assassin watching?"

"No," Ives said, "but something is going on. Can you suit up and make it over there? I've got a bad feeling."

"Yeah," Darren said, rising from the bed. "Give me fifteen minutes to dress and get out there."

Surgical

***

There's only one thing more terrifying than the inescapable threat of death: the inescapable threat of imminent death.

Sergei had never felt anything like this, not even the time that maniacal sergeant in the Czech army had held a gun to his head and threatened to blow his brains out just to make a point. His platoon had gone off book on a recon mission and this was the sergeant's way of instilling greater discipline. He could still feel the cold barrel of the gun against his forehead, could smell the filthy sergeant's BO and the way cigar smoke clung to his fatigues. He could still hear his own heart beat over the silence of the shocked platoon members.

But this was different.

First of all, that sergeant hadn't threatened Sergei's family. He hadn't held a gun to Sergei's wife's head, not that he had even met her at that point. The sergeant hadn't threatened to extinguish everyone and everything Sergei cared about. He only threatened Sergei with a quick, painless death. Sergei could almost get comfortable with that, but not his family, not his loved ones. Second, Sergei could see the sergeant, could look him in the eye. He could face him. The sergeant didn't just cling to the air like some nightmarish ghost, haunting him, mocking him, eroding his sanity. He was real, present, tangible, and if death came, it would have been quick.

The assassin was like a force of nature and Sergei well knew he was powerless against him. He couldn't fight this devil with force of will. He had to count on planning and luck.

Sergei packed his single suitcase as efficiently as possible. He had practiced it many times. He kept one eye on the phone the assassin had ordered him to keep with him at all times and prayed it didn't ring tonight. His wife packed her bag dutifully. She was shaken. She was afraid. She was already mourning the life they were leaving behind, but to her credit, she managed to maintain her composure and soldier on.

A black limo pulled up to the residence. It was the one Sergei had commissioned for his escape, not the usual state car that he was sure the assassin was tracking. Also, this one was driven by Sergei's most trusted man, not the usual state lackey assigned to him. All this needed to be planned to the last detail.

Sergei heard the phone ring and almost panicked. Fortunately, it wasn't the assassin's phone but the signal to come down.

It was time to go.

Sergei took one last glance at the assassin's phone on the nightstand, picked up his bag, and ushered his wife down the stairs.

There was no turning back now.

***

"Anything?" Darren called over the wind in his ear and the sound of the bike in the background.

"No," Ives said. "Darren, I think he is rabbiting. He and his wife have their bags packed and are headed down the stairs. An unmarked car just pulled up to their house."

"I'm just a couple of minutes out," Darren called.

"I'll keep you posted… Oh!" Ives yelped in mid-sentence.

"What?" Darren called.

"He's made," Ives said. "The surveillance wave just kicked on."

"How?" Darren said.

"It looks like the assassin had the Minister's door metaphorically locked," Ives said. "He must've set it up so that the surveillance engaged when the door opened. The sensor Faye planted in his house just rang in."

"How could he have known when the door opened?" Darren asked.

"There are any number of ways," Ives said. "He probably set up a completely different trigger monitor. That'd be the best way to keep tabs on the Minister without the wave on. Either way, the assassin is on to him now."

"And the Minister probably doesn't even know it," Darren said.

"Right," Ives said. "Darren, this is precarious but this is our chance. If the assassin is tracking the Minister, he has to keep the wave on and he has to have it trained on the target at all times. That gives us one of the two points that we need to find him. If we can get a second fix, that'll give us the line that the wave must be following. Track the line back to its source and we've got him."

"Assuming the Minister lives that long," Darren said, and hit the gas.

***

There was always a haunting, dewy silence to the morning at this hour. It always felt a bit unnatural to be moving when the rest of the world was asleep, but then again that was the point. Sergei snuck out the back door to the waiting limo. The driver stepped out and the trunk popped open even as they approached. He took Sergei and Letitia's bags and gingerly placed them in the trunk.

Sergei looked around.

"Where's Matthias?" he asked.

Letitia and the driver shook their heads.

147

Sergei bit down so hard, he almost cracked his teeth. He raced back up the stairs and into the house. He stomped over to Matthias' room and threw the door open. Matthias, whose bag was perhaps one-quarter packed, shrunk away from him and started whimpering. Sergei couldn't stand the sight of a twenty-two-year-old man acting like an eight-year-old boy, particularly when that individual was his own flesh and blood.

Sergei marched over to him and grabbed him by the hair. He yanked Matthias forward as the boy screamed in fear and pain. He kept screaming as Sergei dragged him through the house toward the back door.

In the kitchen, Sergei threw him to the floor and started rifling through the drawers. As Matthias rubbed his aching scalp and continued to sob incessantly, Sergei found what he was looking for: a roll of duct tape. Sergei peeled off a six-inch length and ripped it off the spool. He stomped over to the sniveling thing, pushed up his son's weak chin to close his mouth, and slapped the tape over the quivering lips. Sergei yanked the boy to his feet and fairly threw him out the back door. Matthias, half-scrambled, half-fell down the back steps. He eventually made it into the waiting car, but with the tape over his mouth he did so silently.

Sergei followed a handful of seconds later.

When he entered the car, he saw Letitia holding Matthias and stroking his hair. They both knew better than to remove the gag. Lyly was passed out on the back seat like a sleeping angel.

It reminded Sergei why he was doing this.

***

"Darren, get ahead of him," Ives called. "He's not using his usual car. He's chartered a new one and I don't have a bug

148

on it. If the Minister runs out of my range, I'll lose him. That means we'll lose our contact point and we'll be done."

"Damn it!" Darren breathed and started running the red lights.

The good news was that at this hour there weren't many people on the road. The bad news was that made him a sitting duck for both the local police and the assassin.

"You're gaining," Ives said, "but you have to step on it."

"Darren," Walter came on the line, "I'd bet that he's heading to the airport. Swing north and try to get around him from that angle."

"Ives?" Darren asked.

"It's a gamble, but I'd take it."

Darren swore again and turned left.

He headed for the main highway going north.

***

Sergei reached over to his son, got a hold of one of the ends of the tape, and ripped it off without warning. Matthias screamed like a girl. Sergei grabbed him by the hair and glowered at him.

"If you're not silent in three seconds, I will silence you, so help me."

The boy choked back his last shriek and fell silent, but for the pathetic whimpering.

Letitia glared at Sergei, but knew better than to speak.

They would soon be halfway to the airport and none of them were dead.

Maybe he would get away with it.

***

Darren could name half a dozen of his vehicles that would have put him there by now. This bike he was forced to make do with would sink them if he couldn't get more life out of it.

"Looks like Walter's guess may have been right, Darren," Ives reported. "If he stays on that track, you should get around them in another couple of minutes."

"Correct me if I'm wrong, Ives," Darren said, "but if I get 180° around him and we haven't seen a signal, your theory is shot."

There was a sound on the line that sounded like a yelp from Walter.

"That won't be a problem," Ives said.

"Why not?" Darren asked.

"Because you just got a blip," Ives said.

Darren cut back on the throttle.

"Now what?" he asked. "You have a line, but not a direction."

"Head southeast," Ives said.

"Why?" Walter asked.

"Because that's my best guess, and it's all you've got," Ives said.

"Shit," Darren said and stepped it up again, racing southeast.

"Ives?" Walter asked.

"I can't reach the airport," Ives said, "but I'd guess that he'd want to keep an eye on it. We didn't plan for that contingency, but he may have. Southwest would have a better position to watch both the government capital buildings and the Minister's residence and still be close to the airport."

"That's a lot of assumptions," Walter said.

"I'm open to better suggestions," Ives said.

Walter and Darren were silent.

"Darren, drift east. When I tell you to, swing back south. We're going to try to weave in and out of the beam and track it back to the source."

"In other words you want me to step right into the line of fire," Darren said.

"Yes, but he won't know it unless he's looking for you, and as long as he's focused on the Minister, it's unlikely he'll be watching two targets at the same time."

"Says the one of us that doesn't have a gun pointed at his head," Darren said.

"Now," Ives said, "you just passed it on the far side. Swing south until you find it again. The Minister is almost out of range. Once he's gone, you're all we have."

***

When the charter jet came into view, Sergei could almost taste his freedom.

Matthias had stopped whimpering, but Lyly hadn't woken up yet. Sergei stepped over to her and checked her pulse and breathing. She smelled like a hospital ward, but she was fine. It was probably better this way. Any protest would just be disastrous anyway and the chauffeur could carry her onto the plane easily enough.

By the time the car rolled to a stop, the pilot was already starting the engines. That was good. He knew his instructions. Sergei stayed in the car while the attendants took the bags from the trunk and loaded them onto the plane.

Logically, it didn't matter if he was in the car, on the plane, or dancing a jig on the tarmac. If the assassin knew where he was, it wouldn't make one iota of difference.

***

"Darren," Ives said, "the good news is you've come about half a mile from the intercept point and the trace is perfect. The beam is just a couple of dozen feet wide."

"And?" Darren asked.

"The bad news is that the Minister's car is out of my range," Ives said. "He's probably at the airport but I'm blind to him from here on out. You're all we've got."

"Great," Darren said.

"Darren, you just stepped out of it again. Swing east and get it back."

Darren pulled east slowly.

"Darren?" Ives sounded confused. "East."

"I'm going east," Darren said.

"Move!" Ives said.

Darren slowed and turned as close to east as he could determine from the dash compass.

"Shit!" Ives said.

"What?" Darren called.

"We lost it," Ives said. "We lost it. I don't see anything. He must've turned it off."

There was a moment of silence.

"No!" Walter said. "He passed it! Darren, look back. Try to find something that could house the generator."

Darren looked back in the direction he'd come. There was a large semi-trailer parked by the side of the road. Darren peeled toward it, raced past then cut a sharp turn and ran a tight circle around the site.

"Only one blip, Darren," Ives said. "That's it! Leave the bike in the beam and get inside the truck."

Darren jumped off the bike and came around to the rear of the trailer. It was locked shut and double bolted, plus the doors were not ordinary semi doors. They were heavily enforced.

Darren chose program 'straight punch' and hit the seam between the doors as hard as the suit could muster.

The doors held.

***

Sergei took a deep breath and stepped out of the car. He pulled Letitia and Matthias out and pointed the driver to Lyly.

"Quickly now," he scolded. "Move. Move!"

He shoved Letitia and Matthias toward the plane and watched as they started to ascend the stairs to the cabin. The driver took Lyly out and followed the other two.

Sergei looked around. The morning was silent and calm, but death was still in the air and he knew it. When the driver finally disappeared through the cabin door, it was time to go.

Each step was both agony and ecstasy.

By all logic, he was home free. Why would the devil wait until now if he knew Sergei had betrayed him? He could have killed them in the car. He could have killed them at any time. Sergei's footsteps sounded a series of hard metallic clanks he could hear above the sound of the readying engines.

At the three-quarter mark, he was really starting to believe he had pulled it off.

The glorious exhale was just upon his lips.

In hindsight, that was exactly what the assassin wanted him to think.

It felt like being shot in the knee or at least what Sergei might have imagined being shot in the knee felt like. There was an explosion that almost cut his leg in half and he went down like a big game trophy. He fell back and tumbled down the stairs in a merciless avalanche. He smashed his shoulder, twisted the ankle he still had, cracked two ribs, and suffered a nasty gash on his forehead.

All that was nothing compared to the agony of dragging his maimed knee down in the fall.

He landed on the tarmac at the base of the stairs, still screaming.

Then it happened again, this time in the eye.

It felt like the assassin had blown his face off. The horror was beyond anything Sergei could have imagined. Then it occurred to him.

Why?

The cabinet aide had gone quickly and painlessly.

The assassin could have, should have, just killed him with one shot.

Not this.

Not like this.

Letitia and Matthias appeared in the cabin door and started down the stairs toward Sergei.

"No!" Sergei screamed. "No! No! Go back!"

***

Darren chose 'loop' and punched the doors in blindingly rapid succession. The seam between the two doors opened up as a sound like a jackhammer echoed through the street. When the hole was big enough that he could grab the corner, he reached both hands in, set his foot against the bottom beam, and pulled.

Still the door didn't come open, but the hole was almost big enough to fit through.

At this point, he expected shots to start flying through the rift he put in the door, but there was nothing.

Darren trained his flashlight into the darkness. There was a lot of high-tech equipment, but no movement.

"Ives, is there anyone in there?" Darren asked.

"No, damn it," Ives said. "It looks like a remote unit."

***

Letitia and Matthias kept coming. They ran down the stairs and came next to Sergei.

Then it happened again, but for the love of God, this time to Letitia, and right in front of Sergei's remaining eye.

A bright blue spark exploded on her right cheek and knocked her back several feet. She landed on her back on the hard runway. From the event, Sergei could tell she would be scarred for life. Not dead, disfigured.

"No!" Sergei screamed. "No!"

The driver now emerged from the cabin door. He had to come the full length of the plane after carrying Lyly to the sleeping compartments in the stern. He bounded down the stairs with his gun drawn.

He was dumbfounded to find no assailant, just three terrified family members, two of whom had been mutilated.

Sergei was still screaming. He held out his hand to the driver.

"Give me your gun," Sergei demanded. "Give me your gun!"

The driver hesitated but finally turned the gun around and presented the hand grip to Sergei.

Then it happened again. This time at the elbow as Sergei reached to receive the driver's gun. Sergei's arm was nearly torn off. It went dead below the elbow and flopped to the ground at a gristly inverted angle. Sergei screamed.

155

"He's not going to stop!" Sergei begged. "He's not going to stop! Kill me!" He ordered the driver. "Kill me before he kills you, too!"

***

"Darren, you need to shut that thing off!" Walter said.

Darren bent the second door aside to make a crawl space that would accommodate him then he scrambled inside, stood up, and scanned around. It looked a lot like Ives' equipment right down to the off switch, at which Darren took an educated guess.

As he flipped the switch, there was the very distinct and familiar sound of electronic equipment powering down.

"You got it, Darren!" Ives said. "The signal went dead."

***

Bang!

The driver shot Sergei right between the eyes. All life went out of his smashed body as the gunshot echoed along the airport runway. He heard Letitia crying, he heard Matthias whimpering as he waited for more retribution from the god Sergei had clearly angered.

It never came.

***

The news of the Minister's death didn't reach them until the following day.

"Damn it!" Walter screamed.

He kicked a chair and sent it flying across the room.

Darren shook his head and gritted his teeth.

"How close were we?" Darren asked.

"We don't know," Ives said. "It happened at the airport. There's no way to know exactly when because he was out of range. The official report is suicide, but inside sources describe the Minister's condition. It wasn't suicide. Also, his wife is in the hospital with some sort of facial injury that sounds suspiciously like the assassin's weapon. I'd guess it all happened before we turned off the surveillance generator, but the truth is we just don't know. He may even have had a second surveillance generator, so who even knows if turning one off helped at all."

"God damn it," Darren said.

"What about the kids?" Faye asked.

"The kids are fine," Ives said.

Faye seemed to take some comfort in that.

"And now the trail is cold," Darren said. "We have nothing."

Ives nodded.

"It's worse," he said. "We've tipped our hand. He knows we are looking for him, and he knows we found his generator. He's got all the cards now and there's no way to find him."

Another pause.

"There's one," Walter said. "Only one."

They looked at him.

"He'll come back for me," he said.

Faye muttered something. The others were silent.

"What options do we have?" Walter asked. "I will not hide from this bastard for the rest of my life."

"Killing you is one thing," Ives said, "but look what he did to the Minister."

"He wants something," Walter said. "More specifically, he wants something from me. I don't know what it is and it doesn't make sense to kill me before he's made it clear. If he makes a set of demands and I betray him, then yes, he probably would take me apart piece by piece, but he has a move he hasn't made yet. Otherwise, he'd have done the job in my office in the first place. He wants something. We've got to draw him out, make him come to us. It's the only thing we can do."

"But he knows you're after him now," Faye said. "The Minister told him. That at least has changed. So he may very well just kill you at his next opportunity."

"That doesn't change the fact that he is still after something he doesn't have yet," Walter said, "and honestly, it wouldn't matter if it did. I'm just not going to run from this asshole."

"So what are you suggesting?" Ives asked. "What do we do?"

"We don't do anything," Walter said. "I go back to the States and wait for him to make a move. I stand right in his gun sight and see what happens."

Darren sighed.

"I hate this plan," Darren said, "but, unfortunately, I don't have a better suggestion."

CHAPTER
13

It was back, this cancer of his.

It was like a relapse of the scourge, like returning to the condition where the disease consumed his entire life and by which he defined every aspect of his existence. It was lurking in every shadow, waiting in every corner. It would show itself, but Walter never knew when, and that anxiety, that uncertainty, was almost worse than the disease itself.

He had good days and bad days. Some mornings he would come into the office strong, determined, brave, and ready to meet whatever came at him. Other days he felt like a mouse walking into what he knew was an armed mousetrap, tiptoeing under this tense coil that could trip at a breath and end his life in the merest fraction of an instant.

Some days his office was that of a general on a grand and just mission; other times it was a torture chamber, and every tick of the clock was agony.

Today was the latter.

Walter paced the office, trying to hang on to the conversation he'd had with his team a week ago, when they'd just returned from the mission in Czech, weak, defeated, carrying the burden of failure and out of options.

He was their only lead, the only thing left to draw the fire of the assassin.

Logically, he shouldn't be afraid. The assassin didn't work like that. It was unlikely that he'd kill Walter with this next shot. Logically, Walter knew it would probably be another warning shot, another prod herding him in the direction of the killer's bidding. The early shots were never kill shots, unless the target was an example, unless he wanted to kill you to make an impression on someone else, and Walter couldn't fathom how that would apply to him.

No, it had to be another warning shot. Logically, there was no reason to be afraid.

Somehow, that didn't help.

It was a source of constant frustration and fascination to Walter that no matter how often he went over it, no matter what invincible argument he used, no matter how he arranged and presented the data, reason did not work in altering his emotions, not with fear, not with worry.

He'd worked on it all his life in all kinds of situations and emotions, even love.

It just never worked.

Failing that he used a different weapon: courage.

He couldn't reason his way to not being afraid, but he could control what he did with that fear, how he acted upon it. It was the only thing that mattered anyway. He could grit his teeth and put one foot in front of the other, grinding out the minutes, hours and days until he reached the goal.

The window.

That was where it happened last time and that personified Walter's fear. That flat pane of glass felt more like the jaws of a monster than the infrared, filtered, bulletproof shield it was designed to be. Walter walked over to the jaws of the monster. He came to within about a foot of the surface and looked out over the city. He could almost feel the breath of the beast on his skin. He took a deep breath and tried to relax, tried to show courage in the face of this sadistic thing.

He did this every day, every time he could muster the will to stick his neck in the lion's mouth. Not so often that it was conspicuous, but the goal was to invite another shot, so offering the opportunity was necessary.

He'd done this for over a week now. He didn't know if they'd been good days or bad days.

He turned from the beast.

Then it happened, a loud bang right where he had been an instant earlier. Walter ducked involuntarily and rolled away. He regained his composure enough to move in the direction of the closet they had lined to insulate the inside from radio waves. Walter knew that if the assassin chose, the closet was irrelevant. Walter would be dead before he reached it, but that didn't stop him from trying.

He launched toward the one safe place as quickly as he could, but even as he did so he called to the comm link on his lapel.

"Ives?" Walter asked.

"Got him!" Ives reported.

It was a window.

Before Walter had ever begun coming to the office on a regular schedule, before he presented himself to the assassin for bait, Darren and Ives had covered the outside wall of the office, including the windows, with broad spectrum radiation sensors. Each detector was only about the size of a pinhead, so it was hard to see from a distance but very effective.

They had set the trap, but the assassin still needed to bite. Once the detectors picked up the energy of the attack wave, they could detect the intensity and direction of the incident radiation, and with that Ives could use his surveillance techniques to track the signal back to its source.

"Down the block, about one hundred yards away on the thirtieth floor," Ives reported. "It looks like he's got a line-of-sight shot at your window."

Walter continued to scramble for the closet.

"It looks like he's packing up, Walter."

"Darren?"

"On it," Darren said. "Ives, don't lose him."

Darren, waiting in the garage of Walter's building, peeled out on the bike. The building was just up the street. It may not have been far, but the bike was still the best way to get there. Besides, Darren had been expecting to have to go more like two miles.

Short distance notwithstanding, it was almost thirty seconds before Darren was off the bike and headed for the building.

Operating in the daytime was both less familiar and less effective. Darren had to disguise the suit as a biker's leather gear and helmet and go without the usual coat and hat. That wasn't the problem though. The problem was that he couldn't look like he was skulking around.

The shadow routine was easy to pull off at night and even if someone did get a glimpse, the tendency was to run. During the day, the prospect was completely different. There were no shadows to hide in and suspicious movement tended to draw attention rather than repel it. Darren had to look like he was one of the crowd and move like a common pedestrian. He couldn't go zipping and jumping around trying to catch the sniper. It would draw too much attention.

It was maddeningly slow.

"He's quick, Darren," Ives said. "He's in the elevator headed down."

Darren picked up the pace and climbed the stairs to the building's main entrance at what appeared to be a casual trot.

"Third floor," Ives said. "Passing the second floor now."

Darren walked through the building's main lobby and headed for the stairs. It was not likely the sniper intended to exit on foot from the main floor.

"Passing first floor," Ives reported. "Headed for the parking garage."

Darren found the stairwell entrance and headed down.

There were still people in the stairwell so he needed to keep it to a plausible human speed. Even at that, too many eyebrows were going up.

"He's off on the third basement level, Darren," Ives reported.

It took Darren another eighteen seconds to get to the third basement level and come out into the parking garage, which was packed with cars.

"Northwest corner, Darren," Ives said.

"Which way is that?" Darren called back.

"Left!" Ives said. "Left, then right at the end of the lane."

Darren checked around for other people as he ran, again at human speed. He didn't see any, but one could pop out at any second.

"He's getting into what looks like an SUV," Ives said. "He's moving."

As Darren rounded the corner, he saw a black SUV pulling out of parking space, apparently in a hurry.

"That one?" he asked.

"Yes," Ives said as the black SUV turned in Darren's direction and accelerated.

"Are there any people here?" Darren asked as he glanced around for incidental pedestrians.

"No!" Ives said. "You're clear for the moment, but don't let him get to street level."

Then Darren ran straight at the two-ton projectile.

The driver turned on the high beams and leaned on the horn to warn Darren off, but he kept accelerating.

Darren kept charging the oncoming vehicle.

There was a last loud blast on the horn just before what would have been impact. In the last instant, Darren hit the ground and slid under the vehicle. As the vehicle passed over him, Darren grabbed the rear axle near the differential. There was a modest impact before the vehicle started dragging him on his back across the pavement. Sparks started flying off the battery casing from the friction with the garage floor.

There was a program for the suit called 'dead left.' Darren wasn't actually sure how much it could deliver, but he set it to maximum. With his hands already on the axle, the suit curled up and placed its feet against the undercarriage. Just that act alone lifted the vehicle enough that the left rear tire came off the ground, but the driver continued to urge the machine forward. The suit applied every iota of force that the hundreds of thousands of drive elements could muster. There was a moment's hesitation and a modest creak of metal before a deafening crack, and the axle came away from the vehicle chassis.

The rear end of the SUV, propelled by Darren's feet, leaped off the ground and slammed into the roof of the parking garage. Darren and the rear axle tumbled across the cement floor behind the now two-wheeled vehicle. All three skidded for about twenty feet and slammed into the far wall of the garage.

"Jesus Christ," Darren heard Ives scream in his ear.

It took Darren several moments to extract himself from his entanglement with the axle, get to his feet, and approach the driver's side. He came around the vehicle, but it was already too late. The driver's door was open and the seat was empty. Darren turned around and saw someone sprinting away from the accident.

"Told you he was quick," Ives said.

That was accurate. The figure was nearly at the stairwell door before Darren saw him.

"Shit!" Darren swore and took to the chase.

By the time Darren entered the stairwell, the target was already more than one flight ahead. He could see the shape and his hand moving on the railing about fifteen feet up. Fortunately, the center shaft of the stairwell was wide enough to accommodate a leap because Darren had had enough.

"Ives, is the stairwell clear?" Darren asked.

"Yes," Ives replied, "up to the main floor. Go ahead."

Darren hit 'leap' and shot up the barrel of the stairwell about twenty feet. He gave himself enough distance to be sure he would land ahead of the target. He vaulted over the railing and landed on his feet just as the fugitive came around the next corner.

Finally, Darren was able to get a look at him firsthand. He was a military operative if ever Darren saw one, mid-twenties, close-cropped hair, clean shaven. He wore combat boots and dark, loose-fitting clothes, as practical as fatigues, but more the look of street clothes so he could blend in.

He carried a large pack, but didn't seem burdened by the weight. He was probably 250 pounds and less than seven percent body fat; not someone Darren would ever want to meet without the suit. When the man saw that his escape route had been cut off, Darren expected him to make use of his advanced training and charge forward like the living weapon he clearly was. Instead, the man stopped in his tracks, dropped the pack, and raised his hands.

"Compromised, sir," the man said, apparently speaking to a third party through the headset he was wearing.

Darren approached gingerly. It was possible that this was a ruse to bring him closer. He was sure that if the man decided to move, he would be so fast Darren would have trouble responding. He may make it past the one-man blockade. Of course with Ives guiding him, Darren could just catch him again, but he didn't want this one making it to the street. That would complicate matters.

"Acquired," the man said again to his headset.

Darren would have preferred he not talk at all, but wasn't ready to knock the man out as long as he was standing with his hands in the air. Darren hit him with a gentle sonic blast just to get his attention. The man recoiled from the attack, but kept his hands in the air.

"No more talking to the headset," Darren said. "Remove it."

There was a pause in which Darren guessed the man was listening to a voice through the headset.

"Sir, if I may," the man said, this time apparently speaking to Darren. "My commanding officer would like to speak with you."

"Would like to speak with me?" Darren asked. "The feeling is mutual."

"May I put him on speaker?" the man asked.

Darren hesitated.

"If you even twitch the wrong way, I'll put you down," he warned.

"Understood, sir," the man said.

The strange thing was this guy must have known who Darren was and what he could do. He had recoiled at the sonic attack but he wasn't surprised by it and although Darren didn't have anywhere near this guy's stature or mass, the man seemed to know Darren could take him handily if pushed to it.

Whoever he was, he was well informed.

The man slowly lowered his left hand to his belt, all the while keeping eye contact with Darren, or at least close thereto because, with Darren wearing his helmet, this guy didn't know exactly where Darren's eyes were. The man touched a button on one of the boxes on his belt and brought his hand back up level with his right.

"Dr. Kiel," a voice sounded from the box, "I'm sorry to be meeting like this."

"We haven't yet," Darren said.

"Of course," the voice said. "This is General Richard Leighton."

"Is that supposed to mean something to me?"

"No, but at least you have a name."

"How about two?" Darren said, and nodded at the man with his hands in the air.

"Sergeant Neil Engels 6711248," the man said crisply, but remained still with his hands in the air.

"Ordinarily, I'd be furious with the sergeant for allowing himself to be compromised, but that would be a little contradictory in this case."

"Just another lackey?"

"Hardly. We value Sergeant Engels quite highly, but he had something of a difficult assignment today."

"Yes, his target is still alive."

"I should certainly hope so. That kind of mistake I would not forgive. Speaking of which…"

Then Darren heard the general dial the phone. There was a ring on the other end and Darren heard someone pick up.

"General Leighton?" the other voice said.

Darren recognized it immediately.

It was Walter.

"Hello, Walter," the general said. "I think it's time we have a little chat."

"Actually," Walter said, "I'm in the middle of something at the moment."

"Yes, I know. I have Dr. Kiel and your assassin on the line as well."

"What?"

"Walter?" Darren asked.

"Darren?" Walter said.

"What the hell is going on?"

"Why don't you tell me?" Darren said. "Do you know this guy?"

"How do you?" Walter asked.

"All right, all right," the general said. "Let's just back up for a second. Walter, I know you're being targeted. I also know you're fine, because we did the targeting."

"You what?" Walter said.

"You were in no danger," the general said. "We had to do it this way."

"Do what?"

"Make you think you were targeted."

There was a pause.

"Look," the general continued, "you know what happened in Moldova and you knew what was going on in the Czech Republic. Think about it for a second. We couldn't get involved, even if we wanted to, but we had to address it somehow."

"Wait a minute. Wait a minute," Walter said. "You have been targeting me? Terrorizing me?"

"Two events," the general said, "before Czech, and today. Yes, I'm responsible for those."

"Are you out of your fucking mind?" Walter yelled.

"Put yourself in my shoes," the general said. "I have terrorism with global implications. I have people, leaders of their countries, dying and nations under threat. I have an assassin I couldn't catch even if I had carte blanche on another nation's soil, and I don't. I can't even set foot there.

"Then I have you. I know you have some, shall we say, unusual assets, and I know you can operate on foreign soil if you apply yourself, if you call in a few favors. That's a really compelling scenario for me, but I have a problem with your motivation. You're not going to get involved without a big push, so we provided that. We made it so that you thought you were being targeted by the same threat, so you would get personally invested and work on the problem.

"We had one other ulterior motive," the general said. "We've wanted to speak to Dr. Kiel for some time, but he pretty much dropped off the radar after L.A. We heard some chatter about him being in Europe, but the reports were sporadic and we were pretty sure we wouldn't be able to get a good lock on him without making too much noise. The chances were also good that he'd have no interest in talking to us if we did catch up with him. So, again, the better way was to have you, Walter, find him and encourage him to come back. You have a better chance of convincing him and once back, we might have the opportunity to have the conversation we were looking for."

Darren said nothing.

"Let's talk about that later," the general said. "Right now we still have the problem at hand."

"I don't believe this," Walter spat.

Darren nodded at Sergeant Engels. The man lowered his hands and clasped them behind his back, at ease.

"Look," the general said, "your next question is 'Why didn't I come to you and ask?' But we both know the answer to that question, don't we? If I had asked, whether in an official capacity or not, that would compromise me if things went wrong. It was plausible deniability. Frankly, Walter, I was surprised and disappointed you didn't take the initiative yourself, given the circumstances."

Walter said nothing.

"But given the fact that you chose not to move on your own," the general said, "I decided some extra motivation, a little push, was in order, and this seemed the best way to do that."

"General, if you were in front of me right now..." Walter began.

"Yeah, being manipulated like that must make you want to take a swing at someone, Walter," Darren cut in.

Walter was silent.

"Listen, General," Darren began, "bullshit aside, I have a few questions."

"Go ahead."

"First," Darren said, "your guy was one hundred yards away with a line-of-sight attack. Why that close and why all the way up on the thirtieth floor? I would expect with this technology you could be two miles away and at ground level. Did you want us to catch him?"

"With the assassin's technology, he can be two miles away and at ground level," the general said, "but we don't know how he does it, and we don't have that technology. We had to simulate the assassin's attack and the only way we have to generate that kind of effect is an infrared laser. We could get a wavelength that would make it through Walter's windows, but not through solid objects. Since we also can't see the target through solid objects, the line-of-sight attack was necessary. Basically, this was what we had, but it seemed adequate to the task of convincing Walter he was in danger."

"Secondly, why now?" Darren continued. "I can understand pushing Walter to go after the guy in Czech, but why now? The Czech minister is already dead."

"But the assassin is not," the general said. "Nothing has changed as far as I'm concerned. I still need you on the job."

"Where?" Darren asked. "The trail is cold."

"The trail isn't cold," the general said. "We have recent intelligence reports that he's in Bucharest, Romania. Walter, you'd probably know that if you had looked into it, and you'd probably know it next week anyway, but a week has already gone by and we didn't see you jumping on it, whether for lack of knowledge or choice, so it was time for us to push.

"Anyway, now you know: Bucharest, Romania. And it's not the minister this time, it's the president. That may be why the intelligence is taking longer to get out. They're keeping it under a pretty tight lid."

"Let me get this straight," Darren said. "After the train wreck in Czech, you want us to go to Romania and stop an assassination attempt on the president?"

"I don't want you to," the general said, "I need you to. Nothing has changed. I can't involve myself in the affairs of another nation state, and I wouldn't have the tools to address this problem if I could."

Darren said nothing.

"Look, why did you go last time?" the general asked.

There was no answer.

"To prevent the assassination from eroding stability in Western Europe. Nothing has changed," the general

171

concluded. "Whatever the reasons were, the situation is the same. The stakes have just gone up because he's much closer to his goal and much more dangerous. On the other hand, can I assume you've learned a thing or two?"

More silence.

"Walter?" Darren asked.

Walter said nothing and the line carried dead air for several moments.

CHAPTER
14

A plane ride is a hell of a lot nicer when you own the plane, Darren thought as he eased into a butter-colored high-backed leather chair and marveled at the benefits of privilege.

They had boarded Walter's private jet about three hours ago and the accommodations of this transport were palatial in comparison to anything Darren frequented. Even on the rare occasion that Darren did fly, he always did so low key, jammed into the back of the coach cabin like one of so many sardines in a can. It was one of the many sacrifices he made to avoid distinguishing himself from the crowd. He didn't even indulge in first class for fear of standing out that far.

This ride was entirely different. There were about one tenth the number of chairs than any common coach cabin or, for that matter, even any first-class cabin. The space felt more like a living room or hotel lobby than a jet bound for Romania. The only clear difference was the height of the ceiling, which was constrained to a semi-cylindrical eight feet rather than the cubic ten or twelve you might expect in a ground-based living space. But the appointments more than made up for that. The hardwood trim that seemed to adorn every surface, the open bar with cut lead crystal glassware, the strategically placed conversation pits, all contributed to the feeling of pampered, nurtured advantage.

There were sleeping compartments in the back that made Darren drool. Six-hundred thread-count sheets, crisp down bedding, and sound-proofing made him look forward to burying himself and hibernating for the balance of the trip.

But it wasn't only the creature comforts. The absolute convenience was striking. They had left within hours of having made the decision, and it might have been a fraction of that time if they had desired. There were no passport issues or lines to wait in and Darren didn't have to explain any of the equipment he wanted to bring along. There was a pronounced efficiency to the process, a reduction of the common barriers that might impede productivity, and Walter made use of it.

Darren got up and walked to where Ives, Faye, Walter, and Brigham were huddled around a conference table. There was a map showing the Romanian president's office and the surrounding area.

"How are we going to approach it this time, Walter?" Faye asked. "If we go anywhere near the president, it's over. The assassin will know we're after him again. He'll get us in his cross-hairs and we'll all be dead."

"I know," Walter said. "One of you may even get away with it once or twice, as far as we know, he doesn't know you, but if I even set foot near his next target, he'll know exactly what's going on and it'll be game over."

"Then what?" Faye asked.

"I don't want to go straight at him this time," Walter said. "We'll need to be smarter. If we can stake out the president's office with Ives' detectors, basically set up a perimeter around the grounds, we can pick up the signal when he's watching and get a direction, because we'll have two points up front, the office and the perimeter sensor. Then we won't be dependent on getting lucky and having Darren drive around looking for the second signal at random. We'll be quicker."

"But that's only the surveillance wave," Darren said. "That'll probably just lead us back to another remote generator."

"True, but at least we'll have that and we'll be able to turn it off at a time of our choosing," Walter said. "That may give us an edge."

"Unless he has a back-up," Ives said, "which I'd bet on."

"First things first," Walter said. "There's no reason to keep the president under the microscope twenty-four hours a day, not to mention the fact that doing so would increase his chances of being caught. So I'm hoping there are breaks in the times when we'll detect the signal. Ideally, he'd keep to a set schedule, but that'd be too much to ask. If we watch for a few days, we should be able to pick a time when it would be least probable he's watching."

Ives gave a cautious nod.

"I can schedule an audience with the president during one of those times. Again, there is some risk, but I think that would be our best shot."

"Do you really think you can get in there? He is the president, after all," Faye asked.

"I'll need to call in some favors, but yes, it should be possible."

"Then what?" Faye said. "He could rat us out, just like the Czech minister did."

"My best information is that this guy is cut from a different cloth," Walter said. "My mistake last time was not doing enough homework to investigate the Czech minister, his background, his history, his skeletons. In hindsight, I should have known from the start that he would rat us out. The Romanian president looks like a better candidate for us, stronger, solid, and more trustworthy. I'm hoping we can convince him that we can help, that he should cooperate with us. If we can get him to collaborate, that puts us in a much better position."

"How?"

"We can be privy to his schedule. We can suggest patterns to his movement. We may be able to get him to discuss what demands are being placed on him and how the assassin is communicating. We need to get some data on how this guy is operating."

"Then what?"

"Then it gets a little more dicey," Walter said. He seemed to drift away for a second then he said in a quiet voice, almost a whisper, "That weapon of his is devastating. We've got to figure out some way to cope with it."

"Just a few points to consider," Darren said. "It may, and probably does, operate on a completely different wavelength from surveillance. It won't be easy to detect because it's focused on one place. The surveillance wave is made to blanket an entire area so it's much easier to pick up with a generic detector. The weapon targets one pinpoint location, so it will go through a detection net much more easily."

"So what are you saying?"

"I'm saying we'll need to lay down a much finer grid to see the weapon once it's activated," Darren said, "and we won't be able to do that from two blocks away. We'll need to have access to the actual residence grounds."

"Shit!" Faye said.

Walter rubbed his temples.

"I'm sorry about this, but it gets worse," Darren said. "Even assuming we can detect the weapon, we'll need him to fire it first. Until he actually fires it and it hits a target, we've got nothing to go on."

"Double shit," Faye said.

"Firing it doesn't mean killing anybody," Walter said. "It could be a warning shot."

"True," Darren said. "Then there's the problem of direction. We don't want to just detect it. We'll know that he fired it easily enough from the president telling us so. We need to detect directionality. I'm not sure how we can determine *where* it's coming from."

"He could be doing that remotely as well. I certainly would. He could be in Timbuktu and just controlling the equipment from there."

"Well, how the hell we going to catch him if he's in outer Mongolia and controlling everything with a joystick?" Faye asked in a raised voice.

"For the moment, he's not the target," Walter said. "The equipment is. If we can disable the equipment, I'd call that progress."

"Then we're back to the problem of direction," Darren said.

"Leave that to me," Ives said. "If you all can figure out the rest, I can manage a directional detector, but be aware, it's likely that there are several pieces of equipment. Darren mentioned earlier that he might be crossing beams and using a multidirectional approach for both surveillance and attack. We need to find them all and we need to disable them all. Any one of them could still be lethal."

"Anything else?" Faye said.

"Yeah," Ives said. "It could be mobile too, contained in a van or truck bed and driving around the city. Again, that's how I would do it. That makes it harder to track."

"No shit," Faye spat.

"First things first," Walter said. "Let's get to the president and get closer to the problem."

"On that," Darren said, "a word of caution. If we let the president know how the targeting works and he decides to lock himself away in a radio secure location, that will tip off the assassin and let him know something is up. I'd recommend advising the president to stick to the same schedule, or even not telling him about this at all."

"I'll have to get a read on him before making that decision," Walter said.

***

It was nearing 6:00 PM when Walter's plane touched down at the Otopeni International Airport just outside Bucharest. Unfortunately, that was 9:00 AM in Los Angeles and their bodies were still on West Coast time. They were all reasonably well-rested thanks to Walter's accommodations, but given the hour, most of the group was staring at a pretty serious bout of jet lag. It was less of a problem for Darren, who preferred to operate at night anyway. For him, the timing was perfect.

"So, listen," Walter began as the plane rolled up to a private gate and they made preparations to exit, "this is the last time we'll see each other until this is over.

"I can't afford to be seen, and you can't afford to be seen with me," Walter explained. "I've set up secure quarters for myself and accommodations for each of you separately."

He handed them each a key card and an address card, all from different establishments.

"These are each pretty secure," Walter continued, "but don't take any chances. I would advise you all to spend as little time together as possible. We can communicate via a cell phone and video whenever you like, but there's nothing to be gained from sticking together, and everything to be gained from keeping separate. Each of these locations is close to the president's residence, but distributed around the perimeter evenly."

They each took their cards from Walter.

"Ives," Walter continued, "we brought your equipment, and there's a truck for you."

He pointed out the window to a flatbed truck, waiting to receive the cargo container Ives had loaded before they left.

"We'll get you loaded and see you off," Walter said. "I expect to see you least of all and hear you most of all."

Ives glanced out the window and nodded.

"Faye," Walter said, "I'll need you when I go to the president's office, whenever that turns out to be, but for the time being, stay out of sight."

He paused.

"The usual way," he added. "Until then, both you and Darren can help by getting supplies for Ives. Here's a shopping list."

He handed Faye and Darren each a list of components.

"You want me to go shopping?" Faye asked.

"Ives will need these to build the detector sets," Walter said. "It'll take some time for him to set up the surveillance operation here. In the meantime, you can make yourselves useful by picking up what he needs for the next step: detection. These are pretty common items, but the leg work will help."

Darren took the list from Walter. He glanced at it then back to Walter.

"No problem," he said then looked at Faye.

Faye rolled her eyes and took the list from Walter without comment.

"Darren," Walter said, "in addition to getting the equipment, there's one more thing that I want you to do: nothing. I'd like you to stay off your usual activities until this is over."

Darren opened his mouth to speak.

"I want you to stay focused on this and I don't need you distracted or stirring anything up while this is going on," Walter said.

Darren closed his mouth.

"You can put a hold on it for a week or two," Walter concluded.

Darren nodded reluctantly.

The plane rolled to a stop. The door came open to a set of stairs leading down to the tarmac.

It had been several months since Darren had been in Bucharest and he welcomed the lung full of fresh air with a hint of moisture from the river. The air in the plane was clean and pleasant enough, but it wasn't fresh air. The filters and conditioners hadn't been developed to replace that just yet.

Darren descended the stairs and helped the porters load his equipment and suitcase into the waiting beige sedan. Usually, Walter would have ordered a set of black stretch limos, but it was time to stay low key, not indulge.

On the chauffeured ride to his quarters, Darren used the laptop in the back seat to locate the stores that sold Ives' components. He sketched out the path he'd take to gather the list together and sent Faye an e-mail to coordinate with her list.

Surgical

The next few days were going to be a bit tedious.

***

"Shit, these things are heavy," Darren said to his earpiece. "Did you ever hear of microelectronics?"

"They are as small as I could make them this fast and with what I could get my hands on," Ives said. "Besides, most of the weight is in the batteries."

"Christ," Darren said, adjusting the backpack strap on his shoulder.

"Why didn't you wear the suit and have it help you carry them?" Ives asked.

"I suppose I would have if I'd known. I just didn't think it would be this much of a pain in the ass."

"Well, carry a few less next time and make a few extra trips."

"How many did you make anyway?"

"About 200. I figured one every thirty to fifty feet around the perimeter, that's 1500 feet on a side."

"Jesus!"

"We can't get much closer to the President's residence without pushing the security risk. Besides, the longer the perimeter, the easier it is to find places to plant them. We can't have the ground patrol finding them peppered about the place."

"How many have we done so far?"

"Fifty."

Darren grunted.

"We'll be done by the end of the day," Ives said.

As Darren lugged his seemingly increasingly heavy burden down one of the streets surrounding the P.M.'s residence grounds, he watched for inviting locations to stow the next detector. It was not a trivial exercise. He couldn't drop them in the sewer. They had to be at street level, but not much higher. They had to be concealed from sight, but not so deeply hidden that the location might block the radio waves they were trying to detect, and he had to find a fitting place every thirty to fifty feet. If he stretched the distance, Ives squawked at him like a mother duck herding her brood.

Darren placed the next sensor, about the size of an apple, in a flower box on the sidewalk across the street from the Romanian equivalent of the White House.

"Feel free to take several laps," Ives said. "Placing something every thirty feet repeatedly could raise suspicion."

"Easy for you to say," Darren complained. "You don't have to walk the laps carrying this bag of lead."

He adjusted the strap again.

"Holy shit!" Ives cried.

"What?" Darren stopped walking and held a hand to his ear.

"Holy shit!" Ives cried again.

"What?"

"We've got a hit!"

"What? Where?"

"Numbers zero through eight. It looks like he's watching right now."

"You're kidding?"

"No, I get this spike at the southeast corner and it's pretty broad. It looks like he's coming from that direction."

"Can you triangulate on it?"

"No, these are not directional. They're just quick and dirty. They let us know when he's watching, but not much more."

"Are you sure it's him?"

"Well, no, but I would bet on it. A sudden jump in the radio wave spectrum around the residence and it just happens to be around the band that's perfect for this kind of work. We'll know more when you finish placing the rest of them, but it's pretty promising."

"That was quick."

"Unfortunately, it bodes poorly. If we got a hit this fast, it might imply that he's watching frequently. That'll make it harder for Walter to schedule an interview."

"Mark the time. We need to start mapping out when he's got eyes on."

"Done. Now c'mon, let's get the rest of them set."

"4:00 AM," Ives said. "We've been watching the spectrum for a week, and the safest time is around 4:00 AM."

"Perfect," Walter grumbled.

"I could choose a different time," Ives said, "but the risk would go up."

"No," Walter said, "it'll have to be 4:00 AM. Now it falls on me to arrange it."

He closed the connection.

***

The milling masses of humanity.

Ninety-nine percent useless.

Someone once said 'Life just wants to be'; in the case of humanity, one would hope for a greater aspiration, but for ninety-nine percent of the population, that was as far as it went.

It was loathsome.

It was reprehensible.

Anyone can do better than to simply exist. Everyone must aspire to more if they seek to be included among the ruling species of the planet. These vermin should not be considered so.

Marcus Cahn walked among them, more to gloat at his superiority than anything else. For ninety-nine percent of the people who passed him on the sidewalk, their thinking didn't extend past their own noses, the next hour, the next meal, the next source of stimulation.

He watched them come and go, from homeless waif wearing torn and filthy clothing and smelling of urine and wretched squalor, to supposedly refined aristocrat wearing tens of thousands of dollars in diamonds and jewelry, painted and manicured nails, primped coif, and supposedly designer clothes.

And what more purpose did one serve than the other?

An argument could be made that the former had greater merit. At least the homeless didn't consume resources and hoard ten times what they returned in real value.

Show me one, Marcus thought. *Show me one of these scampering weasels that actually had some thought of tomorrow that didn't involve one and only one central figure, themselves, in a purely selfish and rapacious capacity.*

"Yes, I have a plan for a better tomorrow. I'm saving to buy that cool car I've had my eye on." And that was the best of them. Mostly, it was just one minute to the next.

It made them small. It made them meager, inconsequential, superficial, but, above all, this repugnant lack of higher brain capacity and planning, this abhorrent absence of aspiration, made them powerless.

They were powerless in the world, powerless over their environment, powerless over themselves.

Marcus had known powerlessness in his life.

Surgical

He never wanted to see it again.

He was twelve, old enough to remember it clearly.

He was working at his father's car repair garage after school. He often did, particularly between midterms and finals. Mostly he did janitorial work, kept inventory in the back and made sure the shelves were stocked full in front. His father didn't want him interacting with customers and he didn't want Marcus in a position where he could make any serious mistakes, so it was mostly clean up.

Marcus was taking auto shop in school at his father's insistence and he suspected that his father would eventually put him to work as a mechanic. Marcus had no objection just yet. He wasn't old enough to have that discussion with a primary authority figure.

He was sweeping behind the counter, virtually at his father's feet, when a man, an ordinary man, not much bigger than Marcus himself, walked into the store.

The man wore a dark blue knit cap and sunglasses. He had a tattoo of a dagger on his left cheek. He moved quickly and aggressively, not at all like the customers Marcus usually saw. He marched up to the counter like a dog rushing on a rabbit, took a gun out of his pocket, and yelled at Marcus's father.

It was so loud it almost knocked Marcus over.

His father asked, "What?" clearly in terror.

"All the money now," the man yelled, his verbal attack as effective as any physical act could have been.

Marcus watched his father unlock the cash register for this man. He was shaking like a leaf and fumbling with the buttons of the machine, but finally the register came open. Marcus rarely saw the cash drawer from this perspective. It was bulging with tens and twenties. Marcus's father thrust his hands into the drawer and began pulling out fistfuls of money and giving them over. The man still had the gun, this dark black piece of metal, pointed at his target.

He stuffed the cash in his pockets and shirt until the cash register was empty then bolted out of the store and away.

They never saw him again.

Marcus's father was still shaking and pale. He staggered back and sat down on a stool just a few feet behind him. If the stool hadn't been there, Marcus was sure his father would have collapsed to the floor, still shaking. Marcus saw him reach for the phone and dial a number, obviously the police. He proceeded to report the robbery in a shaky and confused voice.

The police came a short time later. There were flashing lights and questions. There were strangers in blue uniforms and unfamiliar activity. For Marcus, it all seemed a blur. He was still fixated on the image of his father shaking with fear in front of this total stranger; compelled to follow his orders without question, forced to hand over everything he and the rest of the garage employees had worked for all in an instant, and just at the whim of the stranger.

Everything they valued so highly had been whisked away.

Who was in power here?

Marcus had been used to the idea of his father as the authority figure. This showed the fallacy of that lifelong perception. All his authority, all his power, all his dignity had been stripped from him in an instant by somebody with a piece of metal in his hand. Ordinarily, this 'punk,' as his father might have called him, would have gone at best without notice and at worst with derision, but not now.

Now he was the person with absolute control.

If this useless thug could garner such power, clearly there was an equation here Marcus had failed to calculate. The next question that came to mind was: what would have prevented this? What would have insulated himself, his father, and their world from this kind of violent incursion, this god-awful violation?

If he could kill this man with a thought, if he could have ended him right then and there in an instant and left the man with no defense, no recourse, even no awareness that it was happening—just think 'dead' and the man hits the floor.

Power, Marcus decided, is not an illusion.

It is preparedness.

It is forethought.

It is an exercise of higher brain capacity, and this Marcus had in abundance.

CHAPTER
15

Depression is learned helplessness.

For the first time in a long time, August Chevenyenko wished he could choose not to learn this lesson life was trying to teach him. He'd learned enough. He didn't need another lesson.

Forty-five years ago the lesson had been fear.

At twenty years old, as a lowly infantryman in the Romanian army, life had taught him fear as he watched bombs explode within an arm's length and watched his friends and comrades blown to bits right in front of him. There is no greater horror than that, to watch the bullets rip through the torso of a man standing three feet from you, to see legs and arms and body parts strewn about you. There is no hell like war when you are a twenty-year-old kid. Fear is just as inescapable as the fetid air you breathe, full of the stench of blood and bile and decaying human remains.

After a time, he found that, for him, there was only one response: rage.

It was insanity.

He never denied that.

When he ran from his cramped, filthy hole and charged the enemy, he hadn't been given any orders and didn't have any authority to ask anyone to join him. Hell, he wouldn't have been coherent enough to form the words to do so even if he had. One minute he had been cowering in his hole, on the verge of tears, and just trying to survive; the next minute he was up and out, gun blazing into empty air. He wasn't thinking anything in that moment but rage at the horror, at the loss, at the enemy, at everything.

He had been trained well enough to reload when the gun clip ran empty, but even that moment of practicality didn't dampen his fury. How he even made it as far as the enemy nest he never knew. He was positive that had he tried that stunt a hundred times, he'd have been dead in three seconds ninety-nine of the attempts, but that day... who the hell knew?

So he just kept going.

By the time he reached the nest, his gun was empty and he had no more clips to reload, so he grabbed the nearest weapon he could find and still kept going. Sure, by that time the enemy was so shocked by the raid that he had surprise on his side but still...

What he didn't know at the time was that the minute the rage took him, his entire platoon had jumped up and followed him. He had a wave of starving, desperate soldiers on his heels that were just as frenzied as he was. That's why he never caught one in the back. The sweep just kept mowing down anyone he had missed. When he finally cut the last man down with a rifle he didn't even recognize, he honestly didn't know what to do with himself. By that time, he was deep in the enemy camp and had killed more soldiers than he could possibly count. He looked around, but no one was moving. He searched around a bit, but there were no other targets.

It was only then that he realized he was hyperventilating. He wasn't sure if it was the exhaustion or the mental state. He tried to calm himself and control his breathing, but both were elusive.

He turned around. He supposed the right thing to do would have been to retrace his steps and return to the unit. He hadn't taken his first step when he saw the entire platoon standing among the ruins of his raid, staring at him. He hesitated for a second, on the verge of passing out from hyperventilation. Instead, he gave them a thumbs up.

"Fuckin' A," he breathed.

The raid had been a blur. The next weeks were what he privately called the second blur. He remembered the platoon surrounding him, congratulating him, smiling and laughing with him. He remembered being slapped on the back and feeling the stabbing pain. That was how they figured out he had been shot. No one knew when. He remembered being carried back to the camp and he remembered a few things from the hospital stay. It wasn't until months later, when he was back in the field with a two-step promotion and a new platoon, now under his command, that the world seemed to exit that blurry state and resume with some new normalcy.

Blurry though it may have been, he never forgot his response to that first lesson when it finally became too much: rage.

Ten years later, life was insisting on a second lesson.

This one was despair.

It should have been safe enough, a three-vehicle convoy from base-to-base. Sure the route was a little close to enemy territory, but that's what the other two vehicles were for. The enemy had other ideas. An RPG took out the first vehicle. A fifty-caliber machine gun perched on an overlook took out the second. He heard a bunch of chattering in Arabic before they reached into the truck and pulled him out. The driver wasn't so lucky. He saw them put a bullet in his head at point blank range.

Apparently, they only wanted the ranking asset.

It was three months and it wasn't like war.

It was personal.

War was indiscriminate. You lived or died out of luck, nothing more. Captivity, torture in particular, was personal. It was against you as an individual. It was configured and adapted to break you as a person, to injure you, body and soul.

He would've sold his soul for war again.

So they worked on him. They ground him down, one unimaginable cruelty after the next. He didn't like to think about the dedication or ingenuity. He was glad he hadn't been younger. He wouldn't have been strong enough mentally. He was glad he hadn't been older. He wouldn't have been strong enough physically. As it was, he still didn't know what kept his spirit alive.

The lesson was despair. Response: hatred.

Hatred's best weapon: patience.

Sometimes hatred can be an asset. It can keep you focused. It can give you resolve. Sometimes it can even give you something to live for. August used whatever worked for those three months, and hatred turned out to be his best asset.

When the rescue team came, he didn't believe it. They had tried that tactic before, giving him hope then snatching it away. It was a common technique and he knew not to invest in it, not to lunge for the carrot when it was dangled in front of him. When he heard yelling and gunshots, he expected it was another ruse. Even when the men knocked in his cell door and he saw they were wearing Romanian army uniforms, he was still doubtful, but when he saw several of his captors dead and some even missing limbs…

That would have been hard to simulate.

They led him to an evac helicopter where he recognized the pilot, but it wasn't until he was back at the military hospital, back home, that he actually started to believe this had happened. That he'd been rescued.

Rescued, yes, but it wasn't over, not yet.

It took more patience, several favors called in, a little blackmail, and even a few threats to bring him his closure. The bad news was there were only three of them left from the raid. All the others had been killed. The good news was, as a result of his wrangling, they were all his. He made use of that. There were no official records of the three weeks that he had custody of the prisoners. Any information he got from them was a fringe benefit and attributed to a random informant.

The official cause of death for the three was suicide: one hung himself, one slit his wrists, one managed to wrestle a gun from one of the guards and shoot himself; the usual. During those three weeks, he showed them what a little imagination and ingenuity could do in the hands of a motivated man.

They'd begged for death, plenty of times. All of them. August had never done that and they had him for three months.

Life showed him despair.

He had learned hatred.

He hoped he'd never have to repeat the lesson. He hoped he'd never need to demonstrate he'd learned it a second time.

Once was too many.

Lesson three: purpose.

Surgical

In the subsequent thirty years, August finished his tenure with the military and began his career in politics. If there was one lesson a thirty-year career in politics could teach you, it's persistence. The waves of resistance are unending, from opponents, the electorate, superiors, political fashion, even allies. It's a long soft war pursued over decades, and only one thing can keep you going through a challenge of that magnitude: purpose. The feeling, the knowledge, that you were working toward something worthwhile, a better government, a better country, a better life for you and your family, security, and, yes, power. You work for decades to achieve something positive, something worthwhile.

If the lesson was purpose, the response was persistence.

Life is cruel.

Lesson four: helplessness.

A month ago, August wouldn't have thought that remotely possible. With all his experience, with all the resources at his disposal, with the technology and military strength of an entire nation at his disposal, how could he possibly be made to feel helpless?

Then this son of a bitch comes out of nowhere and checkmates him in three moves.

It was a beautiful spring day. That's a glorious time in Romania, where the winters can be brutal. In the spring, there is a feeling of renewal, of rebirth, that is infectious. After a harsh winter, after an eternity locked in the punishing grip of winter, the blossoming process is just magical.

Of course, that was the perfect time for the assassin to strike, the perfect time to shatter August's sense of security, when his guard was down and he felt safe. That was when the assassin chose to enter his life, to reach into August's heart and pull it out with his bare hands. It was the best way to make an impact. The best was to get his point across on a beautiful spring day.

August and his wife, Marie, were outside watching their seven-year-old, Ava, ride her new bicycle around their private drive. She was beaming. She had just learned to ride a couple of weeks ago so she wheeled around with a sense of pride and accomplishment that warmed their hearts. She pedaled her little feet and piloted the bicycle in little arcs on the smooth pavement. Of course, secret service agents were peppered all around. One was never more than twenty feet from August or Marie, and one was never more than fifteen feet away from Ava. They were safe. They were at peace.

The grounds were protected behind twenty-foot walls topped with razor wire and every single inch of the estate was covered by video surveillance and patrolled by armed guards. One would have thought that would have been enough.

One of the secret service agents' phones rang. It was set to vibrate, but August heard the buzz. It was very unusual that one of the agents would allow an intrusion like that, but it was nothing compared to that agent stepping up to August and saying, "It's for you, sir."

August glowered at him. Even the suggestion that he would break protocol like this would cost the agent his job. August merely shook his head and waved him away.

"Please, sir," the agent said. "He threatened my family and he claims he can threaten yours. He said if I didn't get you on the phone, there would be consequences."

The agent, whose name, August recalled, was Williams, looked terrified.

"Sir," he continued, "I am confident the threat is genuine or I would never ask you to answer the call."

"It is your job to eliminate threats," August reminded him.

"Sir, I have been unable to address this threat," the agent said, clearly a painful personal admission. "I understand I have failed you in that. I understand I likely no longer have a job, but please don't let my failure bring harm to others."

He nodded at Ava.

That got August to reach for the phone.

"This is President Chevenyenko."

"Ah," a voice said, sounding gratified, "Mr. President, thank you for taking my call."

"Who is this?" August demanded. "How have you threatened my former agent?"

"We'll get to that," the voice said, "but please don't be too hard on him. You have to understand his dilemma."

"I understand that we do not negotiate with terrorists," August said.

"Mr. President," the voice said, "watch your daughter."

August's heart froze with a mixture of rage and fear. He'd have killed this person with his bare hands if he'd been able to get his hands on him, but he did look in Ava's direction.

Just at that second she was negotiating a turn on her bike when there was a small explosion on the front tire. It ruptured the rubber membrane and twisted the front wheel so that Ava lost control of the bicycle and fell to the pavement. August dropped the phone and ran to her. The closest agent got to Ava before August could. He had picked her up and was holding her on his knee when August reached her. She was crying and her knees were scraped, but she was otherwise fine. August picked her up and began walking to the house to clean and bandage the injuries.

The first agent, Williams, approached August and handed him the phone again.

August grabbed it from him.

"I can do worse," the voice insisted.

August stopped.

"Look at the tire and think about it for a second."

August turned. The agent had picked up the bicycle and was walking it to the garage, presumably to repair the flat tire. August stopped him and inspected the damage. It looked like someone had stuck a small explosive device in the tire.

"Pick a target," the voice said.

"What?" August asked.

"Pick a target," the voice said. "I can put it anywhere. Pick a target; your daughter's head, for example."

August's chest froze solid. He looked around for something innocuous, something inconsequential. The white fence surrounding Marie's small garden caught his eye.

"The garden fence," August said.

"Which part?" the voice asked.

"Northwest post," August said.

Three seconds later a small explosion charred the top surface of the northwest fence post. August turned white. Apparently that could literally have been Ava's head.

"Would you like to choose another target?" the voice said.

"No," August said.

"Keep the phone and answer it when I call. If you don't answer it, I will take steps to make a more effective impression."

The line went dead.

August looked at Williams.

"I'm sorry, sir," Williams began, but August waved him silent.

"How?" he asked impotently.

"I don't know, sir," Williams said. "I've never seen or heard of anything like it, but it's not a trick. I have seen him hurt people. The threat is very real. I'm sorry, sir. I just didn't know what else to do."

Surgical

The terrifying thing was neither did August.

He can kill anyone, anywhere, anytime. How could anyone respond to that? No degree of rage, hatred, or persistence was of any use here. Nothing August had learned in his sixty-five years could combat this.

It is hard not to feel helpless when you are, in fact, helpless. As that became more apparent, August felt the specter of depression. He could see the signs himself: irritability, erratic behavior, and capitulation to the enemy. And it was getting worse. As the noose tightened and the demands continued to escalate, August was a rat in an ever-shrinking cage.

When the request came that a man, an industrialist, wanted to meet him at 4:00 AM, August's first reaction was "Go to hell," but that didn't seem very presidential, although that would have been consistent with his behavior lately. A 4:00 AM meeting is almost unheard of even under ordinary circumstances, and the circumstances here were nothing like ordinary.

There were a few things that convinced him to allow it.

The U.S. Secretary of State was quite adamant about it, and August didn't know Benjamin to be adamant about anything. The whole idea of insistence is a little politically uncharacteristic itself.

August owed him one. The forced policy changes had been catastrophic to foreign relations and maybe this was one way to reverse the course, even microscopically, without directly defying the assassin's orders.

This was a decision August could make for himself without someone pulling his strings. He welcomed the change, the independence, even if the actual meeting itself was irrelevant. He allowed it because it would probably piss

197

the assassin off, but not so much that he would punish August for the crime. It just wasn't that important.

So, when the time came to meet Walter Rocaena, it wasn't an entirely vile task, just an inconvenient one.

***

"Mr. President," Walter said, "it's an honor, sir."

"Mr. Rocaena," the President said with a nod, "I'm pleased to meet you, but this is a very odd hour and an odd request. How can I help you?"

"I very much appreciate your making the time to see me, sir, and I do apologize for the inconvenience," Walter said. "I was hoping I might be of service to you."

"I'm pleased to make time for our friends under Mr. Gobran's recommendation," the President said as his face betrayed a thin film of impatience, "but I'm not clear on what service you presume to provide."

"Mr. Gobran and I understand you have a unique security threat," Walter said and leaned his head toward the security guard.

"I'm not sure what you're referring to," the President said. "Our security is second to none. Even your president might envy the protections we have here in Bucharest."

"Of course, sir," Walter said. "I meant no disrespect, but the danger I'm referring to is somewhat unique."

"All threats are unique," the President said with a deepening frown. "I assure you our experts are well prepared to handle all of them with thoroughness and efficiency. Our measures are, in every way, equal to those in the United States."

Surgical

"I'm sure your experts are well prepared to handle all those threats of which they are aware," Walter said, meeting the President's frown with one of his own.

"Are you suggesting there are threats about which we are ignorant?" the President said, raising his voice marginally.

"No, sir, I'm suggesting there may be some which only your top cabinet members know, and your security forces do not," Walter said. "Some which may involve, shall we say, stealthy pyrotechnics."

The President's eyes widened noticeably then he collected himself and a scowl of anger boiled to the surface. He looked up at each member of the security detail.

"Leave us," he commanded.

The four men exited hastily. Walter watched them go. When the door closed, he looked back at the President, who shot out of his chair and glowered at Walter.

"You have no idea what you're doing," he said.

"I'm targeted too," Walter said.

The President's eyes widened again.

"Then you know the peril that you bring here to me, to my staff, to my family, just by being here, and even more so by talking about it. You know any one of us could die at any moment, and your very presence goads him."

"To myself most of all, Mr. President," Walter said. "If he wanted you dead, you'd be dead. You're alive because he has a plan for you. My being here would never be part of his plan. If he knew I was here, I'd be in the greatest danger."

"Then why are you here?"

"He must be stopped. This must be stopped. If he is here, if he is threatening you, we've got to take the battle to him."

"We have been trying. What do you presume to do that others can't?"

"Mr. Gobran helped me gain your audience because he has reason to believe we may be able to help."

"I don't agree."

Walter turned his head and appeared to bark a command to someone in the back of the room, but, of course, the room was empty.

"Faye," he said.

At that, the figure of a woman appeared at the back of the room. She materialized right out of thin air and then vanished again in an instant.

"Hologram?" the President said. "An optical trick? I'm not impressed. All you need is a small projector, which I'm sure…"

The President abruptly stopped talking. He felt something decidedly sharp in the small of his back.

"Not a hologram," Walter said, "as I'm sure you now appreciate. Just for your information, that happens to be a letter opener at your back, but I trust the point has been made."

The object came away from the President's kidney region. He looked behind him. There was no one there. He moved his hand to the space that should, by all logic, contain the assailant, but there was nothing. It was like the air had pulled a knife on him.

"I don't see how that helps," the President said.

Walter pulled a handheld screen from his suit pocket and handed it to the President. There was a grayscale image of a room with three people in it. He quickly recognized it as his own office and identified himself and Walter. The third person was about five feet behind Walter and pacing like a cat. He looked at the space and back to the screen. It felt like he was looking at a vampire in a mirror. He simply could not find the person that the image on the screen kept showing him was there.

"Your office," Walter said.

"Clearly," the President agreed, feeling notably unsettled.

"We can see like he does, and we have some unique assets," Walter said.

"Can you find him?" the President asked in a strangely hushed voice, as if whispering could change the outcome. "Can you stop him?

"I'll be honest with you, Mr. President, I don't know, but the very fact that we're not dead right now means that we have a chance."

The President looked back to the image on the screen and back to the office. He still couldn't find the person the image showed. He handed the device back to Walter.

"Keep it," Walter said. "It's a secure cell phone. We can use it to communicate from now on. As you said, the danger presented by my coming here is too great to take the risk again."

The President nodded and pocketed the device.

"Again," Walter said, "thank you for your time. I can't imagine how difficult it is for you. I appreciate your seeing me."

"Actually," the President said, "you may be the only one that does know."

Walter nodded.

"We'll be in touch," he said, as he headed for the door. "I would recommend texting, since it's likely that he has some capability to listen, not just observe."

"Nice meeting you," the President said in a loud voice to the greater room.

"I'm invisible," a voice said right out of thin air, "not deaf."

The President smirked as the door opened and Walter exited. The security team filed back into the empty space and took up their positions. The President pulled Walter's phone out of his pocket and checked the screen.

Only he and his security force remained.

As Rocaena and his compatriot left, August realized that maybe there was one tool he could use to fight helplessness... hope.

CHAPTER
16

Even Darren had to admit that Brigham looked ridiculous in coveralls. They all did, but somehow Brigham managed to look like he was wearing a suit under the white outer layer. He always looked like he was wearing a suit, even when he was wearing sweats.

Faye looked less ridiculous than precarious. She had the wary air of a scared rabbit. Darren wondered how long she could actually go without the cloak. He suspected it wasn't long.

Their escort was arguing with the presidential grounds security personnel, and it was putting them all on edge. All they could do was try to look natural and comfortable, but that was a contradiction in terms for all three of them. Their natural state was never comfortable, it was on edge, and that didn't fit their hourly-rate hired help persona.

On edge or not, they were each far out of their respective elements.

It was a good thing Ives wasn't here. He wouldn't have been able to function at all. Even Darren was having a time with it and he wasn't agoraphobic. It was just infuriating that there was so much riding on such an asinine set of variables.

"I recommend office upholstery," Walter had said out of the blue.

Darren stammered long enough that Walter needed to define it.

"Upholstery for the walls of the presidential office," he continued. "I have it in my study back home. It's a wonderful effect. There's a soft regal feel to the fabric and texture lining the entire room. It also helps with noise reduction."

"Um, what?" Darren had finally gotten out.

Then Walter had come back down to earth.

"We can't lay a net over the entire grounds," he said. "Ives figured out that the mesh needs to be too fine. We need to detect every few inches, so it's just not realistic to cover the whole building. We need to settle for putting a detection grid around the office and maybe a couple of high probability targets, like his bedroom, and his living room. The best way to do that is to disguise it as office renovation, and office upholstery works perfectly in this case. One: detectors have some size to them and they will look suspicious if we just pepper them around the office. Upholstery has some depth so we can hide the gadgetry in the fabric and framework and it will look completely natural. Two: we can prefab the sections that go on the walls. We can weave the sensor equipment into the décor and test it before we put it up. We can take some time to get it right before the installation. If we can do that, there's a significant probability that we'll be able to install them fast enough that the assassin won't even see the activity. Third, it makes a good cover story and, of course, we don't speak Romanian, so we're going to need some help getting clearance. I think this gives us a lot of advantages for getting our counter surveillance in and operational right under his nose."

"We aren't home decorators," Darren said.

"The President has a standard office contractor," Walter said. "He can tell them to work with us, not only to get the gadgetry into the framework but to get us past the ground security, and we can do it without him having to get involved directly, which would raise suspicion."

It sounded like a good plan, until they tried getting through the security gate with a truck full of their framework.

"No matter how well you plan it," Darren said, "it always gets dicey when the rubber hits the road."

Once they convinced the contractor, Vachislov, that the work was under the President's orders, he had been very helpful, but now they were completely dependent on him to get them, and the equipment, past security. Darren couldn't smash his way in. Faye couldn't sneak her way in carrying a truckload of framework. Even Brigham couldn't talk his way in without speaking the native language. They had to depend on an office contractor in Bucharest, Romania.

The arguments ceased and Vachislov walked toward them with a nervous, exasperated gait.

"The three of you do not have clearance," Vachislov said. "Apparently the paperwork hasn't been submitted or the background checks completed. All my usual employees have their clearance, but the system doesn't recognize any of you."

"Shit!" Darren said.

"Have them call the President," Faye said.

"No," Darren said. "He can't get involved directly. That would set off too many questions. Let's do it this way. Faye, can I ask you to cloak and get in your usual way?"

"No sweat there," Faye said, brightening.

"Once cloaked, can I ask you to escort me as well?" he asked.

"That'll be trickier," Faye said. "I'll need to go over a few things with you, and not out here." She gestured to their surroundings.

"All right, we'll have to find some place to practice," Darren said.

Then he turned to Brigham.

"Change into a suit. If you're wearing a suit, the President can invite you in and it won't look suspicious. Once in, change to coveralls and get back to the task. I doubt anyone will ask questions once we're busy decorating the office."

All nodded.

"All right," Darren said, "meet up inside in an hour."

***

"Now, listen to me," Faye said as she pushed the coffee table in her apartment aside to clear the living area of obstacles. "Don't be a fucking klutz, stepping all over my feet and making a racket. Stealth is not simple and it's not free. You have to do your part. The cloak does have some sound insulation but it's not even close to soundproof. If you sneeze or cough, anyone listening will hear it just as clearly as if you weren't inside."

Darren nodded.

"Also, follow me exactly," Faye said, "every move, every gesture. There's not much room inside so you need to shadow me. I hate to draw this analogy but when I escort someone, it's very much like a dance. There has to be a lot of synchronization and a lot of cooperation. Of course, in this case, I will lead so pay attention to my movements and I'll take care of the rest."

Darren listened.

"Have you had any martial arts training?" Faye asked. "Judo, Aikido, Tai-Chi, even yoga, anything like that?"

"No," Darren said.

"Whatever," Faye said. "OK, look."

She walked up to him, turned around, and backed up so her shoulder blades touched his chest.

Darren instinctively flinched and moved away.

"That's exactly what I mean," Faye barked. "If you're uncomfortable being close, this is not going to work. Now get over the coy shit and listen to what I'm telling you."

Faye turned around and backed into him again. This time Darren leaned forward then gently pushed against her to stop her backward movement. It would have been very hard to claim that the warmth of her body was an unpleasant sensation.

"OK, better," Faye said. She held her arms out in front of her. "Now put your arms on mine. It might be best to hold at the wrists."

Darren complied.

"Now, listen carefully," Faye said. "Forget about what's around you. That's going to be difficult when you're invisible. If you react to the environment, it's all the more difficult to avoid detection. You tend to draw attention to yourself if you react to everything you see. So forget about your surroundings and focus on me."

Darren took another breath.

"OK," Faye said.

There was a gentle pressure on his chest before Faye used both legs to shove him backward so hard that Darren lost his footing and crashed into the wall behind him.

Faye turned around.

"This is the klutz part," she said.

"Yes, if you purposefully try to screw it up, you'll probably pull it off," Darren retorted.

"I gave you the cue," Faye said. "You have to pay attention, and sometimes you have to react quickly. Close your eyes if you have to, but pay attention to the cues. I can't be saying 'OK, I'm backing up now.' You've got to read it."

Darren got up.

"Are you pissed off now?" Faye asked.

"Yeah, a little bit," Darren said.

"How often have you danced with someone you're pissed off at?" Faye asked.

Darren paused.

"I don't dance," he said.

"I'm not shocked," she said.

"Ever."

"Learn."

"You're not helping."

Faye turned around and put her arms out in front of her.

Darren stepped up and took his position as before. This time he did close his eyes. He focused on her muscles and her movement. She started by moving her arms, slowly at first, then more quickly. Each time she gave him a cue just an instant before she moved. Darren was able to follow, until he smelled her hair and caught the scent of lavender. Faye nearly flipped him bodily in that instant, but he caught the cue and moved with her.

Navigating the room was more difficult. She couldn't send cues to his legs and feet so he struggled to keep up.

Her dance analogy seemed appropriate so he moved his right hand to her hip. After that, he advanced quickly. The cues were easier to catch and it was comparatively simple to follow her center of gravity. She started stepping and turning more quickly, darting at sharp angles and executing tight spins.

Darren just tried to emulate her, to shadow her; no augmentation, no escalation, just cooperation, just partnership. He couldn't believe they hadn't crashed into the TV or something.

After some time, he wasn't sure how long, Faye came to a stop and stayed still. Darren still didn't move, still didn't react.

There was no cue, so there was no response.

Finally, Faye moved her right hand and tapped him on the left forearm. Darren opened his eyes, came out of his shadow state, and stepped back.

Faye turned around. There was a thin layer of perspiration on her face and her cheeks were slightly flushed. Several strands of hair stuck sweatily to her, one down the center of her forehead and onto her nose. There was an uncharacteristic Mona Lisa-like smile on her face. She looked at Darren and paused before she spoke.

"Ummm... yeah, that'll do," she said with a raised eyebrow before she turned and reached for her cloak.

Faye put on the overcoat, but didn't deploy the cloaking panels. She started for the door and, again uncharacteristically, bumped into the chair on the way.

"Are you OK?" Darren asked.

"Yeah," Faye said, seemingly distracted. "I don't want to ferry you all the way back to the residence. It wasn't as big a deal when I escorted Walter in Prague, but these are much less forgiving conditions. We'll be in broad daylight and indoors. It's a completely different game, so we'll need to conserve a bit of energy and find a good spot to disappear once we get closer to the target."

Darren grabbed the coveralls he'd need once inside and followed Faye out. Unencumbered, it was a relatively short walk back to the residence. Finding a good place to vanish away from any prying eyes and with no video surveillance was less trivial. They had to circle the grounds twice before settling for a back alley underneath a rusty fire escape.

"All right," Faye announced. "This will have to do."

Darren began to change into the coveralls while Faye worked her magic. It took her all of three seconds to unfurl the cloak, let the wings settled upon her, and vanish completely. She left Darren slack-jawed and fumbling with one pant leg.

"C'mon," Faye said, "we're back to the klutz here."

Darren struggled into his uniform and donned the company hat that Vachislov had given him.

"Ready?" Faye asked.

"Yeah," Darren said into thin air.

A rift opened in front of him and rushed in to engulf him. Darren closed his eyes and fought the urge to recoil from the sensation of being swallowed whole. Faye would never have let him live that down.

Once inside, Darren gently reached out for her and maneuvered into the position they had practiced. With his eyes still closed, he tried to return to shadow mode.

It was easier than he thought, aside from being uncomfortably warm in the coveralls.

Faye moved at a gentle, fluid pace. They made very little sound but Darren could hear the noises of the city around them; traffic horns, engines grumbling, wind in the trees and buildings, and people talking. Sometimes the voices were incredibly close. It was astonishing to think that people were within arm's length, but presumably completely oblivious to their presence. They went down and up a street curb as they made their way onto the residence grounds.

Surgical

Then Darren made the mistake of opening his eyes. He gave an audible gasp and froze for an instant. For whatever reason he had expected it to be dark inside the cloak, but it was bright as day. That made him feel exposed and straight-out vulnerable.

Faye stopped and elbowed him with her right arm.

Darren closed his eyes again but he remained frozen.

She put her hand on his left arm to steady him. Her hand was firm, but not stern. She gave him a second to gather himself. Darren took a breath and exhaled slowly. He repeated the exercise then nodded to Faye.

She resumed.

Darren was determined not to make that mistake again.

They moved forward. Darren could hear the gate guard's voice as they approached the entry checkpoint. He was arguing with someone, again. Faye took them closer and closer. Darren could have sworn the guard was talking to them directly. Somehow Faye managed to orbit the guard, maneuver past him, and drift inside the gatehouse. Darren could hear the sounds change as they bounced off the gatehouse walls. They paused for a moment, during which Darren guessed Faye borrowed a couple of security badges, then gracefully drifted back out.

It was no wonder Faye was as silent as a passing breeze. She moved like one.

Then Faye bent at the knee and gracefully shimmied forward, presumably under the guard's traffic rail. They passed effortlessly and moved forward as the guard's voice began to blend with the background noise.

They walked in what Darren guessed was an open field under a strong sun. He could feel the heat on his back and through the cap he was wearing. It was a strange sensation. He'd have thought the cloak would provide shade, but upon reflection, it wouldn't make much sense to see a disembodied shadow moving across the president's lawn.

Darren began to perspire significantly. Two layers of clothing, three if you counted the cloak, and a hat in a hot sun were catching up with him.

"*Well,*" he thought, "*when we de-cloak, I'll look like I've been working. That can't hurt the cover story.*"

They climbed a long set of stairs toward the main entrance as voices drifted around them then they danced and moved until Faye somehow circumvented the metal detectors and entry screening.

Now they were inside.

The next step was for Faye to find a quiet place to de-cloak. Darren shadowed her down a set of hallways toward the President's office. Faye stopped in one place and waited for several minutes as people walked passed within inches of them.

Darren waited.

After a long time, Darren heard a door open next to them and Faye darted past someone to get inside. From the quality of the echo, Darren surmised it was the men's room. Faye touched his hand, which Darren somehow correctly inferred meant 'open your eyes,' and pushed open a stall door.

Faye opened the cloak for a nanosecond to let Darren slither out into the waiting stall.

Darren gave it about ten seconds.

He could hear others in the bathroom so he flushed the toilet before exiting. He didn't know if Faye was still in the room or not so after washing his hands, he went to the door, pushed it wide open, and kept to one side in case she needed an egress. When he entered the hallway, there were more people than he would have liked, all in suits, all eyeing him disapprovingly.

He guessed Faye would need to access the ladies' room next door, but he couldn't stay where he was and wait so he walked as inconspicuously as he could toward the president's office.

It wasn't far, and thankfully Brigham and Vachislov were already there and in character. The panels were set against the walls and they were installing the first set on the north wall.

Vachislov barked something at him and began pointing and gesturing agitatedly while verbally abusing Darren in Romanian. Darren tried to look humble and went to fetch a panel.

CHAPTER
17

Ten minutes later, Faye still had not shown up and Darren was getting concerned. He presumed he'd have heard about it if she'd run into trouble, but it was far too long for her to be delayed.

Something was wrong.

He thought about going to look for her but realized how pointless that would be.

"Ives? Walter?" Darren whispered.

"Yeah," they said in stereo.

"Faye still isn't here," Darren said. "Can you check on her?"

"Ives?" Walter said.

"Just a second," Ives said. "There are a lot of people around so it'll be easier to use the GPS on the cloak."

Almost immediately, Ives reported back.

"Um... yeah," Ives said. "We have a problem. She is holed up in a vacant office on the second floor. She's not doing anything. She's just sitting there in the corner."

"Aww, shit!" Walter said. "Darren, you have to go get her."

"What?" Darren said too loudly. "I'm not even sure I have clearance for that area. What the hell is the problem?"

"She can't de-cloak," Walter said. "This sometimes happens under stress. She's fine if she's cloaked and her missions, usually, keep her that way, but she sometimes has trouble coping out in the real world."

"Walter, we need her," Darren said. "This is a four-person job. We don't have time for this."

"I know," Walter said. "You've got to go after her. Talk her down. Help her get some grounding."

"Can't you do that?" Darren said. "Use the comm link. She'll listen to you better than she'll listen to me."

"She needs someone there physically," Walter said. "Another voice out of the ether isn't going to work."

"What do you mean 'another' voice out of the ether?" Darren asked.

"Never mind," Walter said. "Ives will help you get there, but you have to go coax her down. I don't think she's going to come out on her own."

"Fuck," Darren spat, again too loudly.

Both Brigham and Vachislov glared at him. Construction workers don't whisper into comm links or swear for no reason. Then Brigham cocked his head as if he was listening to something. Walter updated him through the link and he winced. He got a disgusted look on his face before looking back to Darren, nodding, and mouthing the word, 'Go.'

Darren exited the office and walked back toward the bathroom.

"There is a stairwell at the end of the hall," Ives said. "Slow down. There are two guys with shoulder holsters coming down. Don't get there until they exit."

Darren slowed down and tried to act like he was being paid by the hour. There was a water fountain near the bathroom. He paused and took a drink, a longer drink, a still-longer drink.

The surveillance team on the grounds must have thought he was damn thirsty.

Finally, the door at the end of the hallway opened and two men in suits emerged. They turned left and disappeared around the corner. Darren stood up and walked as quickly as he could without looking conspicuous.

"Go, go, go," Ives said. "Still clear."

Darren made it to the stairwell door and pulled on the handle.

It was locked.

"Son of a bitch!" Darren growled.

He pulled again.

No dice.

"Try the badge," Ives said.

Darren scanned the badge that Faye had procured from the entry checkpoint.

There was a confirmation beep and the diode on the door turned green.

The door clicked open.

"Lucky!" Darren breathed.

He darted up the stairs to the second floor. Again the door was locked. He scanned his badge and again the door clicked open.

"That's two," Darren said.

"Wait!" Ives said. "Two people coming toward you on the second floor. Stay there."

"*Shit!*" Darren thought, but said nothing.

"Hold on and let them pass," Ives said.

Darren let the door close and stood still. Several seconds later he heard the stairwell door open several flights up.

"Ives," Darren said, "up the stairwell."

"I see them," Ives said. "Crap!"

Darren heard footsteps as several people started coming down the concrete steps. The voices were loud and getting louder.

"Hold on," Ives said. "Darren, get behind the door."

Darren backed up against the wall as the door burst open and raced up to within about an inch of his nose. Two people came through and started down the flight of stairs to the first floor. Darren held the door open for a fraction of a second, long enough that it would provide cover until the two people were far enough down the stairs that they wouldn't see him standing against the wall when the door closed. Unfortunately, by then the people coming down the stairwell were almost on top of him.

"Now, Darren!" Ives yelled.

Darren whipped around the door just as he saw the feet of the newcomers on the steps up ahead, but he was gone before they came around the corner.

"Left, then left," Ives directed. "It's the second door on the right."

Darren almost ran down the hall. He came to the door Ives indicated and scanned his badge.

The LED on the door turned red and the door stayed locked.

"Shit!" Darren breathed and pulled on the door. "Out of luck."

"Darren, don't scan it again," Ives warned. "You'll alert security if you try more than twice."

"Then how the hell am I going to get in?" Darren said.

"I'm thinking," Ives said.

"Let me try to talk to her," Walter said.

"If you could do that, why the hell am I here?" Darren snapped.

"She doesn't need to de-cloak to open the door," Walter said. "Hold on."

***

"Faye?" Walter said gently through the comm link.

Faye took out the earpiece and pocketed it. She thought about stamping on it and smashing it into dust, but she wasn't that angry, not yet.

After several seconds, she heard him again, this time through the link imbedded in the cloak.

"Faye?" he said.

"Silent." Faye barked the command for the suit to go into radio silent mode.

Another several seconds and Walter pierced her peaceful calm, again, still through the cloak.

"Faye, you know I can override…" Walter began before she cut him off again.

"Silent!" she said more loudly.

Again the cloak temporarily cut the link. This time Walter gave her almost a minute before giving it another try. She was surprised it was that long.

"Faye, I'm not asking you to de-cloak," Walter said.

That got a sliver of her attention.

Walter waited for a moment; Faye said nothing.

"I'm not asking you to de-cloak," he repeated. "Darren is outside the door and it's locked. Can you please let him in?"

Faye didn't move. She took a deep breath and tried to endure the invasion she couldn't turn off.

"Faye," Walter said, "Darren's badge doesn't have security clearance for this area. He's waiting outside the door and I really don't want him to get caught. It's been too long already. Please, can you just walk over and unlock the door? You don't have to de-cloak and Darren won't be able to see you once he gets in the room. I'm saying this is no skin off your nose, but Darren needs some help."

Faye took another deep breath, rose to her feet and walked over to the door. It was clear Walter was not going to leave her alone until she complied so she might as well get it over with. She unlocked the door, retreated to the far end of the room, and sat down.

***

When the door opened, Darren's heart skipped a beat. He pushed on it gently and stepped inside.

The room was, of course, empty.

Darren closed the door behind him and allowed the silence to settle.

"Faye," Darren said gently, "there are probably video cameras in this office too, and it won't do to disappear in front of them. I'm going to crawl under the desk. Can you meet me there?"

There was no response; no breathing, no rustling, nothing. She was good at her job.

"OK, I'm going to get out of sight," Darren said. "Please come meet me under the desk."

Darren walked over to the large oak desk at the far end of the room. He pushed the large leather office chair aside and sat under the desk between the heavy oak drawers on either side.

It was highly unlikely that he was under video surveillance here.

He waited for a few minutes, but no one came.

"Faye," Darren whispered into the comm link, "I'm not wearing my suit so I'm no match for you. Please, come over so we can talk."

He waited.

He was patient.

After another several minutes, a magical veil lifted in front of Darren's hiding place and Faye sat down in front of him. She was still cloaked on three sides and from above, but her fourth side, hidden by the desk, was open to Darren.

He gave a genuine smile and a sigh of relief.

"Thank you," he said. "It's good to see you."

Faye barely acknowledged him.

Darren took a deep breath and crossed his fingers.

"Faye," he said, "we need you out there. This is a four-person job. We can't do it without you."

Still nothing, but there was pain on her face.

"At least tell me to get lost if that's where we're going," he said.

"I'm scared, Darren!" Faye spat. "Is it that hard to figure out? Where the fuck is the genius when you need him? I don't want to do this. Every second I'm here, I feel like someone has a gun pointed at my head and could pull the trigger on a whim. Sometimes I wish they would. Then it would be over. Then I wouldn't have this specter of death hanging over me, mocking me. I can almost hear the laugh when I close my eyes."

"Faye, you've run dozens of ops for Walter," Darren said. "Most of those were more dangerous than this."

"None of them were like this," she said. "Usually the cloak is there. It helps, but now you've taken that away too. It doesn't work with him. My one sanctuary desecrated."

"You're scared?"

"Yes."

"You're afraid?"

"Yes."

"You don't feel safe?"

"No. I feel like I'm falling into some giant abyss, being swallowed up by the darkness."

"Faye, you were never safe."

Faye's face turned an even more bleached shade of white.

"None of us have ever been safe. Ever," Darren said.

She stared at him, but said nothing.

"Life isn't like that. Life isn't safe. It never has been. It never will be. You may think that it is. You may feel safe, but that's an illusion. Think of a time when you felt safe, when you felt warm and secure and happy. I guarantee you the specter of death was hanging over your shoulder right then and there just as much as it is now.

"Whether it's a new stealth weapon, a traditional sniper rifle, a random act of violence, a traffic accident, an earthquake, a bolt of lightning or anything else, a brain tumor, a heart attack, you name it, none of us has ever been safe. It just doesn't work that way."

Faye turned and looked at him, more angry than afraid.

"Count yourself lucky," Darren said. "You live in a time when we have come as close to being truly safe as humankind ever has been. The rate of violent death is lower now than it has ever been. Throughout history, one in seven people didn't make it to die of old age. They were murdered by some violent incomprehensible act, some brutal violation that took their life from them. That has changed, and we're lucky enough to enjoy that, but don't be fooled into thinking you're so privileged that you're safe. You're not."

"No, we don't kill by the knife and the sword anymore," Faye said. "We kill by the gun and the bomb. We kill from afar."

"You think that makes it worse?" Darren asked.

"Yes. Destruction is wholesale, anonymous, easy, cowardly…"

"And dropping," Darren said.

"Bullshit," Faye spat.

"From prehistory until 1945, the number of deaths from war increased exponentially," Darren said.

"Yes, the result of guns and bombs made it easy."

"Until 1945, when it fell precipitously and has stayed constant ever since," Darren said. "From then until now, about one million people per year die in war, an exponential increase until 1945, then it fell and flattened. Why do you think that would be?"

Silence.

"Your hated bomb has put a cap on warfare," Darren said. "It can only go so far until the unthinkable rears its head and stares down the inevitable escalation. The paradox is that the greatest horror ever created by man, the instrument of the greatest human suffering ever perpetrated, has also delivered the greatest peace civilization has ever known. And by that saved the most lives, arguably hundreds of times what it has taken.

"In ancient times, there was an extended period of calm in the Roman Empire. They called it the Pax Romana: the Roman Peace. We live in an age that is the global equivalent, an extended period of calm."

"You call this peace?" Faye asked. "We have a genocidal war what seems like every year. One in seven people own a gun!"

"And yet our rate of violence is the lowest on record. You don't see it that way because you didn't have the experience of growing up in the Middle Ages where someone's arm or leg was hacked off every other day. You also never lived through World War II. You think a million a year is bad? How about five million? How about fifty million?"

"So I'm supposed to be thankful?" Faye asked.

"You're supposed to be thankful and pay your dues," Darren said. "We're facing a new threat, something that can unhinge all of that, something that could potentially bring us a new wave of anarchy, a new dark age. It is our responsibility to stop that. Technology brought us to this place and we are its beneficiaries. Now our great peace is being threatened and we have to stop that threat."

Faye said nothing.

"Faye, I know you're scared. We all are. Don't you think everyone who's ever fought in a war was? Now it's our turn to do our part. We have the skills. We have the tools. We have to use those in defense of that. Please, put aside your fear and your nurtured sense of security. We need to do this or all of what you've enjoyed, all that millions have sacrificed to build for us, could be compromised.

"Faye," Darren said gently, "find something out here that makes you feel like part of this world again. Find a reason to put aside your fear. We all have to. It's the only way we can function."

Faye raised her head and looked at him. There was a pause, a moment of silence, when Darren couldn't read her expression and had no idea what she would do next. She opened her mouth to say something then apparently changed her mind. She closed her mouth then virtually slammed the door on him.

The front cloak panel came down and she disappeared.

"Faye," Darren called as he reached out his hand to where she had been.

The space was empty.

"Damn it!" he breathed.

He was crawling out of his hiding place when he heard the door open. He emerged just in time to see it close again.

"Damn it," he whispered again. "Ives, she's running. You might want to track her."

"Aw, shit!" Ives said.

"Yeah," Darren agreed. "Look, I need to get back. Can you navigate for me and still keep tabs on her?"

"That should be fine, until she leaves the building," Ives said.

"All right," Darren said. "Let's go."

Darren walked to the door and waited.

"Give it about ten seconds," Ives said, "then you should be clear."

"Where's Faye headed?" Darren asked.

"Down the stairs," Ives said. "OK, go. You should be clear."

Darren pulled the door open and started for the stairwell. He didn't look both ways as he instinctively would have. That was Ives' job.

"OK. Go, Darren," Ives said. "Keep going. If you get to the stairwell in the next five seconds, you should be clear to go down."

Darren made it as quickly as he could without running. He flashed the badge through the scanner, fidgeted for the half-second it took to confirm the scan and click open, pulled open the door and darted down the stairs. Ives was right. He could hear footsteps above, headed down.

"Keep going," Ives said. "You're hitting the green lights."

Again Darren scanned the badge, opened the door, and emerged into a temporarily empty hallway. He was well on his way to the office before anyone had seen him, and by then he was out of the suspicious zone.

"Ives," Darren asked, "where's Faye?"

"Yeah, about that," Ives said.

Right on cue, and exactly as Darren approached, the door to the ladies' room opened and Faye, fully visible and in her coveralls and working cap, emerged. Darren almost swallowed his tongue. She barely acknowledged him before turning and walking toward the office.

It was the perfect response for their cover.

Darren somehow managed to keep walking despite his shock. He walked fast enough to get past her. He opened the door to the office and held it for a fraction of a second. As she passed him, he whispered, "Thank you."

She gave no response save for a muted, monosyllabic, "Mmm…"

It was sufficient.

With Faye in place, the operation commenced efficiently. Darren had forgotten how therapeutic it could be to work with his hands and serve as manual labor on a reasonably simple construction project. It might almost have been pleasant, save for the fact that any or all of them could drop dead at any minute. The good news was he had no indication that the assassin was even aware of them. The bad news was they wouldn't know either way.

Ives wouldn't tell them.

Walter wouldn't tell them.

No matter how this went, they wouldn't know until it was over.

That's the way it had to be. In this case, ignorance wasn't necessarily bliss, it was just healthier.

***

The operation was today.

Obviously August knew that. He had rearranged his schedule around the office renovation. They said they'd need at least a day, and maybe two. Halfway through the first day, August was a wreck. This was a big risk and there wasn't a damn thing he could do about it.

It seemed like the best course, but this waiting was agony.

He had to give the team a lot of credit. Technically, they didn't have to do this. They had voluntarily stuck their necks out. That said a lot about them.

August sat in his home office. If he'd been a religious man, this would have been a great time to pray.

He almost jumped out of his skin when the assassin's phone rang.

He took a breath before answering.

They'd rehearsed this.

"Yes," he said in an agitated tone.

"There are people in your office," the voice said.

"Yes," August said, "so what?"

"They're doing some kind of construction," the voice said.

"Office renovation," August corrected. "They do this all the time. They change the decor to maintain fashion and keep a new appearance in the office. A president's office needs to maintain a certain level of opulence." He paused. "Why am I talking to you about this?"

"I made it clear that you were to keep me informed of all scheduled changes," the voice said, rising.

"Do you want me to keep you informed when I wipe my ass, too?" August boomed. "I have a country to run. I don't concern myself with trivial bullshit. Other people have that job. Is there something you actually wanted?"

Click! The line went dead.

Now August really did wish he prayed. He took several deep breaths and just hoped he had one left, then another, then another. As Walter said, logically this just shouldn't be important enough for the assassin to worry about. It shouldn't be important enough to punish August or injure him in a way that would compromise his value.

Why did that logic not help his heart from passing 150 beats per minute?

***

"He's onto them, Walter," Ives reported.

"I know," Walter said. "I just can't believe this is reason enough to kill them if they don't break cover. This is a plausible scenario and an innocuous event. They just need to stay in character."

CHAPTER
18

They made good progress.

They had finished almost a third by the time the day wound to a close. Even more miraculously than that, they were still alive.

Vachislov muttered something in Romanian and gestured at the clock.

It was 6:00.

Darren inferred this meant it was technically quitting time and that working longer might raise suspicion. He glanced at Faye and she left. He looked at Brigham and nodded. Darren exited and went back to the men's room stall to which Faye had originally escorted him.

It was occupied.

"Perfect," he muttered.

Darren washed his hands and procrastinated until he felt a gentle brush against his left shoulder. Then he went to an empty stall, gave it about three seconds, opened the door and slipped into Faye's waiting cloak.

The journey back to her quarters was much like the way in but in reverse. They navigated the exit checkpoint, returned the badges to the security hut, and wound past the gate. The only variation was that Faye did not return to their place under the rusty fire escape. She took a direct route to her quarters, still under cloak. Presumably, with what practice they had, the journey was less strenuous than it might have been the first time.

Darren's comm link rang even as he and Faye were emerging from the cloak back at her quarters.

"Update?" Walter's voice asked.

"It's about one-quarter done, Walter," Darren answered. "We had a few bumps, so it looks like it's going to take another day or two to finish."

"Thanks," Walter said. "I appreciate you all doing this. I'd help but…"

"You're too recognizable," Darren said. "We know."

"Can I treat you all to dinner?" Walter asked. "I have a secure location in mind."

"Thanks," Darren said, "I'm going to pass tonight."

"Darren?" Walter asked.

"No, I'm not going to patrol," Darren said. "We agreed I'd stay quiet. I just want to go check on my workshop. It's about an hour away on the outskirts of the city and I haven't been there yet."

"Can't you do that remotely?" Walter asked.

"I can," Darren said, "I just prefer not to. I'd just like to stretch my legs and pay a physical visit."

There was silence on the line.

"Walter, I have to sleep too," Darren said, "and there is work to do tomorrow. I won't be too late."

"OK," Walter breathed. "Have fun."

It did feel good to have the suit on again. It had been a few days and he may not have been planning to use it, but there was no reason not to wear it when he was going that far. The trip out, mostly by metro train, was uneventful and fortunately the workshop was in great shape. Of course, he already knew that. He checked in remotely almost every day whether he was in Bucharest or not, but it was good to see.

And it's not like it couldn't defend itself with its own countermeasures in the event someone did come looking for trouble, but there's nothing like a face-to-face, even when dealing with equipment.

Darren spent about an hour in the workshop before it was time to leave. He enabled the security systems, double checked them, pulled the door shut then turned the doorknob and pushed to ensure it was locked. It was getting late and he needed to be heading back, but there was one detour he needed to make. He was sure Walter wouldn't object.

Bucharest had two distribution hubs for street drugs. One was relatively close to Darren's workshop. That was, of course, not a coincidence. The other was across town on the northwest side. That wasn't convenient, but it wasn't too bad by metro.

Darren swung through the closest district first. He called it the South End. He didn't know the colloquial term. Whatever it was, it was in Romanian and he hadn't spent enough time listening to the locals to pick it up.

In any case, he had a standard path through it. He had mapped a particular set of back alleys and sewer transfers that kept him out of sight but let him sweep up to eighty percent of the active area in an efficient route. Ordinarily, he didn't like using a predictable path but he hadn't been here in a while and the familiar course gave the most efficient coverage pattern.

Not much had changed.

There were plenty of transactions going on. Fortunately for everyone, there was no real violence in progress during Darren's quick pass, just the usual small-time buying and selling. He would've given money to roust a few, but he stayed his hand out of respect for Walter.

"*When this is over,*" he thought.

Darren darted through the South End and shot out near the metro station on the far side. He took off his mask before entering the station and rode the train as an ordinary mask-less but anonymous passenger. When he got out near the second hub, he again took to the shadows, mask and signature hat included. He had a standard route in the North End as well, but this time he took it a bit more slowly and deliberately.

It was more likely his target was here and he didn't want to fly right past.

Darren swept through patiently. He let crimes pass that he ordinarily would have tripped up with a sound blast or a little light trick.

He was quiet.

He didn't need to save the world today, just intercept the problem he knew was coming.

It took longer than he expected. He spent almost an hour canvassing the area. He saw hundreds of transactions, but near as he could tell no one saw him. He was about to pack it in, hopeful that he'd misjudged the situation, when, unfortunately, his vigilance paid off.

A man in a full-length coat, trying to look like he belonged here and failing miserably, came in from the east. He tried to stick to the shadows and look like a local street consumer, but his gait was too precise and his coat was from

Brooks Brothers. He might as well have been wearing neon. To his credit, he approached the right huddle of vendors from the right direction and at the right speed.

These were all signs that he was a little too practiced at this.

"You lost, bitch?" the vendor asked through a thick accent. At least he knew his customer base.

The customer shot something back that Darren didn't catch. It sounded like Romanian. At least the customer had done his homework. Then he held up a short stack of cash.

"Double that," the vendor demanded, again in English.

"Double this," the customer said in English, extending his middle finger.

He spun on his heel and started walking. The vendor let him go five steps before calling, "One hundred and fifty."

The customer kept walking. He looked both ways before stepping into the street on a trajectory toward the vendor's competitor.

"OK, whitefish," the vendor called.

The customer turned around, walked back, and extended the cash. The vendor reached for it, but he pulled it back. The vendor produced a small plastic bag and the parties made their exchange. The customer set to a brisk walk in the direction from which he had come.

Darren followed until they'd left the north end district for a more savory atmosphere. Then he took a position he knew was on the target's return path.

When Brigham passed within about five feet, Darren called to him. "Walter asked me to behave."

Brigham almost jumped out of his skin.

"I assume he meant you should too," Darren said.

"Jesus fucking Christ," Brigham spat. "What the fuck are you doing?"

"I'd ask you the same thing," Darren said, "but we both know."

"It's none of your fucking business," Brigham shot back.

Darren said nothing.

"How long have you known?" Brigham asked.

"The better question is: how long has Walter known?" Darren said.

"Walter doesn't know," Brigham said.

"Really?" Darren said. "Walter doesn't know! We're talking about Walter Rocaena, right? That Walter? Are you honestly that deluded that you believe Walter doesn't know about this? Jesus, Brigham!"

Brigham scanned the ground to avoid eye contact.

"Look," Brigham said, "you have no idea what it's like working for Walter every day. You cross paths with him once in a while. You don't have daily contact. You don't know what it's like trying to sustain that kind of pace."

"Is that the excuse?" Darren asked. "Is that when it started?"

"You have no idea," Brigham said again.

There was a pause.

"If Walter thought you needed it, you wouldn't be working for him," Darren said. "He never would've hired you in the first place. The fact that he has tolerated it for this long without getting rid of you means you bring something to the table that he values."

Brigham said nothing.

"That being said, if I had to guess, I'd say you're running out of time," Darren continued. "He won't tolerate this kind of risk during an operation." Brigham looked up. "If you want to get clean, go to him and tell him you want to get clean. If you don't want to get clean, don't expect anyone to stick around, least of all Walter."

Brigham looked down at his clenched fist. He opened his hand and studied the small plastic bag. He closed his fist again and looked up.

He saw only blackness.

Darren had moved on.

The trip back was mostly uneventful. One purse snatcher did run into him and bounce off like he'd just hit a brick wall, and, OK, maybe Darren had arranged the impact, but it was nearly uneventful.

Darren stepped off the train around 3:00 AM, took a walk around the President's residence to reflect on the work they had done that day then took a circuitous route back to the quarters Walter had arranged. The accommodations were better equipped than a hotel and more secure. Ives and Faye had something similar, but they were located at two other strategic points around the perimeter of the main residence. Darren, of course, had no idea where Walter was: another secondary redundancy.

***

When the phone rang, it jolted Darren out of the first real night's sleep he had gotten in days.

"Damn it," he groaned, glanced at the clock, and picked up the receiver.

It was 7:24 AM, just a few minutes before he'd set the alarm to wake him.

"Darren, it's Vachislov."

"Yeah," Darren said.

"It looks like the security checks cleared. We can meet you at the front gate at 8:30."

"Something finally went right?" Darren muttered. "OK, thanks, we'll see you in about an hour."

He hung up the phone and called to the comm link.

"Faye, Brigham," he called.

"Need a lift?" Faye said with what sounded like a smile.

"Actually, no," Darren said. "Thanks, but it looks like the security clearance came through. Can we meet at the front gate at 8.30?"

"OK, good," Brigham said.

"Yeah," Faye said more mutedly.

The second day went smoothly.

The guard at the front gate gave each of them a dirty look when he handed over the badges, but that was probably his job. The screening at the service entrance was mostly innocuous. Faye had stacked the cloak in with a set of drop cloths and they didn't check carefully enough to notice the difference. Technically, she didn't need it today, but Darren wasn't going to argue the point.

They got to the office and went to work without so much as a word. Vachislov directed them well enough that they could remain mute most of the morning.

Right around lunch hour, Faye flashed Darren a look and he nodded at her. She picked up her cloak and left. Darren, Brigham, and Vachislov ate the lunch the company had prepared for its usual labor force then went back to work. Faye returned after about an hour. Darren handed her a sandwich that she choked down while carrying the various panels back and forth.

Progress was steady, but still slower than they would have liked. The job required a bit more precision than they had estimated and Darren guessed they'd need one more day to finish the job. That wasn't optimal, but they seemed to be pulling off their cover. There was no wrangling from the security side and the assassin himself had, apparently, been silent.

The exit was at least as innocuous as the entry. Even the guard at the front gate seemed more interested in ending his shift than strictly following the exit protocol.

By the time Darren packed away the last of the gear, took off his hat and coveralls, and bade the others a good night, he was cautiously optimistic about their prospects.

CHAPTER
19

Darren came back to the apartment through the front door lobby and took the front stairs. There was no reason not to. He wasn't wearing the suit and he had done nothing to attract attention. If the security team at the president's grounds wanted him or suspected him, they would have detained him on the spot. There was no reason for them to follow him. He was as secure and innocent as he could get. Granted, that wasn't saying much where Darren was concerned, but it was still relevant.

When he unlocked the door to his quarters, he wasn't expecting any surprises and in that first moment there were none, but something wasn't right. He noticed it didn't feel quite right. It wasn't the temperature. It wasn't a scent or anything else in the air, but there was something. He didn't detect any sound or see anything unusual immediately.

It was something intangible, something ineffable, like there was a presence in the room that he couldn't detect with his five senses. He didn't believe Faye was here, but it was the only thing he could think of that would set off his paranoia.

"Faye?" he called into the room.

There was no answer.

"Faye?" he called again.

Silence.

Darren stepped into the room gingerly He rounded the entryway corner and looked into the living space.

The armoire, the cabinet in which he stored the suit; the door was ajar.

He had not left it that way.

Darren ran over and threw the door open.

The armoire was empty.

At the last moment, there was one resounding, almost deafening, order firing every nerve ending in his cerebral cortex.

"Duck!"

Darren dropped halfway to the floor as fast as gravity could carry him. The instant his head left the space above his shoulder height, Darren heard a loud crack just above him. He dropped the rest of the way to the floor, shoulder rolled toward the door, and came up running. There was another firecracker explosion about two feet behind him. Darren bolted out the door and threw himself down the first flight of stairs.

He was halfway down the first leg when he screeched to a halt and bent backward like he might if avoiding a limbo bar.

The move was well considered.

Another spark went off about eighteen inches in front of his face.

If you can anticipate my path, you'll nail me, Darren thought, *but if I keep it chaotic, keep jerking around so you can't lead me, there's a chance I can shake you at least for the moment. Of course, I can't keep this up forever, but first things first.*

Darren started running again.

As he passed through the position of the last explosion, he smelled the ozone, the telltale report of the radiant discharge. It would have made him nauseous from fear if his mind wasn't otherwise occupied.

He kept running.

He grabbed the railing at the base of the first leg of stairs, whipped around and leaped seven stairs at once.

Another report came three feet behind him.

Darren jumped the rest of the way down the stairwell. The impact sent a stinging pain to his feet and his shins. He pushed past the pain and ran out the front door.

Darren kept bobbing and weaving as he made his way down the street at a brisk jog. He would have run like a bat out of hell, sprinting as fast as his feet could carry him, but he was only going to stay alive as long as he could keep running, and he couldn't do that forever. Evading the assassin was going to be a distance run.

That was if he was lucky, and his luck was running out fast.

Now what? Darren thought as he lurched forward, then pulled up short and backed up half a step before ducking to the ground and sprinting forward again.

He heard another firecracker go off behind him, but the street noise drowned out the sound. With all the commotion in the city, no one would think anything of him dropping dead on the spot; just another heart attack.

Darren saw a sign for the subway station dead ahead.

How about this, asshole? he thought to whoever was watching but in all likelihood couldn't hear.

Darren sprinted toward the subway entrance, tracing a chaotic path as he went. He scanned the crowd drifting this or that way on the sidewalk and kept watch on the commuters spilling from the subway entrance.

He chose a likely target about twenty yards ahead, a kid of about sixteen with headphones in his ears, holding the source of the music in his hand. The boy bounced his head, presumably in time to the music, and stared at the ground as he walked. Darren got to within about fifteen feet then accelerated. He grabbed the youth's music and headphones and dove down the mouth of the subway entrance without looking back.

Sorry, kid, Darren thought, *but I'll need to borrow these.*

Darren heard a commotion behind him, most assuredly the boy chasing him and pushing his way past the crowd to pursue.

Darren ran down the subway stairs and vaulted the entrance turnstile. He glanced back. Darren had put some distance between himself and his pursuer in the first handful of seconds after the grab, but his victim had quickly shaken off the surprise and was gaining on him. Worse still, his violation of the subway fare collector hadn't gone unnoticed. Several security guards were after him now.

Darren heard a crack right next to his left ear.

"Son of a bitch," he spat. Then he stopped, backed up and started running diagonally in the hallway. Of course that only brought his pursuers closer.

Darren sprinted for the metro train tracks. He vaulted a garbage can, ran up on a bench under which a homeless person still slept, and dodged several imaginary metro line patrons, all to keep his escape path as chaotic as possible.

Just as a security detail was within arm's reach, Darren leaped from the subway platform to the tracks below.

The guards hesitated.

Darren kept running.

He watched both right and left as he picked his way across the live train tracks. He heard the telltale oncoming rush from his right and ducked behind a support beam as the train raced by with a blast of air and sound.

"Duck," the voice in his head cried.

Darren couldn't tell if there was another discharge over the noise of the passenger train, but he didn't wait for the next opportunity. He ran parallel to the train to the next support beam until the train passed.

Now it was time to get more focused.

Still bobbing and weaving, Darren picked his way toward the door that he knew led to the lower levels of the subway line system. Neither the security guards nor the youth were pursuing him now, but his breathing was getting labored and his legs were beginning to feel like lead from the prolonged exertion.

Darren put the ear buds from the music player he had stolen in his ears and searched for the radio receiver. Almost all these music players had a tuner, even though the owners rarely use them. The circuits were just too small and cheap to exclude. The particular model he had chosen was no exception. It almost certainly had one.

He got lucky.

This unit had both an AM and an FM tuner. Still running, he set it to the longest wavelength it could reach and listened for a station. He heard babbling in a language he couldn't understand and, unfortunately in this case, the signal was clear and free of static.

Darren was huffing and puffing and sweating when he reached the service entrance and leaped down the gray metal stairs. The distance was too much for his tired legs and he fell forward. He slammed into the cinder block wall and fell to the floor. Yet another spark missed him, but he felt the attack singe his hair just at the base of his skull near the neckline.

He pushed off the wall, came to his feet, and ran down the next set of stairs. Darren steeled himself, stopped again, and forced his exhausted legs to climb back half the flight of stairs then he spun and descended again.

His legs were burning now; his breathing coming in short, desperate gasps. The radio was beginning to show the slightest steady static interference.

Darren continued his descent. He bounced back and forth between the railing and the wall like a ball bearing in a pinball machine and kept descending. He reached a connection gangway that he knew led to the next sub tunnel. He came out onto the gang and forced his legs to carry him on.

Halfway across, he made a move that could best be described as 'sliding into second' then saw a blue spark ignite directly above him. Whether it was his imagination or the sound from the radio drowning out the report, Darren thought this time the spark was weaker, smaller, diminished.

That hope brought him renewed strength. He jumped to his feet and redoubled his chaotic trajectory. By the time he got to the next level, Darren's radio was giving pronounced static and it was hard to believe the strength and the sniper's attacks hadn't been beaten down.

They were still lethal, but they were weakening.

He kept diving, winding his way deeper into a labyrinth underneath the city, putting layers and layers of concrete and machinery between himself and the sniper until the radio signal could no longer register at all. The attacks had decayed from an explosion like a large firecracker to a discharge one might get from rubbing one's feet on a shag carpet, to nothing at all. Importantly, the last several attempts were diminished in both intensity and accuracy. They were weaker and farther away from Darren each time. That meant the sniper was losing his bead on his target.

By the time Darren reached the lowest sublevel of the long-forgotten access tunnel deep beneath the city, he collapsed in an exhausted heap in the dust and paint chips that had probably gone undisturbed for decades. He waited for the next attack that he prayed would not come.

One minute, ten minutes, twenty minutes; he was still alive and his breathing was beginning to return to normal.

The sniper couldn't reach him here and, perhaps more importantly, he couldn't see him either.

Darren stayed in the tunnel for a long time. He took off the headphones that were now playing nothing but static and turned off the music player. He wished he could return it to the owner with a sincere apology, but, unfortunately, that wasn't going to happen.

He wiped the sweat off his face, caught his breath, and stretched his legs. The latter were likely accumulating lactic acid in real time. Unfortunately, no matter how much he stretched, he was going to be sore tomorrow. Fortunately, he was still alive so there would be a tomorrow.

Eventually, Darren stood up, subconsciously crouching to stay as far away from the surface as possible. He walked a few hundred yards in the sub tunnel and found another sub tunnel, which he followed for another few hundred yards. He kept winding his way along the deepest subterranean routes he could find to put as much distance between him and the sniper as possible.

He had gone a few miles before he even began to ascend, and even then he tried to target the most crowded area he could think of; the subway construction site on the east end of the city.

When he emerged, he garnered a set of dirty looks and admonishment in Romanian. Undoubtedly, they were telling him he shouldn't be here because it was an active site and he didn't even have a hard hat. Darren nodded respectfully and kept moving. Somehow he made it to the street level without getting arrested, and started walking south.

Again, fortunately, even after he reached the surface, he was still alive.

Once the sniper had lost sight of him, there was no way he could know where Darren was going to emerge. Even more importantly, it was virtually impossible to locate him among the six million inhabitants of the city. So, as long as Darren could maintain his anonymity, he could avoid being a ready target.

But there was a problem. How had the sniper identified him to begin with? He supposed it was possible that he could have followed Darren back from the president's grounds, but that was a little hard to believe since they had taken steps to blend in.

Why would the sniper follow a contractor back from work?

But if he had…

Darren dialed Faye's cell phone.

She picked up.

"Darren?"

"Faye, are you OK?"

"Yeah, I'm fine. Why?"

"The sniper found me. He stole my suit and equipment and tried to kill me."

"What? How?"

"I don't know how, but if he can find me, he can find you and Brigham. You've got to get out of there."

"I just talked to Brigham. He's fine. Where are you?"

"On the move."

"How are you still alive?"

"I'll explain that later."

He heard rustling.

"I'm going. I'll call Walter and have him set up a new location. I'll call you when I'm set."

"Tell Brigham to move too. I don't know how but we've got to assume he knows we're all in this."

"I'll tell him. We'll talk to you soon."

The line went dead.

What did I do? Darren thought. *I worked at the president's grounds. I came back. I put on the suit. I went to the workshop. Shit!*

Darren dialed the workshop on his phone. The video feed came to his handheld screen. The shop looked undisturbed. He checked the perimeter cameras and the electronic locks on the equipment cabinets. He called up the central computer and checked the system files. They didn't look like they had been hacked. Everything appeared to be in order at the workshop.

Then either he's baiting me and waiting for me to show up so he can target me again, or he doesn't know about the workshop, Darren thought. *OK, let's trace it out again. I put on the suit. I went to the workshop. I came back and circled the president's grounds then I went back to the quarters.*

I suppose that's possible.

If he picked me up on patrol around the grounds, if the suit has a recognizable signature to his surveillance radar, it might have tipped him off enough to follow me back to the safe house. When I left to go to work on the net, he could have come and cleaned out the whole place. He would have known exactly where I was. There really couldn't be another way. If he knew about the workshop, he already would have raided it. He wouldn't have left it as bait because he didn't know I was going to evade him in the first place. We'll call that a working theory and pray. If he can't see me now, if he lost me in the tunnel, it should be safe enough to go to the workshop and re-equip.

Darren caught a metro train south, got off the station nearest his workshop, and walked one and a half miles to complete the trip. He approached the den warily. If he was wrong, he was an easy target and there was no subway tunnel to dive into to escape out here. This was an all-or-nothing bet.

He walked up like any other pedestrian then made a quick move to the side entrance of the warehouse. He keyed in the access code and stared at the retinal imager to release the outer lock. When the latch opened, he darted inside and made for the workbench.

He had seen Ives make plenty of the sensors for the surveillance net. He scrambled together a few similar components and grabbed a few batteries from a nearby drawer. He waited and rechecked the device.

It appeared to be working, but it was not detecting any surveillance activity. Again, it seemed the sniper did not know he was here.

"OK, asshole. Now, where the fuck is my suit!"

Darren pulled one of his spare exo-suits from the storage cabinet and put it on. He suspended the suit, with himself inside, from a harness designed for just that application. He remotely accessed the suit the sniper had stolen and synced the suit he was wearing to the movements of the missing twin.

It was black until he turned on the connection and the eye sets on the remote suit came on. It was disorienting at first because he didn't know where the suit was, how it was oriented, or what he was looking at. He could be in a closet, a gutter, a dumpster, or anywhere else for that matter.

When the eyes came on, it showed a blank tile surface, presumably some sort of flooring, about eighteen inches in front of his face. He activated the rest of the body, raised the head and extended the arms. The arms stopped in mid-motion, restrained by something.

He looked at the wrists.

There were chains binding him to the floor.

Then he heard a voice.

"Dr. Kiel, I presume," the voice said.

Darren looked up. There was a large video monitor in front of him and a video camera mounted at the top of the monitor. The image of a man comfortably seated in a high-backed chair was on the video feed.

He was thin, mid-forties, he wore a goatee and his hair was thinning on top. His eyes had the steady intensity of the chess grandmaster.

Darren looked down at the chains.

"You have me at a disadvantage," he said.

The man wrinkled his brow fractionally.

"Do I?" he asked.

If he was feigning confusion, he did it well.

"I haven't had the pleasure," Darren said.

"Honestly?" the man asked, again making a good show of it.

Darren waited.

"Forgive me," the man said, "I assumed Walter had briefed you, but maybe that was a mistake on my part."

"Walter?" Darren asked.

"Now you are kidding me," the man said. "Really? C'mon, where should we begin then?"

"How about your name?"

"Let's make it Marcus."

Darren held up his hands to show the chains.

"Is this necessary?"

"Not even close to necessary," Marcus almost laughed, "and all but irrelevant. I know you can escape that any one of a dozen ways, including snapping the chains. I just preferred the psychology of it. You know, waking up in chains. It just felt right to me."

Darren said nothing but deactivated the drive elements beneath the elbows on both arms of the suit then he pulled his arms away so the limp sleeves slid through the chain manacles. The chains hit the floor with a rattle and Darren reactivated the now free arms and looked back to the video screen.

Marcus shrugged.

"I just wanted to see it." He smiled.

"How do you know Walter?" Darren asked.

"The same way you do," Marcus said. "I guess you'd call him my father figure, at least insofar as my uniqueness is concerned."

"You've worked with him?"

"More like he's worked with me. Jesus, Darren, didn't he tell you any of this?"

"Let's assume not."

"Where do you think Ives got his start?"

CHAPTER
20

"Remote sensing," Walter frowned. "That's clever, Marcus. That really is. How long has this been going on?"

Marcus smiled with pride. He sat in the chair opposite Walter's desk and looked self-satisfied.

"You mean the harmonics effect?" he asked. "We talked about that three months ago."

"I mean the root wavelength," Walter said sadly. "When did you alter the wavelength?"

Marcus looked confused.

"What do you mean?" he asked.

Walter spun the monitor on his desk to face Marcus. It showed a grayscale image of a conference room with about a dozen people inside. Marcus's face lost the smile and the smugness.

"Did you really think we wouldn't monitor you at all?" Walter asked. "We have capture feeds on every video screen in the company. We know what everyone is doing with company assets."

Marcus said nothing.

"When did you change the root wavelength?" Walter asked again.

Then Marcus really did change. He sat back in his chair and let go of the youthful, energetic tension in his body. He seemed to transform right in front of Walter from a bright, innocent protégé to a repugnant adversary with a dangerous amount of information on Walter and his company.

In that instant, Walter understood he'd been played. Marcus, everything Walter knew of him or thought he knew, had been an act.

"The day I walked in the door," Marcus said with contempt and even a hint of relief, "from day one. I knew you wanted your remote chemical sensing and I was just as pleased to give it to you, as long as I could have access to the lab and develop a tool that was actually useful."

Walter gestured at the monitor with the grayscale image. "This is the boardroom of Krynotech Analytics. They are a competitor of ours. That's espionage."

"Right under your roof," Marcus said. "That's what remote sensing is, Walter. I just put it to a useful purpose."

"How many others?" Walter asked.

"If you've had a capture feed on my monitor, why don't you look for yourself?" Marcus asked with disdain. "I might recommend a file that's titled 'women's locker room'.

"Walter, use your imagination," Marcus said. "Actually, let me do it since you don't seem to have one. You say you want to develop these tools for military applications and homeland defense. You get on your soapbox about how critical it is to be able to checkmate an adversary in the name of defending yourself, but you forget that the best defense is a strong offense. Do you have any idea how much money I've made in the last three months, just gathering and applying a little information at the right place and the right time?"

"We haven't rifled through your personal records on a whim if that's what you mean," Walter said.

"Well, if you had, you'd have a lot more information than you have now, wouldn't you?"

"I don't disregard every right and dignity of every person I meet. I might if I were a sociopath, then maybe you would understand that."

"That's just a word that the weak use for a person who makes different choices with the options presented."

"And I clearly have presented you with far too many options. My failure."

"Which you probably wouldn't have made if you were a little less myopic and a little more imaginative. That's my point."

"Well, let's start here. Let's work on remedying my shortcomings by understanding exactly how busy you've been and how much damage you've caused."

"And how do you expect to do that without 'disregarding my every right and dignity'?"

"Marcus, my mistake was not understanding what you are, giving you too much freedom and trusting you. That gave you the regrettable opportunity to infect too much. How much we don't know yet, but we will."

"I still don't see how without violating your own weighty ethos."

Walter indulged in a wicked smirk then gave Marcus his steeliest glare. There was a marked satisfaction in seeing the smugness drain from Marcus's face, along with several shades of color.

"You don't have to dissect an animal to understand its physiology. 'Remote sensing,' remember? Marcus, I can be more imaginative than you think, but let's not get ahead of ourselves. I think we're in a 'need to know' situation here. I'll tell you what you need to know and you can 'make your different choices with the options presented.'"

At that point, two very burly security guards entered Walter's office upon the bidding of the under-desk call button he'd pressed five seconds before. They moved in and took up positions on either side of the chair Marcus occupied.

"Let's escort Mr. Cahn to a less comfortable room," Walter said to the guards. "He'll be leaving our employ presently, but there are some debriefing and exit protocols we'll need to cover before he leaves the building."

Marcus stood up, still staring at Walter. He said nothing as the guards escorted him away.

Fifteen minutes later Walter was still seething from the revelations and struggling to bring his heart rate down and emotions in check. He was spinning his meditation balls when the room went dark and the emergency lights came on.

Power to the building had been cut.

Walter could barely speak the words through barred teeth. "Marcus," he growled.

It only took fifteen minutes to find the problem, a power shunt planted by you-know-who for a well-calculated contingency. By the time the power came back on, Marcus was gone.

***

"I did the original work on the radio wave surveillance system, under Walter's auspices, of course. I did the original research and developed the initial two-dimensional technology. When Walter and I parted company, he recruited

Ives to continue the work. Obviously he ran with the ball. I'll grant you he seems to have taken it a little further. He seems to be able to see holographically. That's something I never was able to manage in the early days, but then again he had more time. It's a nice trick. I'm a little busy putting my effort into a different application."

"Murder."

"I'd call it activism."

"Now there's a euphemism."

"An accurate characterization."

"I guess the next question is why? You're clearly intelligent; that usually implies an affinity for order, but you seem to be craving anarchy. Why?"

"Asks the rich boy."

"That doesn't answer the question."

"I suppose you would be blind to the shortcomings of the status quo."

"You obviously don't know me as well as you think."

"Because you trot around among the dirty masses and play savior? I know about your hobby well enough, but that's all it is. It makes no difference in the long run and the only reason you do it is so you can have your anonymous comfort and not feel guilty for living above the rest of them. You are a self-appointed judge, but you obviously view the society you serve with derision."

"So murder, terrorism, anarchy, and war are your gifts to mankind?"

"The only way to win against a stacked deck is to reshuffle the cards. From there, let's just say, I'll play some role in restacking the deck."

"This is what your brilliant mind aspires to? You think the rose garden is going to grow out of your scorched earth?"

"If you know where and how to plant the seeds. I'm very judicious in where I apply my craft."

"Clearly."

"I do have to hand it to you. No one has ever evaded me once I decided to pull the trigger. That was a clever move, sounding like that."

Darren said nothing.

"Let's be clear," Marcus continued. "If you get in my sights again, you won't be so lucky. I won't give you a warning next time and, as we know, your suit is no protection. I can shoot you right through it."

"That does beg the question: why didn't you in the first place?"

"I was curious," Marcus said. "A set of unannounced contractors working in the office was a little too convenient. I watched for a while and saw you and that woman exit under some kind of cloak. I presumed, from the way you were moving, that it rendered you invisible to everyone but me. That had Walter written all over it, so I followed you to her quarters and followed you to yours. Once there, I saw you put on this strange suit and go out again, more of Walter's fingerprints. I was a bit disappointed when you got out of my range but I knew you'd be back, so I could afford to be patient."

"I'm still not clear on why you didn't pull the trigger when I got back," Darren said.

"I just had to get my hands on that suit," Marcus said. "If I had killed you there, Walter would have swept in and cleaned the place before I could get to it. So, I let you go back to work and borrowed it while you were gone.

"When I got a good look, it was pretty obvious what it was. I didn't have time to do a detailed study, but I figured you'd be able to remote control the exo-suit. I certainly would have engineered that option. So I made your surrogate comfortable and waited for you to dial in. I didn't see it, but I assumed you have a homing system on it so I figured I'd dial in remotely as well."

"And once you had it?" Darren asked.

"I wanted you to know I had it," Marcus said.

"So, basically, your hubris and sadism saved my life."

"For the moment."

"You'll end up regretting that."

"Unlikely."

"I'm disappointed you didn't try it on," Darren said. "It can be very exhilarating."

"I'm sure," Marcus said. "Also a little dangerous if you dial in while I'm wearing it and, shall we say, constrict the chest until I pass out. I don't take you for a spinning-the-head-around-until-my-neck-breaks kind of guy."

"In your case, I might make an exception."

"I'm flattered, but I'll pass. Oh, one more thing."

Marcus hit a button on his console and Darren lost all control of the suit. It collapsed in a heap like a hamper full of dirty clothes thrown to the floor. Through the static that nearly drowned out the eye sets, he saw the floor rush up and smack him in the virtual face. The hand of the suit fell in front of him and lay there twitching like a fish gasping for air.

Marcus had cut his strings.

A few seconds later, Darren regained control. The suit regained its shape. He found his footing and stood back up.

"Anything that can operate remotely can be jammed," Marcus said. "You probably would have figured that out anyway, but it was just something I wanted to see."

Then there was a pause. Marcus got a look on his face like he had just remembered something, but this time Darren could see that he was only acting, playing his game.

"Oh, and speaking of seeing," Marcus said as he turned back to his console and executed a few commands, "who was that woman with the invisible cape?"

Darren's heart rate shot up and a bitter taste came to his mouth.

"From where I was sitting, she was quite pretty," Marcus continued to work his console. "After you evaded me, you called her and told her to move. That was a prudent move, but irrelevant. I just followed her to her new place, just for future reference. You understand."

Darren curled up his fists and ground away until his nails nearly pierced his palms. Unfortunately, so did the surrogate suit.

"More than a passing acquaintance, I see," Marcus said. "Well, let's see what she's up to, shall we?"

Darren saw a grayscale image of a room come up on the monitor screen behind Marcus. His tormentor even moved aside and pulled the screen up toward the video feed so Darren could get a better look.

"How's that?" Marcus asked. "Can you see well enough? I wouldn't want you to miss this."

Darren shut off his voice link and dialed Faye's cell phone.

It started ringing.

"She's not in the living room," Marcus reported as the image walked through Faye's quarters. "She's not in the kitchen," he continued as the voyeuristic ghost freely examined the private space.

The phone kept ringing.

Darren opened another channel and dialed Walter.

"Hmm," Marcus continued the search, "it's late. Let's try the bedroom. Maybe she turned in early."

The image walked right through the door to Faye's bedroom. The bed seemed undisturbed but some clothes had been thrown on top of it.

"Hello?" Walter picked up the phone.

"Walter, Marcus is in Faye's bedroom. He has her under surveillance. He's targeting her."

"How do you know Marcus?" Walter stammered.

"Walter!" Darren yelled. "She's not answering her cell. You've got to get to her!"

"The shower?" Marcus taunted. "Do we dare? Oh, why not? Who is it gonna hurt?"

The image walked through the bedroom toward the bathroom door.

Darren heard a clamoring on Walter's side of the line.

"Walter!"

"I'm working on it!" Walter said.

The image pierced the closed portal and entered the bathroom. There was the figure of a woman in the shower. The shower door appeared transparent and the surveillance technology showed the spray of water as a strange pixilated mass flowing over her body.

"My my," Marcus drooled. "Well, that is nice."

Marcus leaned his head in front of the video monitor. "I almost hate to interrupt her, but let's get aligned."

Marcus started working his controls. Darren saw shadows move in the room behind Marcus and reflections drift across the video screen that watched Faye like some perverse phantom.

"Walter!" Darren yelled.

"I'm trying!" Walter yelled. "There's an emergency alarm in the cloak. If I can set it off remotely, Faye would have to hear it. She'd be more attuned to it than a ringing cell phone. To her it would be like the sound of her infant crying."

Marcus continued to tune in his equipment. Darren could even see the graphics and targeting readouts on the video screen, zeroing in on Faye, locking onto the mark.

Then something happened.

Faye's head jerked to the left, the way it might if she had heard something in the other room. Then she leaped out of the shower in one deft move. She didn't reach for a towel. She didn't shake the water on her body. She simply darted out from under the spray and lunged for the bathroom door. It took her all of one-half a second to throw the door open and sprint across the room. Darren could see her clear as day. Unfortunately, he could also see the targeting graphics, and they still had a lock on her.

Faye jumped onto the bed from halfway across the room. She grabbed the corners of whatever was lying on the mattress and rolled forward. She wrapped herself in what was presumably her cloak and tumbled forward onto the floor.

She was right.

It didn't work at this wavelength.

She was no more invisible to Marcus than anyone else. With the cloak on, Faye righted herself and came to her feet. Darren could see her adjusting it around her and searching for Walter's emergency channel.

"Good night, sweet princess," Marcus called and pushed a button.

Faye froze in mid-motion. There was an instant of stillness before she fell forward like an ancient oak with its roots cut away. It was a long way down, slowly at first, then accelerating without letup. She made no gesture to protect herself from the impact. She just toppled over. Her arms were still at waist height when she hit. Her face smashed into the hardwood floor with a sickening impact. Darren was sure she'd shattered her teeth and broken her jaw. Her head bounced twice before settling. The way it looked, she could possibly have broken her neck as well.

Thank God she was at least spared that pain.

There was silence on the line for a moment.

"Darren?" Walter called.

"She's dead, Walter," Darren reported.

Another moment of silence.

Darren watched Faye's body on the screen. There was no movement at all, only stillness.

After another few seconds, the envelope around Faye's body dissolved. Darren surmised Walter had triggered a self-destruct order on the cloak and it had disintegrated into sand and useless components.

"And that's what happens," Marcus said. "I know you were after me in Prague. I know…"

Darren wouldn't hear one more syllable from this thing. He hit the self-destruct on the surrogate suit and the eye sets went black. He was quite sure Marcus's captive dissolved into dust before his eyes. Darren came down from his suspension harness, sat down, and removed the mask.

There was some time before he even stood up again.

CHAPTER
21

"Why didn't you tell me?" Darren yelled. "What the hell were you thinking? You asked us for our help. You ask for our trust, but you hide something like this. If I could get my hands on you right now, I'd kill you myself."

"It wouldn't have changed anything," Walter said.

"Faye's dead."

"That had nothing to do with whether I told you about Marcus or not. There's nothing I could have told you that would have changed that. As far as the mission is concerned, you knew everything I did."

"And how the hell are we supposed to believe that?"

"Why do you think I didn't tell you? Why do you think I would hide something like that in the first place?"

"Guilt!"

"That's probably a big piece of it, but that's not the reason. What would have happened if I told you about this at the start?"

"We would have been better equipped to handle the threat."

"No, you'd have been no better equipped to handle the threat, but this threat would have had an advantage."

"How?"

"You might not have come. You might not have helped. You might have said 'No, sorry, Walter, but this is your mess. You need to clean it up.' And how was I supposed to do that? I didn't tell you because it would have increased the risk of your saying no and I couldn't risk it. None of us could."

"Did Faye know?"

"No, no one else knew except Brigham because he helped me recruit Marcus."

"And this is the product of your incubation, your recruitment? This is what you accomplish by nurturing your outliers to their full potential? Did your carefully planned psychiatric evaluations tell you that Marcus was a psychotic nut job?"

"When do you think we started doing psychiatric evaluations?" Walter yelled. "Marcus taught us that. He was the first one to go rogue. It was after him that we started doing psych evaluations on all candidates to try to screen out the potential for this kind of thing. Before that, we didn't foresee this possibility well enough."

"Brilliant."

"It's easy for you to sit there and judge, but you haven't been there and played the game from the beginning. Things aren't always as obvious as they seem in retrospect."

"What else aren't you telling us?"

"A lot, Darren. You don't know everything about our operation, and you don't need to. I'd be lying if I said I've told you everything or that I ever will. I doubt I know everything about your operations, do I?"

"Insofar as this case is concerned, I'm not hiding anything from you or putting you at risk."

"We've already established that I'm not either. None of this changes anything."

"So you claim, but without complete information, how do we know that?"

"I guess you don't, but absence of evidence is not evidence of absence. Just because you know something now is not evidence that I'm hiding anything else."

"Fuck your arguments, Walter. I think you're missing the most important part of this. How can we trust you? If you withhold information, if you hide things from us, from all of your 'assets,' how are we to trust you?"

"Darren, I have never betrayed you or put you at more risk than you shoulder yourself every day on your own. I admit I did manipulate you, all of you, but it was not and has never been for personal gain. I've done what I've done and made the choices I've made because it was necessary. You had to come. I needed you. This country needed you. The greatest good is served by your helping with this mission. I did this to ensure your cooperation, not because it made me happy, because it was required. I couldn't risk you saying no just because I sold it poorly, which I would have done by saying 'Darren, I really made a mess of this one. Can you clean it up?'"

Darren rubbed a hand over his face, took a deep breath, and counted to ten. "We're not done with this," he said.

"I'm sure," Walter said, "but we need to finish this first."

Darren took another breath. "Did you know that he is in Bucharest?" Darren asked.

"What do you mean?"

"I mean, did you know that he is physically in Bucharest? He's not operating the targeting equipment remotely. He's here."

"What? How?"

"Did you know?"

"No, I didn't know. I don't know how advanced this system is or if he can control it from anywhere on the planet. What makes you say he's in Bucharest?"

"When he went after Faye, he showed me the surveillance feed on a video link. When he went to adjust the targeting equipment to zero in on her, I saw equipment moving, shadows, reflections, stuff like that. If he was operating remotely, the equipment wouldn't need to move around at his location. He's got to be operating it first person, hands on."

"Are you sure?"

"Pretty sure. I can't think of any other reason his apparatus would require moving parts, unless he was in the room with the weapon itself."

"Holy shit!" Walter breathed.

"At least that narrows our radius. That makes it more likely that he's within five or ten miles of the president's office."

"Darren, that's excellent."

"Only if we catch him. Then you and I are going to talk."

***

"OK," Walter began, "what have we got?"

"The net is about half done," Ives said. "Think of it as a half sphere covering the west side of the grounds."

"And we're not going to be able to finish the second half," Darren said. "If any of us go near there again, it's game over."

"So now what?" Walter asked.

"Well, it's not ideal, but there is a possibility," Ives began.

"I'm listening," Walter said.

"The problem with half a net is that you don't know if the pulse is coming or going. I was hoping to have a complete map so I could tell when the pulse came in and when the pulse went out by measuring the timing between the entry and exit points. Then I'd be able to determine the absolute direction and trace it back."

"And now?"

"Well, we know where the focus is, right?" Ives asked. "It's right where the discharge happens, and I'll be able to detect one of the points on the half sphere. With those two points, I can determine the line. I just won't be able to determine the direction because it won't have accurate enough timing on the discharge point."

"Get to the point, Ives," Walter said.

"I could try both," Ives said. "Again, it's not ideal, but I could trace the beam back in one direction and see if there is a targeting lab on the other end. If not, guess what; I'll try the other direction. I mean, it has to be one or the other, right?"

"Unless he's using two or three intersecting beams," Walter said. "In which case you'd have to chase down four or six possibilities."

"True," Ives said.

"How long will it take?" Walter asked.

"I don't know, but it's basically all we have so we're just going to have to make do."

Walter exhaled.

"So I have to convince the President to goad the sniper into attacking, but do so knowing we have a dicey way of measuring the attack."

"Kind of," Ives admitted.

"Terrific."

***

"You want me to what?"

"We need you to defy him," Walter said. "We need you to provoke an attack so we can get a read on where he's attacking from."

"Out of the question!" the President said. "Mr. Rocaena, you don't know what you're asking."

"Sir..." Walter began.

"First of all, it's not just me," the President continued. "It's my cabinet. It's my family. It's anyone and everyone, so even if I provoked the attack you're asking, there's no guarantee that he will attack on the residence grounds where you have the net set to catch him. He could attack the cabinet members at their own residences, or one of my children when they go to school."

"Sir..." Walter tried again.

"And second," the President continued, "I have no intention of playing roulette with the lives of any of my colleagues and loved ones on the off chance that this scheme of yours might work. It's ludicrous."

Walter rubbed his eyes.

It was 2:30 AM and they were both tired. That gave Marcus the advantage. The more tired they were, the less rational, the less chance he had of convincing the President of what had to be done. But there wasn't much of an option. Ives had determined 2:30 to be the optimal window. Walter just had to deal with that somehow. Add to that the fact that the President was wearing down to begin with and it made Walter's job almost intractable.

Yes, Marcus had the advantage. Walter had to neutralize it through sheer will.

"Mr. President, you are in day 169 of war. That was when the first attack happened, wasn't it: 169 days ago? Ever since then you have been living with the specter of death every second of your life. It's exactly like war on the front lines."

The President nodded.

"You have been at war before, sir," Walter continued. "If I understand correctly, that was how you started your career. That may seem like a long time ago. In a sense, this is much worse than war because you don't know when it's going to end. In war, there are generals managing troop deployments and rotations. They know the toll that war takes on men and take those considerations into account when making their decisions. That's not the case here. He'll run you until you drop. Your fatigue and stress will continue to increase until you collapse mentally and physically."

The President straightened.

"That's not a challenge. You know how this works. You've seen the effects of war on soldiers. It's all the same, and the conclusion is inevitable."

The President relaxed slightly.

"I've studied the campaigns you led when you were in your twenties and thirties," Walter continued. "Some of your decisions were bold, even bordering on reckless. Your own commanders commented as such in your field evaluations, but your strategies worked.

"I understand what we're asking you to do is bold. It might even be bordering on reckless, but I need you to see the wisdom of being aggressive and attacking before you lack the strength to do so. I understand it's risky for everyone, but this is the time to make a move. Before he ends this game his way and a weaker, more obsequious leader takes your place.

"Please, sir, help us nail this son of a bitch before he slips away again like he did in the Czech Republic, like he did in Moldova; before he kills you and moves up the chain again.

"We have a plan.

"We can bring him in.

"Forgive me, but we need the right bold and reckless bait."

The President took a breath and rubbed his eyes.

"I understand that your agreement with your secretary of state is that you will bring him back to the United States for trial," the President said.

"Yes, sir."

"That deal is off," the President said. "You will bring him to me and I will deal with him. If I take the risk, I get the prize."

"Done," Walter said.

***

Brigham could barely face it down.

He couldn't imagine how the President was managing it.

All Brigham had to do was stand in the corner inconspicuously like half a dozen other security guards in the President's office and hallway. He even had the advantage of the earpiece so Ives and the others could keep him apprised in real time.

That was both good and bad.

The President suspected the assassin was monitoring him.

Brigham knew it for sure.

That knowledge was not comforting. He felt like he was standing helpless while someone held a loaded gun to his head. Yet, here was the President looking solid as a rock, defiant as a steadfast soldier. He actually did have a gun pointed at his head. Even worse, the gun was invisible, so he couldn't even look his assailant in the eye.

Brigham was amazed.

This was a leader.

"There's been a change," the President said to several key cabinet members he had called to his office for the announcement. "We're no longer going to follow through with the troop deployments we discussed last week."

He belted out the order like he was just daring the assembly to argue with him and, in fact, he was.

"What?" his Secretary of State asked.

"I would have thought the statement was clear," the President said.

"Clear, yes, but inexplicable," the Defense Minister said.

"That suggests that I would need to explain the decision," the President goaded. "That would be a misconception."

"Mr. President..." the Secretary of Parliament began.

"Also," the President continued, "the trade embargos with Moldova and Ukraine: lift them. That has changed, too."

"Mr. President," the Secretary of State breathed in a whisper.

To Brigham it was clear: he knew. He wasn't arguing with the policy decisions themselves. He knew about the assassin and the terrible risk the President was taking.

Brigham pressed the signal button on his earpiece.

"Not yet," Walter responded.

The President looked at his minister of foreign policy.

"I want to schedule meetings with the ambassadors of Moldova, Ukraine, and Bulgaria," the President said. "We have some issues to straighten out, so please arrange it."

The minister nodded.

"After that, I'll have another list in both Eastern and Western Europe," the President said.

"Yes, sir," the minister said in a shaky voice.

She knew too.

"Brigham?" Walter said.

Brigham waited.

There was a pause.

"Now," Walter said.

Brigham leaned down and pressed a button on his briefcase. Then he ran full speed, right at the President.

***

"You son of a bitch," Marcus said as the screen went white, overloaded by some interference right at the surveillance wavelength.

He was blind.

His hands flew across his console in a controlled rage.

"If that's the way it is…"

***

Brigham knocked two ministers and two security guards aside before anyone could react. He threw himself bodily over the intervening couch and tackled the President as unceremoniously as a common purse snatcher.

Then it started.

It was unlike anything Brigham had ever seen or could have expected. There was a spark in midair where the President had been. That wasn't surprising, but it was followed by another and another and another.

One of the security guards raced for the exit. When he reached the portal, he suddenly went limp and collapsed to the floor. The sparks appeared throughout the room like so many fireflies, but concentrated around the exit doors in greater profusion.

Then it got angrier.

They came in greater numbers and with greater force, each explosion louder than the last. The cabinet ministers in the room sought cover. They scrambled this way and that to avoid the random bursts.

Brigham grabbed the President's arm and dragged him toward the far corner of the office.

Mistake.

Something hit Brigham in the arm, like someone had set off an explosion in one of the bones of his forearm. He yelled and hit the floor, taking the President down with him.

Then it looked like Zeus himself had lost all self-control and brought his rage down on the assemblage.

The sparks came in vicious strings, exactly like a lightning bolt would. The bolts ripped through the air, crackling like they were tearing the room apart.

One of the flashes went right through the Minister of Defense. It raced toward him, hit him in the back, went silent for an instant; it tore through his heart and lungs then reappeared, exited his chest, and continued on. The minister fell to the ground in a ragged heap.

Over the pain, the noise, the screams of agony and confusion, and the flashes of light, Brigham called to his earpiece.

"Walter?"

"Darren?" Walter called.

"Ives?" Darren said.

"Start northwest," Ives began.

Darren peeled out.

Traffic was the biggest problem; again that was probably not an accident. With this guy, few things were. Darren rode a motorcycle so he could weave in and out of the lanes, but he still wasn't breaking twenty-five miles per hour.

"We have a fifty-fifty chance that this is the right direction," Ives explained. "I'm tracing it back, but it will take a few minutes."

"Make it faster!" Walter called.

CHAPTER
22

Brigham struggled to concentrate.

That was a problem when he'd just been shot in the arm, but his life and that of the President depended on it. He stayed on his back next to the President for a moment and watched the chaos in the office.

It was a nightmare; lethal bolts cutting through the air, people screaming and in panic, two dead bodies already, and, it seemed sure, more on the way.

But Marcus couldn't see them. Brigham was reasonably sure of that. Ives' briefcase covered a pretty broad spectrum, and more than that, the bolts seemed random, thrown into the room in a rage if Brigham was any judge.

No. If Marcus could see them, they'd all be dead. That was certain. He was shooting at them wildly, picking them off by weight of chance.

Brigham forced himself to study the nightmare, to watch for an opening, to meet Marcus's threat. It was horrifying, yes, but, he concluded, not chaos.

Marcus would not shoot wildly. He wouldn't do anything without focus, without a plan.

Even in his rage, the storm was not random.

It was a pattern.

Now Brigham could see it.

The bolts guarded the door. That was clear. They pelted the area around the escape routes about once every three or four seconds: the time it might take someone to rush the egress and get it open. By guarding the doors, Marcus kept them bottled up, contained. From there, he swept the rest of the office, covering one section at a time, isolating and closing in on his prey.

Brigham saw one of the ambassadors crawling on the floor toward the far corner of the room. She kept low, seemingly trying to go unnoticed by the malevolent tempest. One of the bolts cut, scythe-like, right through her. It entered the back of her head and exited her right cheekbone. Her arms collapsed under her and she crumpled to the floor in a lifeless heap. Brigham could see her hair still burning at the site of the entrance wound.

That was the critical data point.

Marcus was assuming, quite effectively, that the targets were staying low and ducking for cover, cowering from the attack. The sparks and flashes were tending toward the floor. Ninety-five percent of them were grouped below the four-foot level.

Brigham picked the tallest item of furniture in the office, a seven-foot wooden cabinet behind the main desk and yanked the President in that direction.

***

Darren had finally hit a relatively clear patch. He was still weaving in and out of traffic, but at least he had sustained something over twenty-five miles per hour for the last minute. He was about a mile from the residence when Ives chimed in.

"Darren."

"Yes."

"Bad news," Ives said. "I got up to five miles and I didn't see a thing. It's hard to believe he's that far out. I'm going to start in the other direction."

"Son of a…" Darren gritted his teeth. "What do you want me to do?"

"Your guess is as good as mine," Ives said. "I'm sorry, but I'm doing the best I can."

Darren pulled to a stop.

He hesitated for a moment then turned the bike around.

***

Brigham felt something slice his left flank. It came right through his clothes like a red hot brand and slashed about an inch along his rib cage. He yelled at the shock and pain and pushed the President forward.

"On the desk!" he ordered.

The President leaped, rolled onto the desk, and came to his feet on top of the surface. He kicked the lamps and paper files off and held a hand out to Brigham.

Brigham was reaching for the assist when the President collapsed.

***

"Darren," Ives called.

"Here," Darren said.

Surgical

"Got him!" Ives said. "The beam originates in a lab about one and half miles to the southeast. I can see Marcus from here. I wish I could shoot the son of a bitch myself."

"Good. Get me to him," Darren said as he rounded the next street and came to a screeching halt.

It was thronged with people, and traffic was at a dead stop.

***

The President came down on all fours, obviously in agony.

"Mr. President?" Brigham called.

"Right leg," the President said through barred teeth. "Just above the ankle."

"Can you get to your feet?"

"I *will* get to my feet."

The two struggled to a standing position on the desk and eyed the tall cabinet.

"I'll climb down and give you a boost to the top," Brigham said.

"No," the President said. "Open the doors and drawers and climb to the top like a ladder. Then I'll follow."

***

Darren picked a youth from the crowd, threw him the keys to the bike, and left it behind.

The bodies of a continuum of stationary cars form an extremely uneven surface but they do a form a surface and, more importantly, a surface free of pedestrians and other traffic.

That surface was Darren's best route to Marcus.

Jumping from hood-to-hood and roof-to-roof was trivial.

Doing so at any velocity without losing his footing and tumbling to the street: that was the hard part. But Darren had spent a great deal of time in the suit and he knew well how to steer it.

Of course, a man running over a street full of cars and leaping twenty feet at a time in a crowded city tended to attract attention, but Darren would be gone before the attention gathered would slow him down in any way, so it was irrelevant.

He began cautiously, taking care to keep his balance, treading as he might on a gigantic collection of cobblestones. He heard the complaints, the traffic horns, and the curses as he cleared the first several dozen vehicles.

By then he was going almost twenty-five miles an hour.

Then he hit the gas.

***

Six-year-old Elian Chenowitz held his mother's hand as she examined vegetables on the street vendor's stand. The street was too crowded and the sidewalk too teeming to trust that he wouldn't wander off or be swept away in the river of the masses. He was bored and fidgeting while her full attention was on her task of choosing just the right rutabaga from the dozens in the basket and negotiating with the owner to reduce the price. He didn't even have a toy to play with to amuse himself; no plastic gun, no diminutive truck.

He fashioned an imaginary weapon by extending his forefinger and bringing his thumb to a right angle with the make-believe barrel. He set about targeting and pulling the trigger on unsuspecting passersby. He was aiming at a long shot across the street, holding his hand steady in his best sniper's bead, when something came screaming up from down the street.

Before Elian could even react, the object whipped across his line of fire. He looked up from his imaginary scope to see a figure, a man in a light coat and rain hat, running on top of the cars in the street.

He was unimaginably fast.

He flew along the top surface of the immobile cars, seeming to barely touch the surface. The effect reminded Elian of the Jesus Christ lizard he'd seen at the zoo: an almost magical defiance of physics and gravity.

Then, like a flash of lightning, he was gone. He was probably 200 yards away before Elian even blinked.

He lowered his forgotten, make-believe weapon.

His face went slack.

The fidgeting had stopped.

***

Brigham grabbed the President's hand and hoisted him up to join him on top of the wooden cabinet from where they had a horrific view of the carnage below. Half a dozen of his staff members were immobile, presumably dead. Another half dozen had scrambled to areas they prayed were safe, but those were clearly shrinking as Marcus closed in and continued to eliminate potential hiding places.

There was another disturbing reality.

Having swept the majority of the low-lying areas, Marcus began to raise the level of his lethal zone.

He was up to six feet.

***

Darren had cleared the congested area and was back at street level. There were plenty of cars to duck, dodge, and vault, but he was making good progress.

"Shit!" Ives swore.

"Ives?" Darren called.

"He saw me," Ives said. "I'm blind. He's got the same flood signal we're using in the President's office."

"You can still get me there?"

"Yes, I can steer you to the lab. I know where it is, specifically that big white spot in my image map. I just can't see inside anymore. I don't know what he's doing."

"Understood. I'm about a quarter mile out."

"Darren, like I said, I can't see him. Be careful."

"Three hundred yards."

***

"I could hold you on my shoulders," Brigham offered.

The President smiled and tapped Brigham on the shoulder. "Or I could hold you on my shoulders," he said. "Let's try this."

The President cupped his hands together, pulled them back to his right side then smashed his left elbow into the wall. He repeated the blow three times before he had beaten a hole in the wall deep enough to get a handhold. He kicked the wall at knee height several times until he had made a sufficient hole in the sheet rock to accommodate his foot.

"Let's see how far we can climb this way," the President said.

Brigham smiled and looked up. The ceiling was only three feet away.

"We can try," he said.

***

Darren raced up to the building at full speed. It looked like an abandoned utility structure. He slowed down just enough to smash through the door but give himself enough time to react to what was on the other side. He stopped about six inches short of slamming into the opposite wall then he bolted to the first flight of stairs.

"Second floor, north end," Ives said.

***

Both the President and Brigham were jammed against the ceiling when Brigham turned to survey the scene. Another two were not moving, but something else scared him even more. Marcus had figured out that if someone had managed to get above the six-foot barrier, that person could not be in the middle of the room. Anyone who had evaded him to this point must be along one of the walls.

That was the only place one could climb so he no longer needed to sweep the volume. He only needed to sweep the area along the inside of the office walls.

The sparks and savage threads started on the wall adjacent to Brigham's position then snaked toward the two men with horrific efficiency.

***

Marcus knew he was coming.

He had to.

If there was any doubt, that ambiguity had disappeared when Marcus blinded Ives.

Why else would he need the blind?

Apart from that, Darren hadn't exactly been stealthy in his approach to the building anyway. So either Marcus knew he was here or he was deaf and stupid, and, of course, he was neither.

So, if he knew Darren was coming, then the element of surprise was off the table. Darren didn't have the time anyway, because Brigham and the President only had seconds left. That's assuming they were still alive to begin with.

Darren hit the door to Marcus's lab the same way he had the outer door: explosively.

The door shattered into a hundred pieces and Darren came up ready.

He looked around quickly, searching for any movement, anything to shoot with his ultrasonics or dodge in the case of attack.

There was no one.

The lab was full of equipment Darren could barely recognize, but there was no operator.

The attack had been set to autopilot.

***

Brigham held his breath as the discharge field wrote a pattern in the air and swept for them. He checked the President's side. It was just a few feet away and moving quickly. One ambitious bolt reached out from the pack and struck toward the President ahead of the main swarm.

***

"Ives," Darren called, "how do I shut it down?"

"Break something!" Ives screamed.

It took Darren just a fraction of a second to smash half the lab into so much high-tech scrap.

***

Surgical

The bolt reaching for the President extinguished mere millimeters from its target.

An eerie, surreal silence settled in the office.

The President slowly turned and looked at Brigham.

His right eyelash had been singed by the latest arc discharge.

CHAPTER
23

"There's really only one place he could go," Darren said and bolted for the entrance to the underground.

He knew from his city maps there was an access tunnel just inside the radius of Ives' blind spot. If Marcus was going to run, that was his best option.

The good news was he had to be close. He couldn't be at street level because Ives might find him. He must be underground, and he couldn't be more than a few hundred yards away. He just didn't have enough time. He couldn't run as fast as Darren, so maybe a quarter mile, but probably not even that far.

The bad news was the underground was a bird's nest in this part of the city. Again, Darren knew that because he had detailed maps at his fingertips, or more accurately the fingertips of the suit. The sewer, power, and subway systems all intersected in a dizzying labyrinth that made it a nightmare to unravel.

That was, of course, not a coincidence. It was almost certain that Marcus had chosen this particular building for exactly that reason. It was perfectly located to provide the greatest possible number of escape routes.

When Darren reached the underground entrance, he skipped the ladder and dropped twelve feet to the concrete floor of the power service tunnel. He looked right then left.

To the right the tunnel split into two smaller service tunnels. Each of those met up with a metro line cross junction about fifty yards out and had access to the sewer line through half a dozen manhole ports in the first hundred yards.

The left wasn't any better. The service tunnel continued for about a quarter mile, but it was perforated with side tunnels and access linkages to the metro line as well as a route to the city's water treatment plant and a plethora of other options Marcus might take.

Darren looked right then left again.

"Ives," he called, "any help?"

"No, Darren," Ives replied. "The blind spot reaches a depth where things get blurry for me even without the jammer. Some of the machinery down there is generating its own RF above the recommended rating. Marcus must've seen that, too. It works to his advantage."

"So radar is out."

"Yes."

"Damn."

You're not far, Darren thought, *but where the hell to start? And of course, if I start in the wrong direction, you'll slip away for sure.*

"No radar," Darren said, "but how about sonar?"

"Uh?" Ives said.

"I'll get back to you," Darren said and cut the channel.

Darren set the earpieces of the suit to filter white noise. As the active noise cancellation countered the hiss and hum of the service tunnel, the space got quieter and quieter. A still hush settled on Darren's ears to the point that he could hear his own breathing.

Then he began pulsing the ultrasonic arrays. Usually, the ultrasonics operated only as a weapon, but today they would serve well enough as a sonic probe. Darren generated a high-pitched sound pulse, basically a loud whistle. He set the microphones of the suit to filter out the sound he was generating. Then, he chopped the signal so he could only hear the sound bouncing back to him about half a second later, the time it took the probe pulse to go about seventy-five yards and return.

Now he couldn't see everything that was seventy-five yards away but he could hear it past all the rest of the noise in the tunnel.

Then he started scanning.

100 yards, 110 yards, 120 yards.

Darren heard only silence.

130, 140, 150.That was about a one-second delay.

Still silence.

160, 170, 180.

Darren kept reaching out, well past where he could see even if the dimly lit tunnel had been straight as an arrow.

200, 210, 220.

Darren's silent scream continued to race down the tunnel, dutifully rounding every corner and bend as it bounced off the concrete walls and searched for a target.

280, 290, 300. Now about a two-second delay.

There were dozens of possibilities now. Three hundred yards out, the options had split into so many permutations, even Darren couldn't keep count. The fourth manhole cover in the second access tunnel? The sixth turn in the metro line junction on the left?

It didn't matter. The sound wave covered them all and kept reaching.

330, 340, 350.

Now came a sound split from the probe pulse. It was shifted by about one-seventieth of the frequency he was using. Three hundred and fifty yards out, something was moving away from him at about 10 miles an hour. The Doppler shift on the signal coming back picked it out like a lighthouse in the dead of night.

"Son of a bitch," Darren smirked then sprinted the suit forward for all it was worth.

Forty miles an hour didn't last long before Darren made it to the first turn and screeched to a halt. He had set the program to lock on the sound, but it still reported a generic 300 yards. When Darren turned the first corner to the right, the number went up.

310.

Wrong turn.

Try again.

He returned to the main tunnel and tried the next option.

290.

"That's the one."

Darren continued his guided pursuit. Down the first tunnel on the left, second access point. Down the third manhole cover, second turn to the left. Third turn on the right then up one level.

He was closing in on the signal all the way.

Darren came up behind Marcus in a stretch of tunnel that gave his quarry nowhere to hide, a fifty-yard segment with a twenty-foot ceiling, no side tunnels and no other features.

It was perfect.

Darren entered the tunnel as loudly as he could, stomping in conspicuous footfalls to make sure Marcus heard him. Marcus, who was about midway through the tunnel, carrying a small shoulder bag and running at a full sustainable tilt, trotted a final few strides, came to a stop and straightened.

He put his hands in the air to indicate he knew Darren was there and he knew he had been caught.

Darren didn't give him a chance to turn around. He focused the ultrasonic beam and hit Marcus with a blast he was sure would knock him out. Marcus flinched ever so slightly, but gave no more reaction than he might if stung by a mosquito.

Darren turned up the volume.

Still no reaction.

Marcus turned around slowly, faced Darren with a smirk, and tapped a finger to his ear.

"I had a chance to look at your tweeter," Marcus said, then Darren could see the earpieces on each side of Marcus's head. "Not hard to filter out if you know the frequency range, particularly with the active noise cancellation."

Darren turned off the ultrasonic.

"Good," Marcus said. "Now maybe we can have a civilized conversation."

"That would require two civilized men," Darren said.

"Honestly, Darren…" Marcus began and lowered his hands.

"Hands in the air," Darren warned.

Marcus put his hands back up and sighed.

"How caught do you need me to be?" Marcus said as he looked around at the featureless tunnel.

"More than you are right now," Darren said.

Marcus kept his hands in the air but fidgeted and shifted his shoulder like he was struggling under the weight of the burden.

"Fine," Darren said, "slowly and with one hand, put it down."

Marcus opened both hands fully and looked at Darren as if to say 'Okay, no tricks,' then he slowly moved his right hand to the shoulder strap and tucked his thumb under it. With his palm still open, he moved the burden off the shoulder, bent at the knees, leaned to the right, and gingerly lowered it to the floor.

"Thank you," he said, seemingly genuinely. "Now, if..."

That was it.

Marcus saw his best chance.

Already bent at the knee, he thrust his hand into the pack.

Darren didn't hesitate. He hit 'sprint' and the suit took off, accelerating to top speed in less than a second. He was up to forty miles per hour, but hadn't covered half the distance when he decided to leap as well.

That probably saved his life.

In that second, Marcus had just enough time to draw something out of the bag, point it at Darren, and fire. Darren didn't know what it was but it hit the suit like a wrecking ball.

First, there was an impact on his left thigh. Darren barely felt a thing, but a patch about the size of his hand failed, disintegrated into its component elements, and fell away like so much sand. Then it hit his left hip, his stomach, his rib cage, his right pectoral, his right deltoid, and made its way up his right arm. All this happened in rapid succession.

The effect was the same in every case. The suit stopped responding to programming, dissolved into so much dust, and blew off the surface like a collection of dandelion seeds.

In just a fraction of a second, Marcus's weapon had cut a swath about eight inches across, right through the center of the suit. The exo-skeleton was all but useless in front, and one more blast would make it completely so.

Fortunately, Darren no longer required it.

Although the weapon had virtually destroyed the suit in one stroke, it had done nothing to cancel Darren's forward momentum. He was still airborne, traveling forty miles per hour in an arc that put him directly on Marcus's jaw line less than 200 milliseconds later.

Darren made full use of that fact.

Of course, when your center of mass is traveling forty miles per hour, your fist may reach up to sixty miles per hour in a full swing. That could break several phalange bones if you hit a solid object, like a human skull. The bones of the hand just aren't that robust.

The elbow on the other hand…

Including his own weight and what was left of the suit, Darren brought more than 250 pounds down on Marcus's left temple. He pulled his blow just enough to make sure he didn't break Marcus's neck, but the target was well unconscious by the time the two bodies had finished the impact and been sent tumbling down the tunnel with residual momentum.

What was left of the suit protected Darren well enough. Marcus picked up plenty of additional cuts and bruises from the fall, but, being unconscious, he was in no position to complain.

Darren skidded across the concrete then rolled to a stop and came to his feet. Marcus only slid about half as far then stopped in a heap of twisted arms and legs.

Darren walked over to him and checked his pulse and respiration. They were both steady. He was out cold, but there would be no permanent damage.

Surgical

Darren retrieved the shoulder strap off Marcus's bag and tied Marcus's limp hands behind his back. Then he stepped back to assess the damage.

It was considerable.

Virtually the entire front of the suit was gone. Elements on the ragged edges of the wound were still failing and flaking off like ashes from a burned oak. The left arm, right leg, and back half of the exo-suit were still intact and were struggling admirably to obey Darren's commands, but they could only do so much. With his torso exposed, any ordinary gun or knife would do the job on Darren now just as well as anyone. Fortunately, his only current threat had been neutralized.

He walked over to the weapon Marcus had dropped when Darren knocked him out, picked it up and examined it. Best guess: an infrared laser pulse tuned to hit an absorption resonance of the control elements. He could probably get a few Watts out of a unit this size, and thirty to fifty percent of the light would penetrate the cover layer of the suit.

Marcus had clearly pulsed it. Based on the timing and spacing of the impact sites, Darren guessed about one hundred Hertz. That kind of power at that kind of intensity could shatter the structure of the suit if the resonance was strong enough.

Marcus had made good use of the time that he had Darren's equipment. He had clearly searched for a weakness and had dug up a very effective way to exploit it. It looked like there was an ultrasound emitter on the unit as well. It wasn't clear what that was for, maybe to increase the efficacy of radiation attack. Either way, Darren was going to study this little toy in great depth.

He made a mental note to try to put a reflective coating on the exo-suit to screen out this wavelength. While he was at it, he'd look for other resonances the control elements might have. He didn't want to get hit like this again.

Darren rechecked Marcus. He was still unconscious and his vital signs were still stable. Darren guessed he might have a concussion, but he doubted it was serious. Either way, he had to get back to the surface.

Darren checked his comm channel. No surprise; there was no signal down here.

Darren put the weapon back in the shoulder bag, put his hand through the handles, and pulled it up to his forearm. He walked over to Marcus, rolled him onto his back, got his hands under Marcus's legs and upper back and accessed the 'carry adult male' program.

He could almost hear the back of the suit groaning as it hefted Marcus's weight without the help of the other half that Marcus had destroyed. Darren just hoped it held out until they got to the surface. He didn't want to have to carry Marcus himself.

It seemed like a long walk, retracing his steps all the way back to the access tunnel under the weapons lab. When Darren got to the final leg, he looked up at the twelve-foot ladder he had bypassed on the way down. He decided that was far enough and put Marcus down.

"Walter," he called to the comm channel.

He heard the channel ring and Walter pick up.

"Darren?"

"Yeah, I got him."

Although Walter struggled to contain it, Darren could hear the jubilation in his voice.

"Oh, you're kidding!"

"No, he's here. He's unconscious for the moment."

"Tie him up, Darren. Don't let him wake up without tying him up."

"No shit, Walter. Listen, I'm in an access tunnel underneath the weapons lab. The suit is pretty badly damaged. Can you send someone to pick him up?"

"Are you OK?"

"Yeah, I'm fine. This clever bastard just didn't make it easy."

"How did he damage the suit?"

"It's a long story. Just send someone to pick him up."

"I'm sure the President will be more than interested. I'll call him. He'll get a team there in a few minutes."

"Good. Again, I'm in an access tunnel under the lab. They'll have to lower a stretcher or something."

"I'll let them know."

There was a pause.

"And Darren?"

"Yeah."

"Good job!"

"Thanks."

A retrieval team arrived about five minutes later, but it took them another five minutes to find the tunnel Darren was in. By that time, Marcus was awake, but uncharacteristically silent. That was a good thing. Darren had promised himself that if Marcus opened his mouth again, he would knock him out without hesitation.

A team of four men in military blue jumpsuits eventually came pouring down the ladder and whisked Marcus away with barely a word.

Just before the last one started for the ladder, he turned, straightened, gave Darren a crisp salute and said, "Thank you, sir" in English.

That was a little strange because Darren still had his mask and signature hat on. This guy couldn't see his face and had no idea who Darren was. This type didn't, usually, let you go without a good grilling, but apparently he'd been instructed to respect Darren's anonymity.

Darren nodded.

The man released his salute then turned and shot up the ladder with practiced speed.

Darren, finally alone, sat down in the silence, took off his hat and mask and took the first breath of relatively fresh air he had had in quite a while.

He was in no hurry to get back to the workshop.

For now, it could wait.

***

A week later, Darren was back in Walter's office in L.A. The meeting was supposed to be a final debrief, a last chance to wrap up any business from the past several weeks. After all that had happened, they hadn't discussed Marcus, but Darren just couldn't leave it at that.

"I have to ask," Darren said. "Will they kill him?"

Walter winced.

"Probably," he said. "To be honest, I hope they do it quickly."

Darren thought he saw something out of the corner of his eye, a wisp of movement or something. He looked in that direction but saw nothing, so he turned back to Walter.

"Will they?" he asked.

"No," Walter said. "I wish it could be different, but we made the deal with the President and we had to keep it."

"Did you at least ask?" Darren said. "Did you at least discuss it with him?"

"No," Walter said. "Once the deal was done, it was none of my business. I had to let it go."

"I agree," Darren said. "I would prefer they…"

Then Darren thought he heard something, a small sound like a foot brushing along the carpet. He looked behind him and scanned the office. There didn't seem to be anyone there. Again he returned his attention to Walter.

"How do you feel about that?" Darren asked.

"Like crap," Walter said. "There was a time, when...well, frankly, there was a time when he was you. I never wanted it to come to this, any of it and in a very real sense this is my failure. My failure to read him, my failure to stop him, my failure to prevent all that has happened."

"He made his choices, Walter," Darren said. "He made his choices, and he was responsible for them, not you."

"This is one of those times when knowing it intellectually doesn't help the emotional side," Walter said. "No matter what he did, I wouldn't wish the fate I damned him to on anyone."

One more time.

This time Darren was sure he heard it, a dull crack, not a mechanical sound, more like knuckles cracking or maybe a knee.

Darren looked at Walter.

Walter smiled.

"She's trying," he said. "She has a way to go, but this is how it starts, with a lot of practice."

Darren looked around the office carefully. It took almost a minute to see it.

There.

Just in the back corner, a small distortion, much the way one might see distortion in the air near a hot object, but very subtle.

"Not bad," Darren said. "No, not bad at all."

He looked at Walter.

"Vanessa," Walter said.

Darren gave a satisfied nod.

"Go on, Van," Walter called. "Go spook someone else."

The door opened and closed seemingly of its own volition.

Darren waited a moment before continuing.

"Now," Darren began, "is there anything else you want to tell me?"

"No," Walter said without looking at him.

"How many of us are there?" Darren pressed.

Then Walter did look at him.

"Do you mean how many of you am I worried about?" Walter said. "All of you. Do you think Marcus was fundamentally any different than the rest of you? He's a human being. He chose his path and it diverged. We are all at risk of that every day, with every decision we make. Before I met Marcus, I doubt he woke up each day thinking 'when I grow up I want to be an international terrorist.' Life just doesn't work that way. He just kept making selfish decisions, one after the next, and kept going."

Darren was silent.

"Do you think Faye could have been trusted?" Walter said. "Would you let Ives loose on the world, with no control, with no checks? I wouldn't, which is why I keep a leash on him. For Faye, it was her possessiveness, her addiction to the cloak. For Ives, it's his phobias. It makes him easier to control."

"What leash do you have on me that I don't know about?" Darren asked.

"Darren, you worry me most of all," Walter said, "because I don't have a good leash on you, and because of that, this is a very dangerous game. You are the riskiest gamble of all, because you have the most autonomy and, consequently, the most power."

"If you're worried about it, why don't you address it?" Darren asked.

"It's a calculated risk," Walter said. "Like I said, we all make our choices. I decided to bet on you a long time ago. I'm standing pat for the moment."

Darren gave a shallow smile.

"But don't think I'm not watching," Walter said.

Darren lost the smile.

"What about you?" Darren challenged. "Who watches the watcher? What makes you the keeper? What puts you above all this?"

"Why do you think you have that autonomy?" Walter said. "Why do you think I take the risk I mentioned? I don't like keeping my eggs all in one basket, even if I'm the one carrying the basket. Call it a diversification strategy, a way to manage risk, mine included. However, I do think there is one thing you're missing."

Darren waited.

"We keep talking about our little corner of the world," Walter said. "Do you really see the world as such a small place? You keep looking around this group with suspicion and a sense of trepidation. Everyone should be focusing on the bigger picture."

Darren felt a punch coming.

"I'm not the first, the biggest, or the best at this," Walter said. "As the world gets more complex, the outliers get more distinct, more extraordinary. The more we learn and grow, the further out there they get. Our little group manifests some physical distinctions, but that's just one small corner of this ever-expanding room. What about other outliers, physical science, bio-technology, nanotechnology, cyberware? Hell, forget about technology, what about economics? What about medicine? What about the manipulation of legal process and politics?"

Darren suddenly felt like he was drowning.

"Any one of these could impact like a wrecking ball when used the wrong way," Walter said. "And I can assure you, not all these outliers have as pure intentions as you or I, or even Faye or Ives, for that matter."

Darren looked away and took a breath.

"And even if they did," Walter said, "even if their intentions were squeaky clean, we all know how the road to hell was paved."

Darren let out that breath.

"My point is," Walter said, "no matter how smart you are, you've got to get a lot smarter. No matter how hard you're working, you need to work a lot harder. It's a great big world, and none of us can keep up with all of it. That's what we develop tools for, and that is threatening to run away from us."

There was a pause.

"Feel like you're drowning?" Walter asked.

"Yes," Darren said.

"Good," Walter said. "That's one of the reasons you're part of the diversification plan. In theory, you can tread water better than most."

Walter gave him another fraction of a second before tapping him on the back and starting for the door.

"C'mon, Darren," he said. "Let's get back to work."

Epilogue

It felt good to be in the States again.

He had to admit it, particularly when he didn't have to constantly look over his shoulder or feel the law was on his heels. It was good to be home and not be a wanted man, at least for the moment, at least if the general was as good as his word.

That was, of course, by no means a given, but it was true for the moment.

And there was good news. Darren kept tabs on the national database of outstanding arrest warrants. A month ago, he was on it. A week ago, his profile had been removed. The general had been true to his word on that point. That didn't mean he could be trusted, but, of course, that applied to everyone. At least he now had one data point.

It was a beginning.

At the moment, Darren was in Detroit. It seemed like a nice place for him and at the right time. He didn't want to wade back into L.A. just yet and it was summer, the high crime season in the north. Things usually quieted down when the cold got too punishing, but summer was, unfortunately, an active time.

He found a good perch on a mostly abandoned high-rise and was just setting up his IR sniper apparatus when the comm channel beeped.

He recognized the number.

"Hello, General," he said.

"Dr. Kiel," the General replied. "I hope I didn't catch you at a bad time."

"No, it's OK."

"We did agree that I got one call for free just to verify the channel was working."

"Yes, and I don't often work during the day, so this is a reasonable hour to try me."

"That was it really. I just wanted to say thanks and verify the channel. We also agreed that I wouldn't call again unless it was more critical."

"Speaking of agreements, I appreciate your taking care of that arrest warrant thing."

"I hope over time we might be able to build some trust between us."

"I hope so, too."

"And hey, maybe world peace will endure and we'll never have to speak again."

Darren smiled.

"One can always hope," he said.

"Of course, stay well."

"You too, sir."

The channel closed.

Darren finished setting up his stealthy deterrent and began monitoring the streets below. From here, with the night vision scope, he could cover close to a quarter of a mile in every direction and see dozens of alleys and corners hiding potential threats. Even at that, he hoped for a quiet shift.

Then again, he always did.

The comm channel beeped again.

"You've got to be kidding me," he mumbled and checked the number.

It was different.

"Hey, Dad," Darren said.

"I know you said not to call," Joseph began," but how do I even know I have the right number if I don't use it?"

"That's a good question," Darren said as he leaned in to his scope and focused on one particular backstreet about 300 yards out. There was movement stirring near the carcass of an abandoned car.

"So I figured I'd call to make sure I got the right number."

"And what would you do if you didn't have the right number?"

"I didn't really think about it."

"Uh huh," Darren said, still monitoring the movement.

"What are you up to?"

"A little busy, Dad. Can we talk later?"

"OK, do you want to call me?"

"I prefer it that way, yes."

"OK, I'll let you go."

"Talk to you soon."

That stirring seemed innocuous enough. Darren pulled back to a wider view and kept watch for sudden movement. Not a lot of violent crimes happened at a leisurely pace, so quick movement was a good detection signature.

After a quiet twenty minutes, Darren decided it might be time to find a different perch or patrol directly for a while, but in that lull he decided to take the opportunity and make a call himself.

He didn't dissect it.

He didn't plan it out.

He didn't script the potential conversation or map the foreseeable contingencies.

He dialed the number before his brain could engage in his natural process.

This time he decided he would just see what happened.

ACKNOWLEDGEMENTS

One of the greatest joys of the creative process is sharing the result with those that have been there to provide support and assistance through the course of the project. It's been said that 'friends multiply our joy' and that adage could not be more operative here, particularly, in my case for those who appreciate and find joy in the end product.

To all and everyone who have both supported the effort and shared my joy in the results, my deepest and most heartfelt Thank You.

If you enjoyed *SURGICAL*,
look for

FIRST COLONY

By
Geoffrey Germann

In the mind of a genius, in the heart of a builder, in the soul of
an explorer, lives a dream, a purpose, a destiny.

Prologue

Even the most blistering heat wave in Hawaii is better than the mildest winter on the outskirts of Siberia so when Andre Cherevsky stepped from his air-conditioned office next to the Highway eleven truck scales in Pahala, he bore the impact of the sweltering furnace with comparative glee. Andre was born and raised in Yerepol, Russia, about 500 miles from the Bering Strait. A stocky, husky man with a barrel chest that was perfect for retaining heat in frigid environments, he looked like he was bred to drag caribou carcasses through thigh-deep snow in the isolated evergreen forests of northern Asia. Stubby fingers on solid, powerful hands rounded out the package that would never really fit in his new home. But as Andre would tell anyone who would listen – he was not going anywhere.

Andre hated the cold, loathed it. He spent the first eighteen years of his life suffering the torture of existence on the tundra before the Berlin Wall fell, the USSR collapsed, and opportunity had come knocking. Most of his compatriots had taken the obvious leap across the straits to Alaska, but Andre had spent all of two days in Nome before jumping on the first ship headed south. He landed in Hawaii two months later and had spent last sixty years in relative heaven.

Recently, a column of forty ton ants had been disturbing his peace.

Andre walked across the tarmac which was hot enough to fry an egg, and approached the latest big rig with the Calvex corporate logo stenciled on the side. Andre had been putting up with dozens of these monsters every day now for months. He didn't know what they were building down on the southern tip of the big island, no one he knew did, but recently they had been pushing the weight limit like a pack of wolves hounding a noble bison. He had to suppress a smile when this one finally tipped over the mark.

"Sorry," he said to the driver, "you're 500 pounds long."

A look of shock, mixed with embarrassment and fear, paled the driver's face as he scrambled out of the cab.

"What?" the kid, who couldn't have been more than twenty, practically pleaded.

"Five hundred pounds, kid," Andre said, still keeping the triumph from his voice. "You're over the weight limit."

The fear grew in the green kid's face and for a moment he looked frozen by it. He stood there for several seconds, appearing to sort through some internal conflict, then looked over his shoulder and spoke to a man seated in the passenger seat of the cab. "Mr. Rhodes?" he called.

For some reason, Andre was surprised and unsettled by the presence of the second man in the cab; surprised because these truckers almost always traveled alone, unsettled because the carriage and demeanor of the second man was just about the opposite of any truck driver that Andre had ever seen in his life.

He was African American, about forty, with mirrored glasses and wearing a pressed, powder-blue linen shirt and khaki pants. When he exited the cab, he did not jump, he sort of glided in a way that made Andre think of a rappelling mountain climber. When he turned to face Andre, he had the imperturbable tone and manner of a man who, if told he was sitting on a nuclear bomb about to explode, would have probably said something like:

"Is there a problem?"

"Sir," the driver said in a crisp but almost trembling tone, "we're over the weight limit. Mr.," he glanced at Andre's badge, "Cherevsky measures us 500 pounds too heavy."

Rhodes actually flinched.

"Hm, Gabe," Rhodes said, "I had a feeling we were pushing it." He put one hand up to his mouth, looked at the truck, and took a minute to ponder the options.

Gabe looked at Andre with a revolting hint of thinly veiled mischief. "Is there any way we can approximate the weight?" he said. "Any way we can stay on schedule?"

Andre had just begun to shift his weight to attack posture, had just begun to position himself to tear this whelp's arms off, when Rhodes spoke.

"No!" he said in a tone that convinced Andre that Gabe had just been demoted. "If we're over, we're over. We'll have to unload one way or another."

There was a brisk anger in his voice that Andre liked, a punishing intolerance that was well placed and well controlled.

"Mr. Cherevsky," Rhodes said, "we'll solve this weight problem then we'll be back and in conformity."

"I'll be here," Andre said.

Rhodes shot a glance at the driver.

"Let's go, Gabe."

The two climbed into the truck cab and backed off the scales. Andre thought that was a little weird. They should have pulled forward and taken the exit ramp to go back where they came from. The truck came to a jerky halt, as if the driver had forgotten something or had been given an abrupt order. A few seconds later, Rhodes got out of the cab, walked around the truck, and climbed into the cargo area.

Andre's attention climbed toward rage.

"*If he thinks he's going to unload on my station, he's out of his frigging mind,*" he thought.

Then something happened that Andre just couldn't compute.

Andre had been working with cargo trucks for decades. He had gotten so he could tell if a truck was going to make weight just by looking at. Now, right before his eyes, over the course of about five seconds, the Calvex truck looked like it lost a thousand pounds. Nothing came out of it and nothing went into it, but to Andre's trained eye, the load on the tires and springs had clearly lessened, even if only fractionally.

Rhodes climbed back out of the cargo area and into the cab. The truck nudged forward and re-entered the scales zone. Rhodes got out of the cab and approached Andre.

"May we try again? We made some adjustments."

Andre didn't need to look, but he motioned to Rhodes to confirm the reading. They were 500 pounds under limit.

Rhodes nodded satisfaction then looked back at Andre.

"Mr. Cherevsky, I know that may seem little unusual."

Andre maintained a suspicious silence.

"May I ask for your indulgence?" Rhodes said. "We do make weight and I can give you my personal guarantee that we will not exceed the allowable limit for the journey to our destination."

Andre a kept stone-cold silence and looked past Rhodes to the truck.

"… and I'm afraid I can't tell you much about the adjustments," Rhodes added.

Andre looked back at Rhodes and his mirrored glasses. Rhodes paused, removed the glasses, and met Andre's assessing eyes. He let Andre hold his gaze for as long as necessary.

"Rules are rules," Andre said resignedly. "I will ask you to walk gently."

Rhodes gave a slight smile that extended well below the surface.

"Of course."

Rhodes got back into the truck. The vehicle pulled off the scales, onto the entrance ramp, and continued down the highway.

As Andre watched it go, he felt something he hadn't felt in over sixty years, something he hadn't felt since just before the Berlin Wall fell; a seismic shift, a redefinition of the rules.

He didn't know exactly how and he didn't know exactly when, but the world was about to change.

9 780985 288839